Too Much Heart To Run

T0126019

SL HARRIS

BELLA
BOOKS

2016

Bella Books, Inc.
P.O. Box 10543
Tallahassee, FL 32302

Printed in the United States of America on acid-free paper.

First Bella Books Edition 2016

Editor: JoSelle Vanderhooft
Cover Designer: Sandy Knowles

ISBN: 978-1-59493-479-7

About the Author

SL Harris lives in rural Missouri with her partner of many years. Her life's work has been helping others as a physical therapist. Writing lesbian fiction has provided a balance to her life that was previously missing. Her debut novel, *Laughter in the Wind*, was published in 2013 and was a GCLS finalist. She juggles health care, writing, family and farming, sometimes more successfully than others.

Dedication

This book is dedicated to the life and memory of Susan Sentell, who lit up the world with her smile and inspired me in ways I'm not sure I can define.

Acknowledgments

This book would not have been possible without the wonderful support of everyone at Bella. My dreams are possible because of you. Thank you.

My friends and family gave me the encouragement and inspiration I needed to make it through writing about some difficult situations. Although I may not always acknowledge how much I need you, I am always grateful for and dependent on your love and support.

Joselle Vanderhooft continued my education as she edited this manuscript, and I thank her for her excellent work and for her patience with this anxious author. May my point of view become more consistent, and active voice triumph in the future.

Ruth, thank you for believing in me. You complete me.

CHAPTER ONE

It was nearly dark when Del pulled up to the gate and stopped her F150. She noticed new sore places in her back as she climbed out of her truck and walked around to open the gate. As she unwound the piece of barbed wire she was using as a temporary latch, she caught the back of her hand on one of the barbs and tore a small notch in her skin.

"Dammit," she exclaimed and made a mental note to move *Make a better latch for the gate* to the top of her to-do list. She found a tissue in her pocket and dabbed the blood away to keep it from dripping onto her good khakis, then finished opening the gate. After retrieving a first aid kit from behind the seat of her truck and placing a bandage on her cut, she climbed inside and drove through onto the rough gravel track beyond. She took more caution when closing the gate and, within a minute, she was crossing the cattle guard that separated her yard from the pasture.

In the road on the wrong side of the cattle guard loomed a massive black bull. He didn't even flinch when she honked in an attempt to get him to move. Del revved the engine, but still he didn't move.

"Shit!" she yelled into the emptiness of the evening. "If one more thing goes wrong today, I think I'll..." She didn't finish the thought, stopping herself from even imagining what she might do if she allowed her control to slip.

Instead, she inched the truck slowly forward until she finally nudged the bull gently with her front bumper. With the slight contact, he grudgingly stepped out of the driveway and into the flower bed she had planted the previous weekend.

"Thanks for nothing," she muttered under her breath as she drove past him and up to the front of the old farmhouse, of which she was the new owner.

Del fished out her cell phone and found her list of contacts. "Gus, where the hell is your number?" she said quietly. Finding the listing she wanted, she pushed the Call button.

The call was answered on the second ring with a simple "Yeah."

She responded quickly. "Hello, this is Del. I have a bull in my yard again. Can you come over and help me get him back through to the pasture?"

"Uh, yeah. I'll be over in a few minutes. Let me get my boots back on."

Del disconnected, then leaned her head back against the seat. What had she been thinking to come back to the country after all these years? Had things really been that bad in the city? She knew the answer to that was a definite yes and closed her eyes, hoping it would all just go away. Life was about to overwhelm her. The old farmhouse needed enough work to tie up every weekend for the next four months just to get it ready for winter. The dilapidated fence around the yard would not keep out Gus's cattle, and she couldn't afford to not lease out the pasture to him. The rutted road needed several hundred dollars worth of gravel spread onto it. Her back ached constantly, and between lifting patients at work and working hard around her house, she had no time to allow it to recover. And now her hand hurt much worse than a small cut should, she thought.

"Oh well. Might as well get out and do something," she reasoned. "I'm not solving any problems sitting here in this truck."

She grabbed her lunch bag and lab jacket from the passenger seat and climbed the three steps she had rebuilt her first weekend at the house, crossed the rickety porch and unlocked the front door. The table lamp in the corner of the living room came on when she flipped the switch inside the front door. Pale yellow light illuminated a narrow room with bare white walls which was filled to overflowing with furniture. She walked along a winding path to the kitchen on the other side of the living room. She placed her lunch bag on the counter, grabbed a Dr. Pepper from the refrigerator and tossed her lab jacket into a basket on the utility room floor on the far side of the kitchen. She downed one cold swig of sweet caffeine before she heard the diesel engine of Gus Andrews's truck moving down the hill toward her house. She grabbed a flashlight from the utility room to fight off the encroaching darkness and headed back to the porch.

Gus and his two teenage boys hopped out of the truck. "We'll get him, Del. I brought some wire to patch the fence too." Gus's tone was reassuring as he hustled past her. They headed out across the yard, cattle sticks in hand, and soon had the bull passing back through the fence where he had crossed earlier. The boys began fixing the fence behind her house while Gus came up to the porch and sat down beside Del.

"Long day?" he asked.

"Guess you could say that." She crossed her arms over her chest, feeling the chill of the May evening settle in.

Twenty-five years earlier, Del and Gus had been fast friends—twelve years old, fishing in the local ponds, playing truck driver in the lawn chairs in Del's front yard, or playing poker for toothpicks under a shade tree behind her parents' house. Then as teenagers they'd drifted apart, and when Del left Devil's Prairie for the city, they nearly lost contact completely. They had been in touch a few times over the past four years, but they had never returned to their easy friendship of childhood. When she'd called him a few months before, she wasn't certain what she'd expected. To her surprise, he and Jenny had jumped at the chance to help. Now she was their neighbor and they leased her pasture for their cattle. Although she still felt a little awkward around them, in the month since she'd moved, she'd found herself letting her guard down and allowing her friendship with the Andrews to grow.

"When do you think you might want to try to replace that fence?" he asked, pulling her from her reverie. "You know the boys and I will help; just say the word."

"I'm nearly tapped out until the first of next month, at least. Then I'll probably have enough to get some posts and wire."

"Have you thought about calling Widow Jennings?" he asked. "She might have some old posts she'd sell you cheap. She tore out a fence row a couple of months ago. She'll quote you a fair price, if she still has them."

"I don't believe I've heard of her. Widow, is it?" Del asked.

"Yeah. That's what everyone calls her. Her name is Felicia, but I've never heard her use that name. She lives over on the old Hammond place," Gus explained.

"Okay. I'll give her a call. The quicker we get that fence replaced, the better. It may not be healthy for your bull to keep breaking into my yard. Next time, I might not bump him so gently."

Gus grinned at Del's mocking tone. "Don't add insult to injury, Del. You'll end up with a busted grille and he'll probably just walk away."

"We're all done, Dad." Gus's elder son, Jim, stepped around the corner of the porch into the illumination of the light. He leaned one hand against a corner post but quickly put it down at his side when the post creaked loudly. "Sorry Del," he said quickly.

"It's okay, Jim. At the rate I'm going, I'll be lucky if I get this place repaired before it falls down around my ears." She smiled to ease his concern.

"I think that fence will hold him out for a little while, but no bets on how long," Jim continued.

"Yeah, we were just talking about that," Gus said, rising from his chair. "Del thinks maybe the first of the month we can start on it. Well boys, guess we better head home. Mom will have supper ready for us. You want to come over, Del? Pot roast, potatoes and carrots."

"Thanks Gus. Maybe another night. It's been a long week, and I think I'll turn in early."

"Okay, but you don't know what you're missing," Gus teased. He turned and headed for his truck.

Del smiled and shrugged, knowing she would not be good company this evening. It had been a trying week at work and nightmares had interrupted her sleep too many times, leaving her exhausted.

She couldn't help but smile at Jim and his younger brother Gary as they rushed ahead of Gus, each trying to secure the prized front-seat position. "Tell Jenny I said hello," she told Gus. "Thanks for coming over so quickly."

"No problem. Hope he didn't do any damage to your yard." Gus peered into the yard, dark beyond the small semicircle of light that surrounded them.

"I think he stomped a few flowers, but they can be replaced," she said, trying to make light of the loss of the hours she had spent building and planting the flower bed. "Good night guys."

"Good night Del," all three of them chimed.

After a salad and another Dr. Pepper, Del settled into her recliner and clicked on the TV. She found nothing of interest on her four local network stations and clicked it off again. Instead, she grabbed an open book from the coffee table and settled back into her chair. One chapter later, she was fast asleep.

CHAPTER TWO

"Hey, honey, how was your day?" Sarah asked as Del came through the kitchen door. Her cheeks glowed with health, and her eyes sparkled with delight to see Del.

"You look great," Del said. She came around the counter and hugged her from behind, nuzzling her neck.

"Thanks. You don't look so shabby yourself. Are you hungry? I'm planning on cube steaks and a veggie."

"That sounds great. Need some help?"

"No, go sit down and rest a little while I finish with these steaks."

"Okay, babe."

"Dee! Dee! Hey Dee, are you in there?"

The beating of a meat tenderizer on steaks changed to the banging of a fist on a door, and Del awoke disoriented, looking for Sarah and their familiar apartment in St. Louis. The furniture looked the same, although out of place, but that was all she recognized in the early morning light of her crowded living room.

"Dee! Are you home?"

"Shit!" Del pried herself up out of the recliner where she had spent the night and stumbled toward the door. She flipped the latch, then pulled open the door. The bright morning sun peeking over the trees caught her fully in the face, and she squinted to see who was standing on her porch.

"About time you woke up, lazybones!" The short, spry woman on her front porch stepped inside and hugged her tightly, not waiting for a response. "You look like hell. What'd you do, sleep in your chair again?"

"Uh, yeah. I guess I did. Sorry Cindy. I didn't mean to keep you waiting out there. How long have you been knocking?"

"Just a few minutes. Don't worry about it. You can pay me back by fixing me some coffee."

"Uh, okay, yeah. I do have coffee." Del walked back to the kitchen, running her hands through her short hair on the way, trying to put it in some semblance of order. "I'll have it ready in a few minutes. Have a seat and I'll bring you a cup when it's done," she called back over her shoulder.

Del heard the muffled sound of the TV from the other room as she waited for the coffee to brew. She hoped Cindy wouldn't give her too much trouble about sleeping in the recliner as she'd been doing for weeks now.

"Cindy worries too much…and I talk to myself too much." Del shook her head in self-reproach.

When Del returned to the living room, she noted her bedding had been piled neatly onto one end of the couch and Cindy was settled comfortably on the other side with the TV remote resting beside her.

"Black coffee," Del announced. She placed one cup on the coffee table in front of Cindy and headed for her recliner.

After a noisy sip of the hot brew, Cindy lifted her cup toward Del. "Good coffee. So, are you up for a weekend of manual labor, old lady?"

"Who are you calling old lady? Last I knew, you were only six months younger than I am. And yes, I'm ready. We'll just see if you can keep up."

Del was glad to see Cindy. Her dream had left her unsettled, and Cindy would help her get her mind on what she needed to get done instead of sitting around and brooding. In St. Louis, she and Cindy had worked together in health care off and on over the past ten years, and they had become close friends. Del and Sarah had helped Cindy get over Brenda when Brenda dumped her for another woman three years earlier. She couldn't count the number of nights Cindy had slept on their couch because she couldn't stand to go home to an empty house. Now she supposed Cindy thought it was her turn. But Del really didn't think anything would help her get over Sarah. The pain she felt now was just as sharp, just as fresh as it was the day she saw the light go out of Sarah's eyes six months earlier. She supposed it always would be.

"Dee, are you still with me?" Cindy's worried expression matched the concern in her voice.

"Oh yeah. What did you say? I was just daydreaming or something." Del rubbed her hand over her face, trying to wipe away ghosts from the past and move back into the present.

"Do you have plans for breakfast? I thought maybe we could run to that little diner up the road and get a good breakfast before we get started. Sound good to you?"

"Sure. Can you give me a few minutes to get cleaned up? I'd like to take a quick shower if it's okay."

"Please," Cindy shot back at her. "I'd appreciate it, especially the shower part if I'm going to be stuck riding in the cab of a pickup with you."

"Oh shut up." Del punched her lightly in the shoulder as she passed by Cindy on the way to her bedroom.

She quickly showered and dressed, then grabbed a cup of coffee to go, shut off the coffeemaker and headed out the door a step behind Cindy.

* * *

"Biscuits and gravy, breakfast of champions," Cindy teased her. "You're going to clog your arteries before you're forty, Dee."

"Oh shut up. I don't know how I survived all those years eating healthy. Yogurt and bagels and all that crap." Del shoved in another forkful of food. After she swallowed, she added, "I guess coming home hasn't been all bad."

"It'll get better. Let's get your house fixed up and you'll have a whole new outlook on it."

"Maybe. Just seems like a never-ending list of things to do, that's all."

"Hurry up and finish eating and let's get to it, then." Cindy had already eaten, and now she turned sideways in the chair, looking at the door impatiently.

"All right, this is my last bite." Del grabbed the ticket and got up from the table, then headed toward the cash register while she was still chewing. "You leave the tip," she called back over her shoulder to Cindy.

A few minutes later, they backed out onto the lazy main street of Devil's Prairie, then drove about a block to a small brick building with unmarked angle parking in front. Del pulled up to the small asphalt curb nearly in front of the single tinted glass door to the local post office. She stepped inside and in five steps was at her post office box. Del shook her head as she compared her experiences in this small town to the city. The conveniences were offset by the main lobby being open only a few hours each day, usually when she was at work. But she seldom needed to do more than check for mail, and this room was always open.

Del was looking down at her mail when she opened the door to step outside. A flicker of movement in her peripheral vision made her stop in her tracks, inches away from a collision. She looked up to see a woman, an inch or two shorter than she was and about her own age, blond hair pulled back into a loose ponytail with several escaped strands framing her tanned face and bright, blue eyes. Judging from her strong arms and the black grease stains on her faded jeans, she was no stranger to manual labor. She stood, patiently waiting for Del to move from the center of the doorway.

"Oh, excuse me," Del said quickly. "I guess I wasn't watching where I was going."

"Most of the time, that's not a problem around here. Traffic isn't really heavy in and out that door, you know."

Del was struck by the strength in her voice and took a closer look at the woman she had nearly run down. "You wouldn't be Widow Jennings, would you?" she ventured on a hunch.

"That's what they call me around here. And you? I think I know nearly everyone in these parts, but I don't think I've seen you before. New to the area?"

"I'm Del, Del Smith. I grew up not far from here, but I've lived away for about twenty years. I just moved back a month ago. I bought the old place just west of Gus Andrews's place."

"Welcome back then, Del. Now if you'll excuse me, I have to get my mail and get back to the farm. Got a busy day planned."

"Sure, yeah, I'm sorry." Del stepped out of her way, holding the door open as Widow passed by her into the post office. She was a little surprised at the brusque response she had received and stared at the door as she allowed it to close again. With a sudden determination, Del turned and went to the truck, where she handed Cindy the mail through the open window. This Jennings woman might be busy, but Del needed some posts and was not going to let the opportunity pass.

"Give me a minute," she explained. "I need to talk to this lady."

"I'm just the hired help. Whatever you want, boss." Cindy smiled at Del's look of annoyance.

Del opened the door again just as Widow reached it.

"Ms. Jennings…"

"Widow, please."

"Widow, Gus suggested I talk to you about some fence posts," Del began. "He thought you might have some old posts for sale. I need to replace the fence around my house before I get mad, shoot Gus's bull and have him for dinner."

Widow laughed. "Don't go to that extreme. If it's the one I'm thinking of, he'd probably be pretty tough, old as he is."

She's got a nice laugh, Del thought.

"Come over when you want to take a look at them. I'll be there all weekend. You know where my place is, right?"

"Yeah. The old Hammond place, Gus said."

"That's it. Well, I'll be seeing you." Widow climbed into her truck. She turned the key, and the old flatbed sputtered to a start. She backed out onto the road and pulled away, leaving Del looking after her.

When Del stepped up into the truck, Cindy gave her a long, sideways glance then started the engine. Del refused to respond to Cindy's interest in her sudden decision to speak to Widow and turned to stare out the window. The reason for this uncharacteristic determination, she admitted to herself, was something she wasn't even comfortable exploring. Cindy backed the truck out onto the road and headed to Del's new home.

* * *

Six hours later, Cindy and Del had put a new, safer latch on the gate at the end of the lane and sealed the old metal roof of the house with a silver sealant. Del stepped down the ladder with a nearly empty, silver-stained bucket in one hand. Cindy was already sitting on the porch in one of Del's plastic lawn chairs.

"Ready for a break, I see," Del said, falling into a chair beside her. "At least it feels like we're getting somewhere. Want a Dr. Pepper?"

"Don't guess you'd have a Diet Coke in there, would you?"

"No. If I'd have been thinking, I'd have picked up some. Sorry about that." Del had risen to go inside for a soda but now decided against it. "Tell you what, let's run to the station and I'll buy you a Diet Coke. On the way back, we can run by Widow Jennings's place and look at those posts."

"Sounds like a good idea to me. Do I look okay?" Cindy asked, running her fingers through the strands of hair the sticky sealant had matted together.

Del laughed. "Good thing you're not looking for a date. Quit worrying about how you look and let's go." Del grunted and rubbed absently at her cheek when she saw her reflection in the truck window. She had a silver streak down the right side of her face, a few silver sprinkles in her hair and a smudge of black in the middle of her forehead. Her shirt and jeans were dirty from the efforts of their day, and the barbed wire at the gate had ripped a hole just above her left back pocket.

The clerk at the station didn't give their scruffy appearances a second look, and many of the other patrons coming and going around them looked as though they had been involved in outdoor tasks of their own. Del headed to the back of the store, leaving Cindy looking at the rack of rental DVDs near the entrance. She bought their drinks and found Cindy where she left her.

Del handed her a forty-four ounce fountain soda. "If that's not enough, I can get a two liter bottle," she teased.

"I think that'll do for a while."

As they headed to Widow's place, Del was quiet and Cindy chose not to interrupt her thoughts. Instead they rode in silence, looking at the passing landscape. If one looked closely, they might be surprised by how rundown most things appeared. Fences lining the perimeters of the pastures were leaning or missing posts, gates were rusty and bent, houses had siding with mold or missing pieces, and the older, more decrepit houses had mobile homes set up next to them either for extended families or because they were no longer habitable. The signs of people struggling to make ends meet were evident everywhere. Occasionally, they passed a nice house, with a new fence and well-tended yard, but these were the exceptions.

When they pulled down the long drive toward the Hammond house, Del finally spoke. "I haven't been to the end of this road since I was a kid. I wonder what all they've done to the old place?"

They came around a corner in the drive, and from behind the trees, the outline of a two-story house emerged. Its mostly glass front looked out over a valley of green, stretching out several hundred yards to a thin line of trees hiding a small creek Del remembered from her childhood.

"Nice." She admired the design and placement of the house, aware that a lot of thought had gone into making it fit seamlessly into its environment. "I guess they had to tear the old house down. It was in pretty bad shape even when I was a kid."

They approached a wide, graveled area in front of a large metal machine shed that was set back farther from the drive than the house. The shed's large, open door appeared to be the center of activity. Widow and a young man—probably her son, Del supposed—appeared to be doing maintenance on a tractor. Widow had a grease gun in one hand and a rag that had probably once been white in the other but set them both down on some nearby machinery when they stopped in front of the shed. As Del turned off the ignition, Widow approached the open window on the driver's side.

"Hello again, neighbor. I wasn't sure if you'd make it out today or not."

"Well, I decided I'd better give my help a break. I wouldn't want to wear her out too much. She might not come back to help again." Del glanced over with a smile for Cindy, who rolled her eyes in response.

"Let's go look at those posts. Del, right? And what's your friend's name?"

"Oh, I'm sorry. Guess I've lost my manners. This is Cindy Collins, from St. Louis. She's a good friend of mine who's crazy enough to give up her weekends to help me out. Cindy, this is Felicia Jennings." Cindy had stepped out of the truck and walked around to stand by Widow.

"Widow. Just call me Widow. Everyone around here does." She held out a darkened hand she had recently rubbed free of grease, but which still showed the stains of her labors. Cindy didn't hesitate to take it, returning her firm handshake.

"Widow. It's nice to meet you. This is a beautiful place you have here. Maybe you can give Del a few tips." Cindy grinned at Del and winked. "After all the repairs we've done to her place, I'm beginning to think we should have just built another house."

Del grunted as she climbed out of the truck, feeling a sharp jab in her back after sitting still for a little while. "Might take the same amount of time and effort, but patching up the old place sure takes a lot less cash."

Widow nodded in agreement. "When we lost the kids' dad, he had a good life insurance policy. That's what made a down payment on this place, including building the house. It's been a battle to meet the mortgage every month, but only four more years to go and it's all mine. I plan to have a big party to celebrate. You'll both have to come."

"That sounds great to me!" Cindy jumped in. "I never pass up an excuse for a party."

"I'll keep you posted," Widow said, smiling at Cindy's enthusiasm. "Well, let's go look at those posts. We stacked them over here behind the shed. Take a look at what we've got and let me know if you're interested."

They followed her around the corner of the building and saw a stack of a few dozen green T-posts next to the shed. "What do you want for them?" Del asked.

"How about seventy-five cents a post? There are forty-six posts. I counted when we unloaded them here. Don't have a calculator or I'd total that for you."

"That's okay. Dee here is a walking calculator," Cindy teased.

Del blushed. She didn't like to come across as a know-it-all, especially around people who didn't know her well. Math was just easy for her. She noticed Widow looking at her curiously, awaiting an answer. "Thirty-four fifty," she answered simply. "You sure that's enough?"

"Yep. I wouldn't have offered if it wasn't a fair price for both of us."

"I'll take them," Del said, digging her leather wallet out of her back pocket. She counted out thirty-five dollars into Widow's hand and after a few minutes of haggling, finally convinced her to keep the fifty cents change. Cindy backed the truck up to the pile, and in no time, they had the stack loaded in the truck bed. Del dusted off her hands on her pant leg, then reached out to shake Widow's hand. She was startled at the warmth that traveled up her arm when she gripped Widow's hand and noticed a look of surprise cross the other woman's face as well.

Del dropped Widow's hand quicker than she had planned, immediately quelling her surprise or any other thoughts that might have reasonably followed. "Thank you." Her voice was steady and calm, her control fully reestablished. "This will be a big help. Now, as soon as I can get some wire, Gus and the boys will come over and we'll build a new yard fence."

"That Gus is a pretty good guy," Widow said. "He and Jenny have helped me out several times over the years. My daughter babysat for their boys a few times when they were younger, and they watched my place if I had to be out of town."

"Yeah, he was a good friend growing up too," Del agreed. "I spent a lot of days sitting on pond banks fishing with him."

"I have a stocked pond up by the road if you're ever interested. Give me a call and I'll unlock the gate for you. You can drive right to it."

Del's eyes widened slightly when Widow mentioned locking the gates. Many of the locals still left their gates open to everyone, and some were offended to find any gate locked. Gus didn't lock his gates, and she had never considered putting a lock on her own.

Widow must have seen her surprise, because she quickly explained, "I put locks on all my gates. Did Gus warn you about the rustling going on in the counties west of here? If they want to steal my cattle, they'll have to work for it."

"No, but that's definitely something I'll keep my eyes open for, and I'll think about getting a lock for mine." Del was concerned about the thought of rustlers running around on her property when she wasn't around, and she knew someone stealing Gus's cattle would be a hard blow for him to absorb. "I may take you up on that fishing too. Thanks, Widow. I'll let you get back to work."

"Come back when we're not so busy and I'll show you around, Del. You too Cindy. You two have a good day." Widow turned and headed back toward the shed, acknowledging their farewells with a wave of her hand.

Within minutes, Del and Cindy were back at Del's house. They unloaded the posts inside her yard fence near the cattle guard.

"Cindy, let's call it a day after this. I'm about to give out."

"Old lady, you say 'rest,' we rest." Cindy grinned at her but added quickly when Del shifted her gaze to the trampled flower garden she had mentioned repairing, "Rest is good though. Besides, this way we'll have some energy left to get your porch rail replaced tomorrow. We also need to eat again sometime. I don't know about you, but I'm practically starved."

"Good, that means I've worked you hard enough. I set out some steaks to thaw this morning. Will meat and potatoes do for you?"

"If you're cooking, I'm eating." Cindy laughed. "Do a good enough job on that steak and I may even wash your dishes for you."

"Sounds like a challenge to me." Del grinned and slammed the tailgate shut on the truck. "Let's go to the house."

CHAPTER THREE

When she walked into the bedroom, the light from the window shined across the bed, illuminating Sarah's profile, relaxed and peaceful in sleep. "Beautiful as the day I met you," Del murmured quietly. "God, I can't believe how much I love you. I must be the luckiest woman in the world to be the one you love."

She stepped quietly into the room and softly sat down on the edge of the bed, careful to not disturb the serenity of the moment. No longer able to resist, she reached out to trace Sarah's features, to run a fingertip gently over the lines of her face. Before Del could feel the soft skin, Sarah melted away, leaving only a dent in the pillow and wrinkled bedsheets.

"Sarah," Del called out, confused, unable to comprehend how she had disappeared. She looked wildly around the room, panic now taking hold. "Sarah, where are you? Sarah?"

"Dee, wake up."

Del was aware of someone grabbing her shoulder, shaking her gently, then rougher. She recognized Cindy's voice in her ear.

"Dee, you're dreaming. Wake up."

The brisk shaking roused her out of her nightmare, but it still took Del several seconds to recognize Cindy standing in front of her. The living room seemed foreign to her, and she looked around frantically for Sarah. "Cindy, where is she?"

Cindy looked ashen at the question, but before she could answer, Del knew. She remembered it all, the months of tests, the doctors, the treatments and the sickness. She remembered watching the life slowly drain from her lover until Sarah could no longer get out of bed without help. She remembered holding Sarah that final day as the last flicker of light left her eyes. She remembered feeling as though her world had crumbled around her, and the pain was just as fresh to her as if it were yesterday instead of six months ago.

Cindy held her as the reality overtook her. Del had thought there were no more tears she could cry, but she had been wrong. They came from the depths of her sorrow, as plentiful in number as her love for Sarah had been deep.

"How am I ever going to make it without her, Cindy? She was my life. I thanked God every day for blessing me with her. Now I don't know what to do without her. I can't even sleep in my own bed. I should have sold it, I guess, because I sleep in this damned recliner every night."

Cindy waited, still holding her quietly as Del let her anguish spill out.

"Maybe I was crazy coming back here. I thought it would be easier here for some reason, but it isn't. I still miss her every waking moment of every day. Is it ever going to end?" She dissolved into tears again, this time with her hands over her face.

Cindy leaned in to hold her again, pulling Del tightly against her shoulder. "Dee, Sarah was special. I don't know any two people who loved each other more than you and she. That's why it hurts so bad that she's gone." She paused as if choosing her words carefully. "You haven't lost her completely. I know you'll never forget her, so Sarah will always be with you in your heart." She leaned back and pushed gently on Del's shoulders, getting her to lift her face away from her hands. Del blinked to clear her blurry vision, her face twisted in pain and confusion.

"Dee, I also know Sarah would be mad as hell if she were here right now." Cindy waited for this to sink in. "She would be mad as hell that you haven't been able to move through this grief. What would she say about you sleeping in this recliner? She would chew your ass out, that's what. I see the way you grab your back every time you get up and down. You know as well as I do that spending the night all crumpled up in that chair isn't helping any." She waited a few seconds, then continued. "And that doesn't mean you can't miss her, you know. You just can't let this grief keep you paralyzed forever. I hoped moving here would get you past these nightmares and get you jump-started again. That's what Sarah would want, for you to live again."

Del nodded and sniffled, then reached over for a tissue and blew her nose. She forced a chuckle, then agreed. "She probably would bean me for not sleeping in the bed."

For several moments, Del allowed herself to remember, to let the memories of their love carry her instead of shutting them out in fear of pain. Finally she arose from the recliner and headed into the kitchen, Cindy a step behind her. She reached up and opened the cabinet door above the refrigerator and pulled down a bottle of Seagram's Dark Honey. Cindy handed her two small glasses from the dish drainer, where Del had stacked their supper dishes only a few hours before. Del dropped a couple of ice cubes in each glass, then poured the golden liquid over them. She returned the bottle to its place over the refrigerator, then grabbed her glass and headed back to her recliner. Again Cindy followed silently.

As Del turned to sit, she saw the look of concern on Cindy's face. "Don't worry, Cindy, I'm too scared of becoming my father to hide in a bottle. I just wanted to make a toast, if that's okay with you. Here's to fifteen years of loving and being loved by an angel." Her voice caught, and she cleared her throat before continuing. "I was truly blessed. And here's to good friends, who help you through the tough times." She tapped the side of her glass gently against Cindy's, and they both sipped the sweet, strong liquor.

Cindy set her glass down on the coffee table, but Del continued to hold hers, watching the remaining whiskey wash over the shrinking cubes of ice as she swirled them gently.

"You're making progress, Dee. I don't know if you remember how messed up you were at first. I'm not trying to minimize your grief now, but you are slowly getting there. You've just got to keep plugging away at it. What is it they say? 'Get up and set one foot in front of the other,' or something like that?"

"Yeah, something like that. I guess I can see that too. It is a little easier than it was at first. Sometimes, though, I'll have a bad dream, or something will trigger a memory and I fall apart again. Like tonight...I just never thought I'd have to learn to make it without her, you know?"

"I've got an idea. I'm not trying to make a pass at you, old friend, but let's go to bed."

Del raised her eyebrows and looked sharply at Cindy. "Maybe you better explain that a little more before I agree to anything."

"You haven't slept in that bed for six months. Let's go in there and get a few hours decent sleep on a good mattress instead of you in that recliner and me on your lumpy couch."

"I don't know if I can, Cindy."

"I think you can, and I'll be there if you need me." She grabbed Del's hand and tugged her toward the bedroom door.

Del allowed herself to be pulled along. She was tired, and her back *was* hurting. Besides, Cindy would be there, and she could leave a light on too.

They compromised on allowing the hall light to remain lit, and both lay on top of the covers, pulling a blanket over themselves to keep warm. Del wasn't sure she could tolerate actually climbing between the sheets.

"Good night Dee."

"Good night Cindy. Thank you."

"That's what friends are for."

* * *

The sun filtering between the wooden blinds hit Del in the eyes, awaking her slowly. She looked up, but the blue, peeling paint on the slat-board ceiling gave her no clues as to her location. She scanned the walls across from where she lay, but they were devoid of pictures or other decoration and gave her no further indication. She sat straight up in the bed and looked around, but all she saw was a depression in the pillow beside her. Her senses were slowly coming to life, and she realized at last where she was. The events of the previous night came back to her, and she fell back onto the bed with a groan.

Cindy came through the bedroom door with a cup of coffee in each hand and set one on the bedside table beside Del. She sank down onto the cedar chest against the wall and sipped her own coffee patiently.

"'Bout time you woke up, lazybones. It's going on ten o'clock."

Del just groaned again, rolled over and put a pillow over her head.

Cindy laughed. "How long has it been since you've slept in, Dee? I thought it might do you a little good, so I let you sleep. Besides, you can't work me if you're sleeping."

Del tossed a pillow at her, and Cindy reacted quickly, lifting her cup out of its path. "Easy there, girl. Don't spill my coffee."

Del, giving up on avoiding the day, rolled back to face Cindy, swung her legs over the edge of the bed and sat up. She reached over for the coffee and tried a sip, then set it back down. "Forgot how strong you like your coffee," she commented drily. "Gotta pee." She padded around the bed and out the door toward the bathroom.

A few minutes later, she joined Cindy, who had taken both cups to the living room. "Had breakfast?" Del asked.

"Yes. I had toast and jelly about an hour ago. I was hungry, so I nosed around in your kitchen until I found something."

"Good." Del sat down in her recliner and sipped the strong coffee again.

"You sure are talkative this morning."

"Dang it, Cindy. I'm only half-awake. What do you expect?"

Cindy grinned widely. "You know I love it when you get mad at me. You haven't been mad at me in a long time. That's more like the Dee I love to piss off."

"Glad I could oblige you," Del grumped. "How can you drink this swill?" she asked after trying another sip from her cup.

"Swill?" Cindy drew her eyebrows down in mock offense. "That's good coffee, now, not like that colored water you like to drink." As if to demonstrate, she tilted up her cup and took a large swallow, then leaned back and sighed deeply, grinning broadly.

"Good thing I didn't put a spoon in it. Probably would have stood straight up."

"Shut up and drink it. Then get your butt in gear. We have work to do, and I have to head back to the city in about four hours."

"Okay, don't get your panties in a wad. I'm working on it."

Cindy grinned and waited.

The good-natured bickering continued as they worked together to repair the railing around the porch. Several of the boards were rotten and had to be replaced, but most just needed to be nailed back to the frame of the porch. The finished product was sturdy, although the mixture of old and new wood made for an unusual appearance.

"A layer of paint or stain and it'll look pretty good, Dee."

"Yep. And now I won't be worried about leaning on a rail and falling off on my head. Thought Gus's boy was going to fall *onto* the porch Friday night."

Cindy carried her tools down to her truck and helped Del put them away.

"Think I'll use the rest of the sealant and hit the roof of that shed this afternoon," Del said. "Then I can quit throwing tarps over my saws."

"If it's all right with you, I think I'll leave that job for you and head on back," Cindy said.

"Sure, Cindy. I can get that by myself. You've been babysitting me long enough, don't you think?" Del appreciated the long days Cindy had sacrificed over the past three weekends. She hadn't felt strong enough to turn away Cindy's companionship when she'd offered. "I'm going to finish that roof, then clean up and go do some grocery shopping. I think I can handle it."

"Just buy some Diet Coke for next weekend."

"Are you sure? I really love the help and the company, but you've been here every weekend, and I know you have things you need to do at home."

"Well, Julie will be at work, and coming here means I won't be going out to the bar and getting into trouble without her." Cindy grinned. "Besides, the following two weekends I can't be here. The first weekend we have that benefit dance, and the following Saturday is Julie's birthday. You should try to come up for that, Dee. It'd be good for you to socialize a little. You could become a hermit out here in the boondocks."

Del laughed. "I socialize. I see Gus, Jenny and their boys, Jim and Gary. I also see everyone at work five days a week. My brother even called me last week."

"Your brother called? What did he want?" Del didn't miss the sudden seriousness in Cindy's tone, or the way her smile transformed into a frown.

Del rarely received calls from her brother unless he wanted something. The last time she had seen him was the previous year at the hospital, when their mother had been admitted after a mild stroke. Their mother had lived alone since their father's death three years before that, and after her hospitalization, she required constant supervision. Glen lived with his drinking buddies or his flavor-of-the-month girlfriend. He wouldn't consider staying with their mother at her home, and he had no place of his own to offer. Del and Sarah were already embroiled in Sarah's battle for her life and couldn't take her in either, so Del had made arrangements to place their mother in a long-term care facility in a town a few miles from the small town of Devil's Prairie and she still resided there. Glen had only spoken with Del on the phone a couple of times since then and had never been to the nursing home to see their mother, leaving all of her care for Del to manage.

"I haven't quite figured out what he wanted. He seemed interested in what I was doing. He asked some questions about whether I was farming or leasing the land and if I was living here by myself or not. It was a really odd conversation, considering it was Glen. I know he doesn't care about how I'm doing, but I can't figure out what he was up to. Oh well, at least he didn't ask me for money."

"Dee!"

"Don't worry. Even if I had money, I wouldn't have given it to him." She grinned to try to lessen Cindy's worries. "I learned that lesson a few years ago, remember?"

"I remember. I was just concerned there for a minute that your memory was failing. I know you have a soft heart, Dee, and would give a stranger the shirt off your back. But he's no good. I try not to talk bad about people's family because I know blood ties can be strong, but he would suck you dry if he could, and you know it."

"Yeah, I know. Well, let's get you on the road before more of the day gets away from you."

They both headed into the house to gather Cindy's things and carried them outside to her truck. Cindy tossed her bags into the passenger seat and lodged her thermos of coffee into the floorboard beside the console. Then she turned to grab Del in a firm hug.

"Old woman, take care of yourself. You're too skinny. And you better start sleeping some in that bed before you get hip flexion contractures sleeping sitting up all the time. Oh, and pick me up some Diet Coke for next Saturday!"

"Be careful Cindy. Don't worry, I'm in no danger of wasting away, and I'll do some stretches to loosen up my hips." Del grinned at Cindy's therapy advice. "Really, though, thank you for everything."

"I'll collect someday." Cindy leaped up into the truck and fired it up, then backed down the drive, turned and headed up the hill.

Del stood with a hand on her hip and watched her go, then walked over to the side of the house to get her ladder so she could seal her shed roof.

CHAPTER FOUR

"Gus, I think that ought to do. The fence looks good." Del turned in a slow circle, scanning the yard-perimeter fence and appreciating the work Gus, his two sons and she had just put into it. It was the middle of June, and she was pleased to see that most of the tasks she had needed to complete were finished. Cindy and the Andrews's help had moved things along quickly.

"I agree. If that won't keep old Charlie out, I'll just have to get rid of him." Gus removed his canvas work gloves and shoved them into his back pocket. "Boys, gather the tools and load them up."

Jim and Gary tossed the tools into a plastic bucket of supplies and picked up the wire stretchers and the roll of leftover wire, then packed it all to the back of Gus's truck.

"Keep that extra little bit of wire, Gus. I'll have to buy a lot more than that before I get started on replacing any more fence, and that won't happen this year."

"Thanks Del. I'll use it to patch holes." He followed her up onto the porch and dropped into a chair beside her. "Got any Dr. Pepper?"

Jim and Gary were making their way to the porch, and they looked as hot and thirsty as Del felt. "Jim, why don't you run into the house and grab a Dr. Pepper out of the refrigerator for each of us, unless you'd prefer a Diet Coke? I think Cindy left a few of those in there last weekend."

"Sure Del. Thanks." He ducked quickly into the house, and Gary sat on the steps to wait. In a minute, Jim had returned with three cans of Dr. Pepper and a Diet Coke for himself.

"Watching your figure, Jim? If I didn't know any better, I'd say there's a girl involved," she teased. She had developed an easy companionship with the boys over the past few weeks, and now Jim blushed at her question. This only piqued her interest.

"Don't be too hard on him, Del," Gus warned, heading her off before she could harass him too much. "He's got him a girlfriend, but he's pretty quick to rile over her. You remember being a teenager, don't you?"

"Oh, all right." Del had been running through a list of questions in her head already, but she backed off at Gus's warning. "Well, congratulations, Jim. I hope it turns out good for you."

Jim grinned and ducked his head to hide his ongoing blush. He sat down beside his brother, and the four enjoyed the cool sodas for a few moments in silence.

"What are you doing for the rest of the afternoon, Del?" Jim asked.

After a pause to think, she answered, "I guess I don't really have any plans. It's been a long time since I've been able to say that. But I think I've done about all I can do around here until late next spring. Then I'll think about siding and maybe a new roof, if I can save up enough between now and then to afford it."

"Would you come fishing with me over at Widow's pond? It's well stocked, and I've got a couple dozen worms I bought in town."

Del looked over at Gus, surprised at the invitation. He merely shrugged.

"Okay, that sounds good," she told Jim. "But you'll have to loan me a pole and some tackle. I haven't been fishing in a few years. Sarah didn't care much for it."

Gus looked surprised. Del hadn't casually mentioned Sarah since she'd moved back, and she was a little relieved to recall a memory easily without being upset.

"Del, I'll loan you mine on one condition. You have to guarantee me you won't reel in backward or twist up my line." Gus sounded as serious as he could muster but chuckled when she punched him in the shoulder.

"If I remember right, you were the reason no one would ever loan us their stuff. You always turned the open-face reels backward or got tangled up when you cast out."

"I don't think you remember right, Del. Like I said, you tangle it up, you gotta untangle it before you give it back." Gus looked as if he was trying not to laugh.

"Guess beggars can't be choosers, but you don't have anything to worry about, old boy. Why, I'll be lucky if I can even cast it, from all the tangles you already have in it."

"If you can't, I'll loan you one of mine, Del." Gary was the peacemaker, like his mother, even though their bantering was all good-natured.

"Well, thank you, Gary. You're a very generous young man. You didn't even attach any conditions like your old man here. Jenny must be really proud of you."

Gary blushed this time.

"Gary, let's head to the house. We'll let Del bring Jim over to get the poles and the tackle. Mom said something about baking an apple pie today. Maybe she'll feel sorry for us and let us sample it, being as we're left behind while the others go have fun." Gus arose from his chair and, after the boys moved from the steps, he followed Gary toward the truck. When he reached it, he turned to look back at Del standing on the porch steps.

"I'm glad you moved back. I forgot how much I enjoyed our friendship." Then, in a lighter tone, he added, "But don't think that means you can tangle my fishing line."

"Thanks Gus. Me too. We'll be over shortly." *I wonder what brought that on. Gus is getting sentimental on me.*

It was a beautiful afternoon for fishing. The weather was in the eighties, there was only a slight breeze and the sky was clear. She found a clear spot on the pond's bank and sat down to fish off the bottom while Jim headed out with a topwater plug to fish for bass around the reeds at the shallow end. She watched him land a couple of good-sized bass and drop them into a large bucket of water. She caught a few small catfish but released them all to grow more. She didn't get up when she heard an ATV approaching but watched as it stopped at the far end of the pond near Jim. She wasn't sure who was aboard but assumed it was Widow or her son. After a few minutes, the rider directed the four-wheeler toward her.

As it pulled closer, her earlier assumptions were confirmed. Del smiled a greeting, but the tip of her pole bent to the ground in the next second, focusing her attention back to bringing in another fish. She reeled in the twelve-inch mudcat, trying to contain her excitement. She stopped short of dancing a little jig but couldn't contain the smile splitting her face ear to ear. She had forgotten how much fun it was to fish, especially when you caught a good one. Jim gave her a thumbs-up from the other side of the pond as she lifted the fish into the air by its bottom lip. She turned to see a grinning Widow watching her from astride the ATV, and Del wondered how she appeared to this woman. A thirty-seven-year-old woman about to jump up and down on a pond bank because she caught a fish big enough to eat probably looked a little silly, she decided.

Del smiled sheepishly and tried to explain. "It's been a while since I've caught a keeper."

"That's why I stocked this pond, so people could enjoy themselves a little bit. We fill our lives with work and stress and forget to have fun." Widow swung her leg from over the ATV and grabbed the empty bucket sitting nearby. She filled it with pond water while Del removed the hook from the catfish's hard lip. After Del dropped it into the bucket, she sat down on the pond bank to bait her hook again. Widow squatted on her heels a few feet from her.

"Did you get your fence fixed?"

Del was so focused on fishing that she was momentarily surprised by the question. "Oh yeah. We did it this morning.

Jim and I are celebrating, I guess. I've got an extra pole lying up there if you want to join us."

"Not today. I can only stay for a little bit. I heard your truck pull in here and just came down to check it out. I figured it was Gus or one of the boys, but I was surprised to see you. Come by the house when you finish and I'll give you a key to the gate, if you want."

"Thanks, I'll do that." Del was pleased at the trust she heard in Widow's voice. Gus had told her Widow was a little cautious in her dealings with people she didn't know. He had mentioned a few scoundrels had tried to cheat her when she was new to the area and she had learned quickly to keep up her guard, so the offer of a key meant a great deal to Del. Del supposed Gus had probably put in a good word for her.

"How's your house coming along? You said you had a lot to do when you were here after those posts a few weeks ago."

"I think it'll do for now. I might do more next spring, after I save up for a few months and the weather is good again." Del chuckled. "Cindy will be glad for the break. I think she was getting tired of spending every weekend here."

"Oh, will you be spending more weekends in St. Louis, then?" Widow asked as she stared out at the water.

Puzzled, Del followed her gaze. Seeing nothing unusual on the pond surface, she looked back toward Widow. "No, I hadn't really planned on it," she said, confused.

Widow looked at her shyly before hesitantly continuing, "I guess I must have had it wrong, then. I thought maybe there was more than just a friendship there."

Del laughed loudly, then tried to stifle it as Widow's cheeks reddened. "I'm sorry to laugh. I guess someone who didn't know us might get that impression." Unable to contain it, she chuckled again, then continued, smiling broadly, "You got it partly right. Cindy and I are both lesbians and we've been friends for a lot of years, but just friends. She's kind of like the little sister I never had. We just look out for each other, you know?"

Del thought about all Cindy had done to help her in the past months. She winced as a shaft of pain shot through her along with the memories. "Yeah, Cindy's a good friend, and I don't know if I would've made it this far without her." Her eyes misted over, and she blinked several times, then stared out at where her line disappeared into the water.

Out of the corner of her eye, she saw Jim make his way up onto the pond bank. "Here comes Jim. Wonder if he's fished out." She changed the subject, eager to turn her thoughts in a different direction, pushing the pain down to the deep recesses where she kept it stored. She reeled her line in and removed the uneaten bait before tossing it into the water for the turtles.

Widow arose from the ground and stood quietly beside her ATV, watching Del gather her things. When Jim neared, she greeted him again, breaking the tense silence on the pond bank.

Del attempted to return to her carefree attitude as she and Jim compared their three fish. Eventually, they decided just three were not enough to worry about cleaning, so they released them into the pond.

They followed Widow back to her house, and she went inside to find a gate key for Del. Widow handed her a small rainbow keychain with a padlock key attached. Del quickly placed it in her pocket, unwilling to infer any meaning from the plastic design.

Widow made no attempt to return to their earlier conversation, and Del led them to decidedly impersonal topics. She knew Widow probably wondered about the sudden change in her attitude, but she had no intention of returning to the painful memories to which her mind had so easily taken her.

"How long have you locked your gates?" Del queried.

"Probably about five or six years."

"Wow! That long, huh. I thought this rustling thing was a fairly recent problem."

Widow looked away this time. "Yeah, well, I started locking them because of a stalker, not because of rustlers."

"Oh." Del mentally shook herself for forgetting she may not be the only one with unwanted memories. "Sorry."

"Yeah, me too. But that was a long time ago, and I just never stopped. Now it seems like it would be foolish to remove the padlocks with rustlers in the area."

"Good point," Del conceded. "What does Gus think about it all?"

Jim had remained quiet until now, and despite Del directing the question to Widow, he interjected, "Dad says if a rustler wants your cows bad enough, he'll ram the gate or cut the fence. He says a lock won't help."

Widow shook her head in disagreement. "It might discourage them. If it turns one rustler away, it's worth it."

"Jim, I think I agree with Widow on this one," Del stated.

Jim shrugged, obviously not willing to take a side.

"Widow, thank you for letting us fish, and for the key," Del said. "I'd better get Jim home before Gus comes looking for him. Come by and see me sometime."

"Bye Widow," Jim added.

"You're always welcome, Del. You too, Jim." Widow waved briefly before walking back to her house.

Jim and Del were silent as they drove away. Finally, he cleared his throat. "Uh, Del?"

Del startled from her thoughts. She looked over at Jim and was surprised to see how uncomfortable he appeared. Unsure of what the problem could be, she pulled over to the side of the road and stopped the truck. "Jim, are you okay?" She put a hand on his shoulder.

He cast his gaze to the floor of the truck. "Yeah, I'm okay. I just wondered, just wanted to…just thought maybe…" Then, in a rush, he blurted out, "I thought maybe I could talk to you about something, if that's okay."

Now she was really puzzled. "Jim, you can talk to me about anything. Is everything okay at home? What's up?"

"Well," he continued hesitantly, "I met this girl, you know, Lisa. And…and… I just wondered if I could ask for some advice."

"Lisa, huh? Tell me about her. Does she go to your school?"

"Yeah, she's a year behind me. She plays volleyball and is really smart, like scary smart." He seemed to relax a little as he described her, and Del could see how interested he was as he talked. "Her mom's an English teacher at my school, and her dad's a lineman for the rural electric co-op. She's really pretty, but all the guys are scared of her because she's so smart. I caught a lot of crap from them when she agreed to go out with me. That was two months ago, and we're still dating."

"Ooh, sounds serious." Del tried not to belittle his feelings, remembering first love and how magnified everything could seem. "So, what's the problem?"

"Everyone at school seems to go from first date to looking at rings. But it's not like that with Lisa and me. We like to laugh and have a good time. We enjoy the same music, the same type of movies and that kind of thing. My buddies keep asking what's up, like are we seeing other people, are we sleeping together. We just don't seem to do things like everyone else, you know?"

Del thought for a few moments, then asked carefully, "Do you and Lisa think there's a problem or just your friends?"

"Just the guys, I guess."

"You know, Jim, I've made some decisions in the past that haven't been popular, and it's never easy. I lost a few friends along the way, but I've learned that the ones that really matter stick with you."

Jim was nodding but still didn't look at Del.

"As long as Lisa and you are happy with the way your relationship is going, I don't see any reason to change. I don't know what to tell you about how to make it easier to deal with your friends. Maybe think about it this way—Lisa is your friend too, and I know what she thinks means a lot to you. Remember, the friends who matter will stick by you even if you don't do what's popular."

"Thanks Del. I knew you'd understand what I'm up against. You're not afraid to be different." This time, Jim did look at her, and his obvious admiration struck her in a way she hadn't felt before. As a lesbian in Missouri in the nineties, and even in the new millennium, she had been reminded many times of how wrong many people felt her differences were. Although she ignored their disapproval, this was the first time she had been so openly appreciated for her willingness to be true to herself.

"Thank you Jim. Thank you." She pulled the truck out into the road again, her mood restored to its nearly carefree level from earlier in the day.

CHAPTER FIVE

The following Friday had been a busy day, and Del was running behind, as usual. She had resisted the urge to work late and now had only a few minutes to make it to dinner at the Andrews's house on time. She placed one key for her new gate padlock on her key ring and the other into an envelope for Gus. She would give Gus his key at dinner and put the lock on the gate the next day. Just as she reached to turn off her lamp, the phone rang.

What now? I don't want to be late.

Del reached for the phone on the end table. "Hello?"

"Hello, is this Del Smith?" The soft, feminine voice sounded slightly familiar, but she couldn't quite identify it.

"Speaking. Who is this?"

"This is Widow Jennings."

"Oh. Hello Widow. How can I help you?"

"Well, we're having a birthday dinner tomorrow afternoon at my house. My daughter Jessie turned twenty-four yesterday. I always celebrate the kids' birthdays with a big meal and invite friends and neighbors over to share the celebration. I know you don't know her, but Gus and Jenny and the boys are coming, and I thought it would be a good chance for you to get to know some of us better."

"Well, I guess I don't have any plans. What time and what do I need to bring?"

"We never do gifts, just food. And we have plenty, so all you need to bring is your appetite, about four o'clock."

"Thanks. Well, I guess I'll see you then."

"Okay, see you then."

Del placed the phone down and smiled. *Dinner two nights in a row. I'm becoming a regular social butterfly. Gotta remember to tell Cindy!*

At Gus and Jenny's, Del handed Gus the envelope containing his padlock key.

"What's this?" He looked puzzled as he peered inside.

"I know there's been a local problem with cattle rustling, and I've decided to lock my gate. You'll find a padlock on it starting tomorrow."

"You're starting to sound like Widow. If a rustler wants to steal cattle, a little piece of metal won't stop them. They'll just tear through a fence, cut the lock or take the gate off its hinges."

"I know Widow locks her gates, but this is my decision, Gus. There may be no fail-safe method of deterring them, but they're going to have to work a little harder if they're going to steal from my property."

"Have it your way, Del. You always were stubborn."

Jenny grabbed Del by the hand and steered her toward the kitchen, where she was finishing dinner preparations. "You know Gus is bullheaded," she said. "It's useless to argue with him. Come and tell me how you've been."

Del hadn't known Jenny well until she returned to the area, but the two had quickly become close friends. She felt nearly as comfortable with Jenny as she had with her closest friends in St. Louis and welcomed the chance to talk.

"Things have been good, Jenny."

"That's all I get, 'good'? How is work?"

"Good."

"How is Cindy?"

"Good."

Jenny tossed a dish towel at her in mock anger.

"Really Jenny. Things are okay. I don't have anything interesting to tell you."

"You look like you've been sleeping better. The dark circles are gone. And you seem more relaxed."

"Well, I think I'm starting to do a little better. I'm not sleeping in the recliner anymore. I still have a nightmare every now and then, but not every night like I used to. I still miss her, more than I know what to do with, but, I guess overall, I'm just good."

"Good." Jenny laughed at her word choice. "Really, I'm glad you're doing better. I don't know if you realize how much it means to Gus and me having you around. The boys too. Gus was kind of lost after his parents passed. He said he felt like an orphan. You coming back gave him back his childhood friend—a sister, almost. And it gave me an ally. All this testosterone around constantly can get overwhelming. You're like a breath of fresh air, and you hold your own against this rowdy crew."

"Thanks Jenny. I'm glad I found such good friends and neighbors in you and Gus. So what's tonight all about? Is this a special occasion or something?"

"I think it would qualify as that. Jim asked if he could invite a friend over for dinner and asked if we would invite you also."

Del looked at her in confusion until Jenny added, "A *girl* friend."

"Ooh, I see. Would this be Lisa?"

"He's talked to you about her?" Jenny turned sharply to look at her.

"Kind of. He just wanted to know how to deal with some peer pressure, that's all." Del summed up the conversation with Jim briefly, trying to be respectful of his confidence in her.

A bustling outside the back door alerted them to the boys coming in from finishing chores. Jim rushed past Del with a quick hi.

"He's got to get gussied up before his girl gets here," Gary informed her in a singsong voice.

"Just wait, Gary. Your turn is coming. He'll be just as mean to you as you are to him," Jenny warned her younger son, and he grinned and dropped his head.

"Okay Mom."

Del grinned at the control Jenny had over her sons. She had seen her settle Gus just as quickly and wondered how this quiet power worked. Sarah had effortlessly wielded the same power over her, she remembered. Del would have jumped to the moon if she had asked. Her heart tripped as she recalled the depth of feelings they had for each other, and she shook herself back to the present.

"So Jenny. Widow called just before I left the house. She said you guys are going to this birthday dinner tomorrow."

"Yeah. We go every year, for both Jessie's and Johnnie's birthdays. Jessie doesn't live at home anymore, but Widow said she still wanted to have a dinner. Why, are you coming too?"

"I guess so. She said not to bring anything."

"She'll have enough food there for an army. We won't be bringing anything. I try to always go over an hour early to help her get ready, but that's all." Jenny bustled around, setting the last of the food onto the table.

"Why don't you let me come by and pick you up, and we can both get there early to help?" Del suggested.

"Okay, sounds like a plan. Now I think I just heard a car pull up outside." Jenny stepped over toward the door. "Jim, I think Lisa is here," she yelled into the hallway that led to his room.

Jim was a nervous wreck through the main course but had settled down some by the time they got to dessert. Del found Lisa to be as smart as Jim had indicated, and she seemed to have a temperament similar to his. After dinner, the young couple headed into town to see a movie, and Lisa suggested they take Gary along, winning him over completely.

Jenny and Del loaded the dishwasher and cleaned the kitchen quickly while Gus carried out the trash. Then the adults gathered in the kitchen for a three-handed card game of hand

and foot. After a few rounds to remind Del of the rules, the battle was on. After the final round, Jenny was clearly victorious and Gus and Del were left by the roadside, licking their wounds.

"Gus, she is brutal. Where did you find this woman?"

"She was sweet and innocent when I married her. I don't know what happened."

"Probably all those years putting up with you in this house full of males." Del laughed and poked him hard in the arm.

"I don't know, Del. You showed very little mercy yourself. And I know you haven't been surrounded by males all these years," Gus shot back at her.

"Oh shut up, Gus. You're just jealous."

"Enough, you two. You argue as much as the boys do," Jenny chided. "I don't know how either of you got along without the other all these years."

Del and Gus looked at each other and grinned. They had squabbled as kids too, but never seriously. At the end of the day, they would always be friends again. Del could only remember one time when their relationship had been strained. They must have been sixteen or seventeen, and they'd attended different high schools, so they didn't see each other as often as they had before. At that time, Del wasn't sure what she wanted, but she knew she never mooned over the boys at school the way her friends did.

Gus had come over to see her one weekend and was acting really strange. They had played cards for a while, then he got up to refill his glass. On the way back to his chair, he stopped behind her and gently moved her hair back behind her shoulders. Del froze. *Don't do it, Gus!* her mind screamed, but she remained frozen and silent. He paused, apparently sensing her apprehension, then walked back to his chair. Del resumed breathing when he sat down, and they continued their game as if nothing had happened. For several months after that, she was cautious around him, and Gus seemed distant around her too. But now Gus was obviously head over heels for Jenny, and he had found out with the rest of the community that Del was a lesbian when she left town all those years ago.

She wondered if he even remembered that day but didn't want to ruin their easy friendship by bringing up awkward memories. Some things were just better left in the past.

Del yawned widely, unable to hide her fatigue any longer. "Well folks. I think it's past my bedtime. Thank you both for dinner. Jenny, I guess I'll see you tomorrow, a little before three." She had enjoyed the evening more than she could remember enjoying anything in quite a while.

"Sure Del. We'll see you then. Have a good night." Jenny hugged her briefly, and Gus walked her to the front door.

"Thanks for the key, Del. I still think it's foolish, but it's your land."

"I know. But I'll rest better if I add the padlock. Good night Gus."

"Night Del."

* * *

Saturday morning, Del attached a chain and padlock around her gate. Then she drove her truck twenty miles north to the county seat, where she worked. Her small town consisted of a couple of gas stations and a post office, but the county seat was larger and had a community recreation center that some of her co-workers had recommended to her and which she'd decided to visit. She dressed in sweats over a T-shirt and shorts, uncertain if she would get in a workout or merely look around.

Del was impressed with the recreation center's lobby, which had comfortable furniture and an eclectic assortment of artwork on the walls. When she read the cards below each painting, she discovered they were all by local artists.

Del spoke briefly to the young woman at the front desk, saying she was interested in a membership. The petite blonde handed her a stack of brochures regarding their services, then left to get an athletic trainer who would take her on a tour of the building. She returned shortly with a squarely built woman wearing shorts, a sleeveless T-shirt, and a whistle around her neck. Her name tag identified her as "J.T. Simon, ATC." Del would have guessed her to be in her late twenties, but she knew from experience she didn't guess ages well.

Del reached out to shake her hand and was pleased by the firm handshake she received. "Del Smith. Nice to meet you, J.T."

"Likewise Del. I understand you're new to the area, and we like to provide a guided tour to prospective members, if you're interested."

"I'd like that very much. I didn't interrupt anything, did I?" She pointed to the whistle around J.T.'s neck.

"No. I was helping to ref a pickup game on the basketball courts, but I'm sure they'll get along fine without me."

The two women spent the next twenty minutes making the rounds of the center. Del was impressed by the way J.T. handled herself. When they'd passed through the ball courts, she had firmly but kindly dealt with some unhappy teenagers squabbling over a foul, and she was knowledgeable about all the equipment. Del also hadn't missed the winks exchanged between J.T. and a woman with well-developed muscles working out with free weights.

As Del filled out the paperwork for membership at the center, J.T. sat quietly behind her small desk, watching through the large windows as the joggers made their circuit around the park. She filed Del's paperwork away, made her a membership card, then calmly asked her out to dinner sometime.

Del froze at the invitation. Although she had a positive first impression of this young woman, she wasn't sure what to say. She was also surprised by J.T.'s openness. She didn't want to seem rude, but a date was not something she was ready to consider.

J.T. suddenly looked flushed. "I'm sorry if I was presumptuous..."

"No, there's nothing to apologize for," Del reassured her. "You just took me by surprise, that's all. At another time, I might take you up on the offer. This just isn't the right time for me."

"Okay, I understand. Well, I hope you enjoy your membership here at the center, and maybe the time will be right in the future."

"Maybe." Del shook J.T.'s hand again and walked out of the building, slipping her membership card into her wallet. She dropped her head a notch as she wondered if she would ever be able to let someone get close again and whether she would ultimately survive Sarah's death. Thinking about it scared her more than she cared to admit.

She stopped at the edge of town at the MFA convenience store for gas and a soda. She grabbed her regular, a Dr. Pepper, from the shelf in the cooler and picked up a bag of peanuts near the counter.

The cashier smiled at her as she stepped forward to pay. "Lunch?" she asked Del.

Del stopped here often on her way home from work, and the staff had become used to seeing her. She frequently had chips and a soda on the way home so she wouldn't have to cook a meal. She knew Sarah would have kicked her butt for eating so unhealthily, but she hadn't managed to start caring whether she was eating right or not again. Now she felt a little silly that her bad habits were becoming common knowledge.

She grinned sheepishly, then admitted, "Yeah, I guess. I'm going to a birthday dinner later, so I'll eat right then." She added the last as a hopeful explanation of her behavior.

"Well, I guess that makes it all right." The cashier gave her a disapproving look that said differently.

Del took the chiding in stride, considering this woman was nearly a stranger. She knew the concern was valid. She had lost thirty-five pounds over the last several months. The first twenty-five were good riddance, but she was ten pounds below her ideal weight and knew she looked too thin. Funny how when she tried to lose, she couldn't, and now she needed to gain. She gave the cashier a smile as she picked up her purchases and headed out. "Have a good one," she called back over her shoulder.

"You too," she heard, just before the heavy glass door swung closed behind her.

On the drive back, Del made herself a few promises. With her new gym membership, she had no excuse not to get back into shape. Now she needed to start thinking about better nutrition. She decided she would pick up some soups and ingredients for a salad. That would be a quick and easy meal after work that would be a step up from chips. She wasn't ready to give up her Dr. Pepper though. Sarah had always told her the soda was the reason she couldn't lose weight. Maybe now, if she began eating more regularly, the soda would help her put weight on.

"One step at a time," she said quietly as she slid out of her truck at the post office. She had been wrapped up in her thoughts, and she startled when someone spoke.

"What?" The one word came from the open passenger window of the truck she had parked beside. When she turned to look, she observed a scruffy man, maybe in his forties, his face hidden behind a thick, dark beard, and a misshaped and sweat-stained ball cap sitting at a slight tilt atop his head. She didn't answer immediately, unsure if he had spoken to her or if he had heard her speaking to herself.

"Were you talking to me?" the man asked, his voice rough and loud, defensive.

"No. Sorry. I guess you caught me talking to myself." Del smiled, trying to be sociable to the stranger. Most people she had seen around town were now strangers, she'd realized. Even if she had known them years ago, they had changed enough in appearance while she had been away that she recognized very few.

"Oh. They say that's bad, you know, talking to yourself." The man's words were friendlier, but somehow his tone of voice and his eyes did not match them.

"Yeah, that's what I've heard." Del waved slightly and turned back toward the post office. Another man she didn't recognize was exiting through the door. He had on old jeans with a tear on the lower pant leg and a faded plaid shirt with the sleeves ripped off. He nodded at Del as he passed, and she nodded in return, the typical greeting among strangers around the area. An irrational uneasy feeling settled over her, and from behind the tinted windows in the post office lobby, she turned to watch them drive away. The white, diesel dually was loud as the driver gunned the engine, and although Del seemed to remember seeing the truck before, she couldn't place it now. It came to her suddenly—their eyes, that was it. There was something about the way they had watched her. She mulled over it as she unlocked her post office box, but quickly forgot the men when she found a letter inside from Julie.

She stepped over to the small counter in the corner of the room and set down the rest of her mail so she could open the envelope. She had begged off going to the city for Julie's birthday celebration. She just hadn't been ready to face everyone yet and could only hope Julie would understand.

The envelope felt as though it contained an invitation of some sort, and this thought gained credence when she pulled a second envelope from inside the first. As she read the card inside, her smile broadened. "Well, I'll be damned," she said under her breath as she read it again.

Julie Nicole Jameson
&
Cindy Jean Collins

Wish to invite you
To their
ENGAGEMENT PARTY
5:00 P.M.
September 6, 2011

Inside was a smaller card explaining the party would be at Julie's apartment and the couple would be traveling to Iowa in the spring to be married.

"I can't believe she didn't call me," Del said, shaking her head in wonder.

She punched in Cindy's number on her way to the truck and wasted no time when Cindy answered. "Something you've been keeping from me, old buddy?" she asked.

"Dee! Guess you got your invitation, huh? Julie made me promise not to tell anyone ahead of time or you would have been the first to know, I swear. Good thing you're so far away or I probably would have slipped up and told."

"It sure is a shock. Are you sure? I mean, I think Julie's great for you, Cindy, but it's only been a few months, hasn't it?"

Cindy answered in a quieter tone, as if hesitant to dispel Del's initial excitement. "Dee, I've been seeing Julie for nine months now."

Del was confused. How had that much time passed? It couldn't be possible. But then she remembered. Cindy had started seeing Julie before Sarah took that last turn for the worse. Julie had been with her at the funeral, had driven Cindy's truck home when Cindy had gone with Del. The flash of memory to the funeral left Del sweating and feeling nauseous, but she tried to concentrate on Cindy's voice on the phone to drag her back to the here and now.

"Dee, you okay? Dee?"

"Uh…yeah. I guess you're right. I guess it has been a while." She took a quick drink of Dr. Pepper and made an effort to inject some excitement back into her tone again. "So, what have you got planned?"

"Well, the party is for all the family and friends. Iowa is too far for everyone to drive to, and organizing a wedding at such a distance is more than I want to tackle. We thought we'd have the party here first and celebrate the anniversary of our first date at the same time. Then we'll go to Iowa in the spring and make it official. What do you think?" Cindy's voice became more enlivened as she spoke, and Del couldn't help but catch some of her joy as she listened.

"Cindy, I'm so happy for you both. Is there anything I can do to help out?"

"No. Just show up. Julie's little sister is a party planner, so she's got us taken care of. That's why you received such a formal invitation. You know me—I probably would've settled for sending a group text."

Del laughed at this, in complete agreement with her. Formality had never been either of their strong suits.

"Dee, I do need one thing though."

"What's that? You know I'll do anything for you."

"I want you to stand up with me, be my best whatever, best woman, I guess. Will you go to Iowa with us?"

"Cindy, I'm honored. Of course I will. Just let me know the date."

"You know, we might have to wait until March or April if the winter is bad. I'll let you know the date and give it to you in writing when we're closer to the time so I'm sure you don't forget it or get it mixed up. I remember who I'm talking to here."

"Good idea. Sarah always kept me on track."

"Dee, I gotta go. Julie's been waiting for me to run to the grocery store with her. I'll call you soon?"

"Yeah. Tell Julie congratulations and wish her a happy birthday for me. Love you both."

"Love you too, Dee. Bye."

"Bye." Del hung up and sat in the truck for a few minutes, staring at the brick front of the post office. Del was surprised Cindy was taking such a big step. After Brenda had left her, Cindy swore off serious relationships and went through a series of women. Del couldn't even remember names to attach to most of them. Cindy would bring them around once or twice, then they'd be gone, replaced by the next one. If Del hadn't been so distracted, she probably would have noticed Julie hadn't disappeared after a couple of weeks. But then, her mind had been on other things, and a lot of the details of life had seemed to slip past her.

She arrived home in time to change into a pair of black jeans and a short-sleeved shirt before going over to the Andrews's to pick up Jenny. Jenny was watching for her to pull into the driveway and stepped out onto the porch before Del could turn the truck off. She tossed her purse onto the center of the seat and stepped up into the truck easily.

"All ready," Jenny said simply. She had on a pair of slacks and a silky blouse, and her hair was swept back into a French braid.

"I feel underdressed," Del said. "Jenny, you look great."

"Thanks Del. But you look fine also. You won't be underdressed, trust me. I just seldom get a chance to dress up, so I take advantage of the opportunity when I get it." Jenny fastened her seat belt and settled in for the ride.

"Gus is crazy, then," Del said. "I need to talk to him. He needs to take you out someplace fancy at least once a month so you can get all spiffied up." She couldn't help but notice the time Jenny must have taken with her makeup and her hair. Jenny was a very attractive woman, and although Del's feelings toward her were purely platonic, Del had a hard time not staring.

"In the beginning, we did go out—dancing, to movies, to parties, you know. But then the boys came along and life settled in. I guess we just got old." Jenny sounded wistful and looked out the passenger window at the passing trees.

"Yeah, I understand. Sarah and I did the same thing until we found out she was sick. Then everything became more urgent. Time wasn't on our side, and we had so many things we wanted to do. Every chance I had, if she was feeling well enough, I tried to make it special for her. She liked to get all fixed up and we would go out to a nice restaurant, then maybe to a show or maybe just for a walk in the park to count the stars." Del was staring ahead at the road, but in her mind she could clearly see Sarah in her favorite dress, twirling in front of her on the sidewalk in the park. She had been so beautiful, it had made Del's breath catch to look at her.

"That's a wonderful memory." Jenny squeezed Del's hand where it rested on the truck seat. "Most of us forget to treasure our special moments until they're gone."

Del felt a tear trace its way across her cheek and reached up to wipe it away. She was surprised to find both cheeks wet and abandoned the unsuccessful attempt to dry her face. "I guess, in a strange way, we were lucky. We knew our time was short and we made the most of it. Some people never get that chance."

"That's right Del. Maybe Gus and I can learn something from you." Jenny gave her a smile as Del turned to look at her. She fished a clean tissue from her purse, then handed it to Del. Del wiped her cheeks and stuffed the damp wad of paper into her pants pocket.

"I'm sorry Jenny. I don't mean to get all gloomy on you. We're going to a birthday party and I need to get happy."

"That's all right, Del. You're getting there."

She remembered Cindy's engagement as she turned onto Widow's road. "I've got some good news! Cindy and Julie are engaged!"

"That's great! Was this a sudden decision?"

"Well, I thought it was. But I guess I'd kind of lost track of things a little." Del grinned sheepishly. "She and Julie have been dating for nine months, so I guess not. I'm surprised Julie caught her. Cindy's been rather free-spirited the past few years, if you know what I mean. There'll be more than a few broken hearts in St. Louis. Many women have tried to land her and failed."

"Good for Julie, then. Well, looks like we're the first ones here." Jenny opened her door after Del parked her truck to the side of the driveway.

Del hung a step or two behind Jenny as they got out, hoping her early arrival would be helpful to Widow as she intended and not a hindrance. She didn't know Widow well, but, for reasons she didn't quite understand, it was important to her that Widow see her in a positive light.

Jenny knocked on the door, and Widow quickly answered. She ushered them both in, and Jenny deftly explained Del was with her to provide additional help in getting ready for the party. To Del's relief, Widow accepted her warmly and led them to the large kitchen, where she had been multitasking so all the food would be ready at about the same time. She quickly delegated tasks to each of them as she kept Johnnie busy in the dining room and living room, setting up card tables and folding chairs to accommodate their expected guests. Del was dumping fried green beans from a cast-iron skillet into a large bowl when she heard the front door open and close.

"That must be Jessie," Jenny said.

"Can you take over stirring this gravy when you get your hands empty?" Widow asked Del.

"Sure." Del set the empty skillet down and grabbed the spoon from her. Widow flashed her a warm smile, and Del found herself returning it. Their gazes held for a couple of seconds, and Del was uncertain of what she saw in the depths of Widow's sparkling, blue eyes. Then Widow turned away and headed to the front of the house to catch up with her daughter.

Del turned toward Jenny when she heard her murmur softly. "Did you say something, Jenny?"

Jenny just shrugged innocently. "No, guess I must have been clearing my throat."

"Oh, okay." Del returned to stirring the gravy without giving it another thought.

In the other room, Widow hugged her elder child.

"Mom, how have you been? You look good. Sorry I'm late, but I had to work this morning. George called in sick."

"You're fine. You're here in plenty of time. How are you? Did you come by yourself?" Widow looked behind her expectantly.

"Yes Mom. And before you ask, no, there is no one serious right now. I promise I'll let you know when there is."

"I know." She tucked an errant hair back behind Jessie's ear. "I just worry about you being alone in this world." Widow frowned in concern for her daughter.

"You've been alone most of these years and seem to be doing okay."

"Maybe. We'll have to talk about that someday, but not now. Come on in. Jenny's in the kitchen, and I'll introduce you to our new neighbor."

"Hi Jessie." Jenny stopped mashing potatoes long enough to step over and give her a hug. Widow waited until Jenny moved to introduce Jessie to Del. Del had glanced briefly over her shoulder at the women but was keeping most of her attention on the unfamiliar task of stirring gravy.

"Del Smith, this is my daughter, Jessie, or J.T. I guess that's what she goes by now. She thinks it sounds more official for work, or something like that. But we still call her Jessie."

"Mom." The one word of obvious complaint went unanswered.

Del stopped stirring and turned to greet the newcomer, trying to place the voice and name but unable to do so. As soon as she saw the squarely built woman standing beside Widow, recognition immediately hit her. She blushed momentarily, unsure how Widow might react to the fact she was asked out on a date by her daughter only hours before. She recovered quickly, however, and hoped she sounded normal when she spoke.

"Hello again J.T. I didn't realize you were Widow's daughter." Del set down her stirring spoon long enough to shake the other woman's hand, explaining to a puzzled Jenny and Widow as she did, "I signed up for a membership at the rec center this morning, and J.T. gave me the grand tour." She picked up her spoon and half-turned back to her pan of gravy, still able to see the others over her shoulder.

"Good to see you again, Del. I didn't expect it to be quite so soon though. I didn't even look at your address on your paperwork or I would have asked if you knew Mom."

"I moved to the old farmhouse next to Jenny and Gus's place a couple of months ago. Gus is an old friend from when we were kids."

"Oh, so you grew up around here, then?"

Del couldn't help but notice J.T.'s eagerness to learn more about her. She didn't want to encourage J.T., so her answer was brief and to the point. "Yeah. I lived here until I was eighteen. Then I left for college and only came back infrequently." Del thought about her rocky relationship with her family and wondered why she had returned home at all.

J.T. crossed the room to lean against the counter beside the stove. "That old farmhouse is still standing? You must have been pretty busy getting it fixed up."

"Yeah, it has. That's why I hadn't been working out anywhere recently. I've been getting my workout doing home renovations." Del allowed a small smile.

"Jessie, come into the dining room with me for a minute and see what your brother has done." Widow waved her daughter toward the door.

Jessie frowned slightly as she pushed herself away from the counter but followed her mother as requested.

Jenny wasted no time and came over to whisper to Del, "Is there something going on here I've missed out on?"

"I just met J.T. this morning, Jenny. But she asked me out to dinner already," Del whispered.

"What?" Del shushed Jenny quickly. "She didn't waste any time, did she? Well, that explains a lot."

"I'm glad it explains it to you, now explain it to me." Del had picked up a note of disapproval in Widow's tone before she left the room and was suddenly worried she had ruined a good friendship before it really got started. "Does Widow even know she dates women?"

"Oh yeah. That's not a problem. By the way, what did you say?" Jenny's tone was nonchalant.

"What did I say about what?"

"The date, of course. What did you say?"

"Oh." Del had thought her answer would have been obvious. "I said no. I'm not anywhere near even thinking about another woman. I don't know if I ever will be. Sarah was my forever, you know."

"I don't know, Del. I think you might surprise yourself."

Del responded with a glare that said it all.

In the dining room, Widow cornered her daughter. "Don't you think she's a little old for you, Jessie?"

"I thought maybe you had gotten her for my birthday." Jessie's teasing tone did nothing to lessen her mother's frown. "Oh, don't worry, Mom. I don't think she's into me anyway. She turned me down this morning."

"You don't waste any time, do you? You just met her and you already asked her out? What happened to getting to know someone a little first? And what if she had been straight and homophobic? You would have stirred a nest of hornets then." Widow shook her head.

"Did you look at her, Mom? Of course she's gay. Maybe if you weren't so cautious, you would have more luck in catching a man," J.T. retorted. Widow immediately turned away from her. "Mom, I'm sorry."

"Jessie, we need to talk," Widow began. She was interrupted by knocking at the front door, followed by the sounds of Johnnie talking to Gus and the boys as he let them into the house. "And we will talk, later. For now, though, let's just have a good day, celebrate your birthday and enjoy our company, shall we?" She turned to smile at her daughter and received a smile in return. "Go see Gus and crew while I rescue the gravy. I'm not sure our new neighbor knows what she's doing."

Widow was correct. Del had just turned to ask Jenny if she should do something besides stirring the gravy when Widow came back in the room. She saw the uncertain look in Del's eyes and quickly intervened.

"Here, let me take that spoon," she said. "This gravy will be so thick it may stand up and walk across the room." She moved quickly to add more milk in an attempt to thin it.

"Sorry," Del said. "I never was much of a gravy maker. I left that to…others."

"Did I hear Gus and the boys come in?" Jenny asked.

"Yes. Johnnie let them in. I think they're all in the living room. Why don't you both go join them while I finish up in here?" Widow suggested.

"I think I'll take you up on that before I ruin more than the gravy," Del teased.

Jenny hesitated. "I'll be right in. You go ahead, I just have to finish with this," she said, adding a few unnecessary scrapes to the side of the pan she had been emptying. She waited until Del was out of earshot to speak. "Del tells me Jessie asked her out this morning. Did you know that?"

"Yes, Jessie told me," Widow stated flatly.

"Well, what do you think?" Jenny persisted.

"I told her I thought Del was too old for her and that she was moving too fast. After all, she just met her."

"That's all true. She turned her down, you know." Jenny said, watching Widow closely.

"That's what I hear."

"Widow, I saw how you looked at her."

"What do you mean?"

"I think you're interested in Del too."

"Jenny Andrews. Watch your tongue." Jenny might be her closest friend, but that didn't mean she could tell Widow how she felt. Jenny didn't understand everything, didn't know how hard it was to make the choices she had made.

"You can protest all you want but I know you, and I know what I saw. And…I saw her give you the same look back."

Widow allowed a small smile in response. She had been intrigued by Del from the moment she nearly collided with her at the post office. Del had seemed self-assured yet wary, a trait Widow understood too well. And the way her hair curled just behind her ears…

"I still don't know what you're talking about, Jenny. Gus and those two boys must have finally driven you completely nuts." *The time isn't right. I have to tear down this maze of deceptions I've created with the kids. Friendship is all I can offer at least until then.*

Jenny snorted. "I may be crazy. However, I'm not wrong about this. I want to let you know, though, that Del has had a rough couple of years. I'll let her fill you in on all the details, but she's pretty fragile right now. Don't be surprised if she's got a lot of walls up. She's really a good person, Widow. Just give her time."

"Well, if I was interested, which I'm not, I'd take that under advisement. Now, if you're through with your matchmaking, I think everything in here is finished. Shall we take it all to the dining room? As soon as everyone gets here, we can eat." Widow didn't wait for a reply but began carrying things out of the kitchen at a determined pace.

* * *

Laughter filled the dining room as everyone enjoyed the meal. Even the gravy received compliments, so Del guessed she hadn't caused it irreparable damage. After a quick cleanup, they retired to the living room, where Widow entertained them with home videos she had transferred to DVD. They showed Jessie and Johnnie in a number of activities—riding bicycles, falling off bicycles, showing calves at the fair, and celebrating birthdays with neighbors, including most of those present. Jokes abounded about the changes in waistlines and hairlines, and everyone enjoyed themselves. Del was unaccustomed to family scenes like this, but she recognized the love between the members of this group as something precious, something that had been largely missing from her childhood and that she had found but lost with Sarah.

Jessie divided her time evenly among her family and friends, and Del was relieved Jessie didn't show her special attention. As the guests began to leave, Widow accompanied them to the door, bidding them farewell with a hug. When Del stood and made her way to the door, Widow followed.

Widow walked with Del out to her truck, thanking her for coming over early to help out. Del's concern that Jessie's interest in her would cause tension between Widow and Del faded when Widow hugged her goodbye. As she drove home, she felt lighter than she had in quite a while. It had been a good weekend, she thought.

Del stopped to wait for a white diesel dually to drive past before she pulled from Widow's lane onto the county road. A small voice in the back of her head told her to take notice of the truck, but her mind was on the events of the evening and she gave it little more than a passing glance.

CHAPTER SIX

Keeping her promise to get back into a healthier routine, Monday evening after work, Del stopped by the recreation center. After a day filled with constant demands on her concentration, the continuous, steady rhythm of walking on the treadmill allowed her to clear her mind. As the burning in her quads steadily built, the stress of the day melted away and she allowed her thoughts to wander.

Much to her relief, J.T. had not been in sight the entire time Del was there. She still didn't know what Widow had said to her daughter, but she was sure she wasn't ready to go out on a date with the younger woman. She found herself thinking about Widow as she walked. She must have kept her maiden name when she married because she had a different last name than J.T. It must have been tough, trying to raise two children on your own in a strange place. And why hadn't she remarried? Then again, the pickings were slim in the area, except for a few you wouldn't want your worst enemy stuck with.

Like my brother, she thought, smiling.

This reminded her of his call a few weeks ago. Since then, she hadn't seen or heard from him, except maybe the previous week when she had met an old truck on the county road with two men in it. The one on the passenger side had turned away as if to look out his window just before she reached them, but she thought the man had looked like Glen. There was no love lost between them, and it seemed he only remembered he had a sister when he needed something from her. She marveled at the striking contrast between their relationship and the families playing and laughing together at Widow's on Saturday evening.

Her memory took her back nineteen years—to the last day her family had all been together in the same room. She was eighteen, just out of high school, and was working as a secretary's assistant. She'd returned home from work as usual and parked her old VW Rabbit next to her brother's rusted-out, black Camaro.

To her dismay, her father's multicolored, dented flatbed truck was parked astraddle the front sidewalk, a mere few inches from the concrete porch that ran the length of the front of the old farmhouse.

"Drunk again," she'd said under her breath. She tried to slip through the front door and into the hallway unnoticed, but didn't count on her brother coming up the hall toward her. She raised a finger to her lips to quiet him, but he grinned maliciously at her and nearly shouted as he greeted her.

"Hi sis. How was work?" The words may have sounded innocent, but they achieved their desired effect.

"Baby girl, get in here!" Her father's words were slurred and angry.

She dropped her head and turned back toward the living room. He was sitting in his old recliner, a Pabst Blue Ribbon in his left hand and a Marlboro in his right. "Hi Dad," she said quietly.

"Where the hell have you been?" He set the beer on the end table beside him and struggled a little to push himself to his feet.

"Work. I got off at four thirty and drove straight here." She was surprised by his question.

"Your brother saw you running around with Mitch Wolfe today, so don't give me that 'work' shit!" He lumbered toward her as he spoke, his feet slapping heavily on the hard floor, and she backed away, step by step. "What are you doing whoring around with that piece-of-shit pothead? You know better than that. You're *my* daughter and I won't have it!"

She raised her hands in front of her, as if to defend herself from his accusations. "Dad, honest, it wasn't me. I was at work. Call my boss. You'll see." Her voice was desperate, willing him to believe, afraid of the outcome if he didn't. She saw a second of doubt in his eyes and began to hope, but with her focus on him, she forgot to be wary.

The slap made her ears ring, and she was momentarily disoriented, unsure where the blow had originated. The angry look on her mother's face quickly reminded her of her mistake.

"Are you trying to say your brother is a liar? You ungrateful bitch!" her mother screamed. As though he was enjoying the spectacle, her father grinned maniacally, adding to the nausea caused by the pain in her head.

She knew better than to argue or try to fight back. Just duck your head and wait for them to get tired, that was the best defense. Her mother always started with a slap but would quickly move on to hitting Del with her fists, mostly body blows to avoid bruises that would show. Tonight was no different.

After a time—it may have been a couple of minutes, maybe more, Del wasn't sure—the punches stopped. Del was leaning against the wall for support, doubled over from the pain, but glad it was over. She dared to lift her head and was relieved to see her mother dropping to the sofa to rest. Taking extra care to move noiselessly, she eased away from the wall and began to turn toward the hall. Her stomach turned to lead when her father's hand landed on her shoulder.

"Hold on there, baby girl. You haven't told me why you're whoring around with that son of a bitch Mitch Wolfe." He was quieter now, and this frightened her much more than his yelling had.

"Dad, I swear to you, I'm not sleeping with Mitch Wolfe." She dared to look him in the eyes.

"Lies—"

"Shut up, Bea," her father shouted at his wife, giving her a look that left her sitting quietly on the sofa. He redirected his attention to his daughter. "Now why should I believe you?"

From somewhere deep inside her, a feeling began to grow until it eclipsed her usual resignation. A spirit she didn't recognize lifted her shoulders and straightened her spine. All her life, she had bent to her parents' wills, afraid of the beatings, afraid of whatever might follow that could be worse. Now she no longer cared what happened next, and when she stared into her father's eyes, she knew he was aware of her sudden lack of fear. His eyes widened slightly, but his hand remained strong on her shoulder.

"I only know one way to convince you, Dad. I'm not sleeping with Mitch. I'm not sleeping with any man. I don't like men, Dad. I'm a lesbian." Until she spoke the words, she hadn't recognized the truth behind them.

His face reddened and his hand dropped from her shoulder in surprise. She took his moment of inaction as her chance to escape. The door was two steps away, and she was out it and off the porch before he moved. She had the car started and in gear before he got out the door, and she never looked back.

The beeping of her treadmill timer pulled her attention back to the present, and Del slowed her pace to a crawl to cool down before stopping. She looked around the room for several seconds, trying to shake the fear and anger that had clung to her as she hurtled back from that other time, a world away from her life now. Then she grabbed her towel and headed for the showers.

The shower and the drive home went quickly, with Del determined to keep her mind from wandering to the past again, and she was at her gate before she realized it. When she got out of the truck to unlock the shiny new padlock, she noticed the tracks where a truck had turned around at the locked gate. *Maybe Gus forgot his key. If so, he's probably still cussing me.*

She fixed herself a can of soup and congratulated herself on working out and eating something other than chips. She balanced the full bowl carefully as she sat down in her recliner, then flipped through the channels and found a show she often watched. Too late, she realized the storyline ran perilously close to events in her own life. When one of the main characters' co-workers was diagnosed with brain cancer, Del quickly flipped the channel to a comedy. She tried to forget the hospital images that had flashed uninvited into her mind and thought she had succeeded.

Hours later, she sat straight up in bed, wildly looking around for Sarah, sweating profusely and weeping uncontrollably moments later when reality caught up with her. She finished the night in her bed but tossed and turned the entire time. When she looked in the mirror the next morning, the dark shadows under her eyes had returned. She considered calling in to work but realized she didn't want to stay home. Deciding she would be better off around people, she showered and started another day, trying to forget the nightmares that had haunted her night.

Thankfully, the rest of the week went better. She worked out at the center three nights and ate a small meal every night. Monday was her only rough night, and by the end of the week, her dark circles had faded again.

Thursday evening, Jenny called and insisted she join them for a music festival in a nearby town tomorrow night. She had four tickets and had invited Widow also.

"After all," she said, "this is your idea, you know. Gus and I are going out on a date, without the boys."

Del scoffed, "But with two chaperones instead? That wasn't exactly what I meant."

"It's a start. Give us a break. Besides, this will give you and Widow a chance to get to know each other better. You need more friends around here, Del."

She knew arguing was futile, so she agreed. Besides, she was intrigued by Widow, and this was the perfect opportunity to further develop their friendship. And it would do her good to go out and be social.

On Friday, she started her day early and was able to be home by five. After hurrying through her shower, she chose a pair of khakis to accompany a nice sweater. She cursed her lack of variety in her wardrobe but knew it was her own fault. She never liked anything new, so, once she found something she liked, she wore it for years in a variety of colors but the same style. Maybe she would talk Jenny into going shopping with her for something new to wear to Cindy's engagement party.

The phone rang, interrupting her inner battle over her wardrobe. She hustled into the living room to pick it up, sure it was Jenny checking on her to make sure she wasn't backing out.

"Hello?"

"Uh, yeah," a man's voice responded. "Del?"

With a sinking feeling in the pit of her stomach, Del said, "Yes Glen. This is Del. What do you want?" She consciously kept her statements to her brother brief, trying not to offer anything that would encourage him to continue their conversation.

"Can't a guy call his sister if he wants to?"

Del wasn't buying Glen's attempt at a joke. "Sure Glen. Now what's up?"

"I just wanted to talk a little, sis. Lighten up."

Del snorted at this but didn't answer, waiting for him to get to whatever it was he wanted.

"Have you seen Mom lately?"

"Yeah, I dropped by after work one day this week. She seems to be doing fine. Said she wished she'd hear from you sometime." Del was sure he hadn't spoken to their mother since the day she left the hospital for the nursing home.

"Maybe I'll get by there someday. Thought if you were going to see her this weekend, you could tell her I asked about her." Glen's voice almost convinced her that he cared about someone other than himself, and she let her guard down a little.

"No Glen, I have other plans this weekend. I'll tell her if I stop in next week though."

"Yeah, thanks. So, got a hot date tonight?"

That question surprised her, and her guard went flying back into place. "Actually, no, not that it's any of your business. I'm going out with friends."

"No need to get your panties in a wad, sis." He chuckled, and she almost hung up on him.

"Glen, if there's nothing else, I've got to go."

"Sure, sis. See ya." The click on the other end was a relief. She mulled over the conversation as she walked back to the bedroom to finish getting ready, but soon dropped it as strange but best forgotten.

Widow pulled up in her driveway while Del was combing her hair. Del invited her in, apologizing for the crowded living room. "We had a large apartment in St. Louis, and I couldn't bear to part with any of the furniture, although I realize it doesn't quite fit here. Maybe next year I can build an addition and make a larger living room."

Widow raised her eyebrows at the word *we*. Her gaze lingered on the two joined wedding bands Del wore on her left ring finger.

Del ignored her guest's apparent curiosity and offered her a drink. "Do you have any tea?" Widow asked.

"Sorry, only Dr. Pepper, milk or water…or honey whiskey." Del remembered the stash still above her refrigerator.

"How about water?" Widow smiled at her.

What a pretty smile, Del thought.

"Thank you."

Del turned to see Widow blushing at the compliment and realized she had said it aloud. She hurried from the room before she said something else to embarrass herself.

When she returned with a bottle of water and a Dr. Pepper, she had decided to tell Widow about Sarah.

"Your water." Del handed Widow the bottle and retreated to her recliner, surprised at her nervousness around the calm, blond woman sitting on her couch.

"Widow, I don't know what Gus and Jenny have or have not told you about me, but I thought maybe this would be a good time for me to explain a little bit about myself," Del started. She paused, trying to gauge Widow's reaction, but Widow merely waited patiently for her to continue.

"I left Devil's Prairie when I was eighteen. I didn't have a good family life here, so I cut most of my ties when I left. I told my family I was a lesbian before I split, and I think they were kind of glad I didn't come back." She took a drink of Dr. Pepper, then continued nervously when Widow only nodded. "Almost sixteen years ago, I met the love of my life, Sarah." Del blinked back her tears, determined not to lose control at this simple admission. "We had fifteen glorious years together, but I lost her last year to cancer." She dropped her head down and sniffed hard once, holding on to her control desperately. A deep breath and a hard swallow allowed her to continue.

"I just couldn't take it in the city any longer without her. Everything there was a reminder of her. So I called Gus, the only friend I had who wasn't from there. The rest, as they say, is history." She attempted to lighten her tone at the end but failed. Her smile was forced, but she had managed to contain the tears.

Widow blinked rapidly and smiled, although it appeared a little forced. "I know it couldn't have been easy to tell me that, Del. I could say I know how you feel, but I doubt that I do." She paused, cleared her throat and continued, "I might as well try to be as honest with you as you've been with me. You see, most people around here think they know my story, but few really do. Gus and Jenny are among the few. There are some things even my kids don't know."

Del's eyebrows lifted slightly in surprise.

"Unlike you, when the kids' father died, I can't really say I lost the love of my life. By then, we were nearly strangers. He was so wrapped up in his work that we seldom saw him, and, truthfully, I was so busy with the kids I didn't mind. I married him at eighteen, and I was pregnant with Jessie at the time. His parents supported us while he finished engineering school. I thought I loved him, but I doubt many of us really know what love is at eighteen." Del watched intently as Widow sipped her water. When Widow turned to look at her, their gazes locked and held for several seconds.

Finally, Widow shifted her eyes to a spot on the wall above the television. She cleared her throat again. "When Jonathan died in a car accident, I felt the loss but I don't know that I actually grieved the loss of love. I moved the kids here to get out of the city. His parents were furious, but they relented when

I agreed to take the kids up to see them every other weekend. Sometimes I would stay there with the kids, and sometimes I would stay with a friend. I found good neighbors here, Gus and Jenny, who were willing to watch my place when we were gone." She stopped, and Del knew she was leaving something unsaid.

"There was no one else, all those years?" Del questioned gently, understanding Widow's desire to talk just as much as she understood the other woman's hesitation. "No love of your life, I suppose?"

Widow chuckled. "There may have been a couple of times when I thought I'd met the love of my life, but when it came down to it, nothing ever seemed to work out. My kids didn't even meet most of them."

Del whistled softly between her teeth. "That must have been tough, keeping two lives going at the same time."

"You have no idea," Widow said. "The two I did allow my kids to meet…my kids thought were just friends."

"Didn't they guess?" Del was sure she would have guessed more than a friendship was going on if her mother had introduced her to a new man after her father passed away.

"No. There was no reason for them to suspect." Widow turned to look at Del again. "They were women, and we were very discreet around them."

Del nodded, suddenly understanding. She swallowed a sudden lump in her throat. "But what about J.T., er, Jessie? Why didn't you tell her?"

"When she was younger, I was afraid she would say something to her grandparents. They had already become suspicious of my friendship with Elaine." She waved her hand as if pushing away undesired memories. "They threatened to fight for custody of the kids and said I was an unfit mother. They had a lot of connections and the finances to afford a legal battle, and I didn't. And nothing was worth losing my kids, so I denied it all and stopped seeing her."

She looked away, and Del was no longer able to see her face, but the long-buried pain was still evident in her voice. "Elaine didn't understand, of course, and I never forgot the pain I caused her."

She paused a few seconds, then swallowed audibly before turning back to look at Del. A glimmer in the inside corner of her right eye contrasted her shaky smile. "Later, when Jessie was older, I was intimidated by her 'take no prisoners' attitude about being a lesbian. She really doesn't care who knows, and she leads her life fully in the open. I've never been that brave, and I don't want her to be ashamed of me."

Del nodded in understanding.

"I told her last week that we need to talk, and I'm going to tell her everything. I just haven't had the opportunity yet." Widow drank the last of her water and set it down on the end table. "I guess that's about it."

"No current love interest?" Del asked.

"No." Widow's eyes caught Del's, and Del swam in their sparkling depths for a few seconds before Widow broke the spell and looked away. "I think we should be going. We don't want to keep Jenny and Gus waiting."

"Yeah, let me put your glass and my soda can in the kitchen and I'll be right out." Del hurried to the kitchen, switched all of the lights off as she passed back through the house, and headed out the door. Del climbed into Widow's truck just as Widow started the engine.

They were both silent until they were almost to Gus and Jenny's. When the obvious finally occurred to Del, a quick chill of dread ran up her spine, and she spoke without consideration for Widow's feelings as she said in exasperation, "You don't think Jenny's set this up as a date, do you? I made it clear to her that I'm not interested in dating."

Widow gently placed her hand over Del's on the seat where it rested. "Knowing Jenny, that is entirely possible. Let her think what she wants, we'll just go as friends and have a good time. Will that be okay?"

Del stared out the window in silence a few seconds. "Okay. Friends."

Widow sighed quietly. The air in the truck was heavy with words unspoken, and they exchanged one last look after stopping in the Andrews's driveway. Del saw the searching look in Widow's caring blue eyes and knew she couldn't disguise the regret in her own.

* * *

The evening passed quickly, and Del surprised herself by having a wonderful time. She laughed with her three friends and even danced with Gus once, mostly avoiding his toes as she tried to follow instead of lead during a two-step. She was glad to see Jenny and Gus exchanging fleeting touches and even one smoldering kiss on the dance floor as the evening progressed, and when they climbed into Gus's four-door truck for the return drive home, Jenny slid over to sit next to Gus. Del looked at Widow and smiled, nodding toward the couple in the front seat and receiving a knowing smile in return.

The quiet ride home in the dark was broken only occasionally by conversation, and Del was yawning by the time they pulled into the Andrews's driveway. "Folks, I had a great time, but I think it must be past my bedtime."

Widow nodded. "Yes, I agree. Del, would you mind if we call it an evening and head on home?"

Jenny started to interrupt, but Del stopped her. "Widow, I insist. Thank you all for a wonderful evening, but I'm about to drop. Gus and Jenny, have a good night. I'll talk to you tomorrow."

Widow followed her lead, not allowing Jenny to break in. "Good night folks. Thank you both for a great time. Del, let's go."

Gus and Jenny smiled at each other and answered together, "Good night ladies."

CHAPTER SEVEN

Widow and Del were in the truck and out of the driveway in seconds. They rode quietly together, comfortable in the silence of their own thoughts. When the headlights illuminated her gate, Del instantly became more alert. She leaned forward in the seat and peered out the windshield, knowing something wasn't right.

"Turn your brights on, Widow," she said. Instantly, the world doubled in size, and Del could clearly see that her gate stood open and hung crookedly from one hinge.

"What the hell…?" Widow looked in confusion at the gate as she pulled through it onto Del's private drive.

"Stop, stop," Del ordered. She leaped out as Widow slowed the truck, her feet hitting the ground while the wheels were still rolling. Based on the bowed appearance of the gate, it must have been rammed by a large vehicle. Her chain and padlock were conspicuously absent, likely hidden in the undergrowth along the fence row after breaking under the strain of impact. She had her phone out of her pocket before she got back to the truck, and dialed Gus quickly.

He sounded exasperated when he answered. "Yeah, this is Gus."

"Gus. This is Del. I'm sorry to bother you, but you better get over here. My gate's been forced. It was standing open when I got here. Don't see any cows yet, but they were down around my house when I left."

"On my way now." The seriousness of Gus's voice only heightened her concern.

"Okay, see you in a minute. We're going down to the house." She closed the phone and turned to Widow. "Let's keep going. Just drive slowly and stay alert. I don't know who did this, but they may still be around."

They proceeded cautiously down the long, narrow drive but saw no vehicles or other signs of life, human or bovine, along the way. When the headlights lit up the front of her house, the front door stood gaping open, a dark hole into which Del was suddenly afraid to enter.

"Del, let's wait until Gus gets here before we go in. He'll be here in less than a minute, unless I miss my guess." Widow sounded as nervous as Del felt.

"Okay." Del's hands were shaking a little, and she thought foolishly that she hoped Widow wouldn't see her fear.

Gus flew down the hill twenty seconds later, and his truck slid to a stop behind them. "Have you seen any of the cows?" he yelled as he got out. He held a large, battery-powered spotlight in his left hand and a twelve-gauge shotgun in the right.

Widow and Del had stepped out of their truck when they saw his lights approaching, and they answered in unison. "No."

"Oh shit," Gus exclaimed as his light picked up the open front door. "They broke into your house."

"Yeah, looks like it. We were waiting on reinforcements before we took a look, just in case there's still someone hanging around." Del tried unsuccessfully to keep the tremor out of her voice.

They moved cautiously up the porch steps, listening but hearing nothing inside. Del reached through the door for the light switch and breathed a sigh of relief to see her living room mostly unscathed. A few pictures on the shelves had been knocked over and the drawers to her desk were hanging open, but otherwise, things seemed mostly untouched. They quickly checked all of the rooms but the intruders had done little in the way of damage. When they inspected the front door lock, however, they found it busted beyond repair.

"We'll have to replace that lock, Del," Gus pointed out unnecessarily.

"Maybe the whole door," she countered. "We'll look at it closer later. Now we need to look for your cows." She turned and strode across the porch, and the other two followed her closely. They jumped into Gus's truck, and he spun it around and headed out of the yard.

"Jim and Gary should be here in Jim's truck any minute," Gus said. "Jenny was rousting them out of bed when I left." He handed Del his phone. "Call Jim, he's number three on speed dial, and tell them to start circling the fence row just inside the gate. We'll work our way toward them."

Del quickly did as he asked, all the while looking out the window where Gus was shining the light, hoping to pick up any sign of his herd. When they met the boys on the far side of the pasture, neither of the vehicles had driven past a cow. They both turned and headed down the draws that crisscrossed the field, but after fifteen more minutes of desperate searching, they admitted defeat. Gus pulled up alongside Jim's truck window and shut his engine off so they could speak easier.

"I think we've covered it, boys. It looks like they're gone. All that's left now is calling the sheriff." The sound of defeat in his voice was hard to hear. "Go on home and get some sleep. Tell Mom I'll be over here at Del's till the sheriff gets done looking around, then I'll be home."

Jim nodded and started his truck, but Gus stopped him with a raised hand before he could drive away. "No, on second thought, I guess I'd better call her and tell her the bad news myself. You boys just head on home."

Jim made a wide circle around Gus's truck, then pulled onto the road and headed toward the broken gate. Del sank down into the passenger seat and barely heard Gus talking to the sheriff, then to Jenny. Her mind was in turmoil with fright, anger, worry about Gus, and confusion about what exactly had happened here.

They returned to the house to wait on the sheriff. Gus and Del sat down immediately, but Widow headed through the living room toward the kitchen. "You said something earlier about some honey whiskey, Del? Where is it?"

"In the cabinet above the fridge. The glasses are in the cabinet to the left of the sink."

Widow returned a few minutes later with two glasses of whiskey and handed one to each of them, then returned to the kitchen for one of her own. A few sips of the strong, sweet drink seemed to clear Del's head a little, and she began to look around her house more. She went carefully through the contents of her desk, trying to recall what had been in each drawer in case something was missing. Then she started picking up the overturned pictures. Tears came to her eyes when she lifted the picture of Sarah and her at a friend's Christmas party two years before. The glass of the frame had been shattered and the picture had jagged tears in it. The image of Sarah had been destroyed.

Widow came up beside her and put an arm around her shoulders. "Are you going to be okay?" She spoke quietly, and her furrowed brow and frown were visible proof of her concern.

Del blinked back the tears. "Yeah. I can get a copy of the picture from Gena. It was taken at her house, and I know she'll have it still. It's just the thought. Of all the pictures here, why did they have to destroy this one?"

Widow looked around thoughtfully. "You know, that's a good question. Why did they just destroy the one? Look, there are others over here of you with different friends, I suppose, and they weren't even touched. That's a little strange."

When the sheriff arrived, they answered questions for several minutes about what they had found. A deputy dusted for prints around the door, the desk and the pictures. He asked them to come to the department the following day to provide prints to eliminate their own from any that might be found.

When the sheriff asked if anyone knew they would be away that evening, Del hesitated, but when the sheriff noticed her hesitation, she spoke up.

"Well, it might not mean anything, but my brother called me today." Gus immediately turned to look at her. "I said I had plans with friends this evening, but I didn't exactly spell it all out."

The sheriff looked a little disappointed at the admission but smiled at her. "Telling your brother wasn't exactly what I meant, ma'am. How about others you might not know so well?"

Gus started to break in, but Del stopped him with a cold stare. "Let me explain it, Gus. He's my brother, after all." She turned to the sheriff. "His name is Glen Smith, Sheriff. You may be familiar with him."

The sheriff nodded in understanding. "His knowing I wouldn't be home may be significant, and so would the pictures that were destroyed. He hated Sarah." She sighed, suddenly filled with an overwhelming fatigue.

"Well, we have his prints on file, and we'll definitely look into it," the sheriff said. "But if he's part of this group that's been rustling cattle, we haven't been having much luck finding where they're hiding them. They're usually not found until they're shipped out to a market somewhere. By then, the rustlers have taken their money and gone. Gus, I hate to say it, but unless we catch a break on this, your cattle may be long gone."

Gus dropped his head. "I understand," he said to the floor.

The sheriff and his deputy left shortly thereafter. Del walked over and sat beside Gus on the couch. "Gus, I'm sorry—"

"Del stop!" Gus snapped. "You have no reason to say you're sorry. If that son of a bitch Glen had anything to do with this, it's not because of anything you did or didn't do. You're the one who insisted on the locks, remember? Now, I don't want to hear you apologize for this again, okay?"

Del had shrunk away from his sudden burst of anger. In all of the years she had known him, he had never raised his voice to her, maybe because he knew how her family had treated her. Now he must have recognized her withdrawal into herself, because he immediately reached toward her, grabbed her shoulders and pulled her toward him in a hug.

"You are not his sister now, Del. I don't think you ever were. Blood isn't everything, you know. You are more my sister than his. Now, get this shit out of your head." He spoke quietly, his mouth close to her ear. "We'll get through this. We are family and we'll get through it."

Del felt as though she were absorbing his strength through her pores. She had taken their friendship for granted for so many years, never acknowledging the bond between them. She blinked back a sudden rush of tears, determined to be brave. "You're right Gus. Thanks for reminding me." She clung to him for a few seconds before he released her. She thought she saw wetness in his eyes, but he quickly turned his head.

"Well, I better get back to Jenny. She's going to be pretty upset." Gus rose from the couch and took a couple of steps toward the door. "Del, where are you staying tonight? You can't stay here until you get your lock fixed."

"Yeah, I guess you're right."

"Why don't you come over to my place?" Widow said quietly. "I've got plenty of room."

"If you're sure it's no trouble…"

"I'm sure."

"Let me grab a few things and I'll follow you in my truck." Del was grateful she would be getting away from the house. Her control had taken a hard hit that night, and childhood fears she had thought forgotten were fighting to come to the surface. Maybe she would settle down at Widow's house. She was sure her own house would be less intimidating in the light of the day.

Within five minutes, the two vehicles were bumping over the cattle guard separating Del's yard from the pasture. The trip to Widow's was uneventful, yet Del was on edge, watching the darkness, for what she didn't know. She was right behind Widow when she opened her front door to step inside.

Both women startled at the greeting they received as they entered. It was nearly midnight, and all the lights had been out, so both anticipated a quiet house. Instead, J.T. met them just inside the door.

"Hello Mom. And Del. Keeping late hours, aren't we?" J.T. had a curious expression on her face. She waited with her arms crossed over her chest, looking from one to the other.

Widow jumped in to explain their evening with Gus and Jenny, followed by the discovery of the break-in at Del's house and the missing cattle. J.T.'s expression changed quickly to one of disbelief, then anger. Del and J.T. followed Widow into the kitchen as she talked, and they sat down around the table.

"Did the sheriff come out?" J.T. demanded.

"Yes, but he didn't sound very hopeful about finding the cattle," Del interjected.

"Do they have any ideas about who might be involved?" J.T. perched forward on her seat, both elbows on the table.

Del puzzled at the sudden look of dread on Widow's face but answered anyway. "I suggested they might want to take a closer look at my brother, Glen."

"Your brother?" J.T. looked perplexed, then slowly her face reddened.

Widow put a hand over her daughter's. "Jessie, take a breath. I just found out Glen was her brother, and Del has no idea about his history with us. From what she and Gus both say, he's a brother by birth only."

"History?" Del was really confused. "J.T., er, Jessie, I have probably seen Glen twice in the past twenty years. I only share parentage with him, nothing else. He pushed me out of his life when I came out twenty years ago. He certainly wasn't much of a brother before then, and, based on what others have told me since then, I have even less reason now to care about him."

J.T.'s hands shook and she clenched her jaw tightly. "If that son of a bitch shows up here, I'll shoot first and ask questions later. And Mom, I expect you to do the same. If you don't like it, Del, you're welcome to leave."

Del nodded in agreement, but before she could respond, Widow spoke up in a voice that allowed no room for argument. "No one is leaving anywhere tonight. Ladies, we will finish this discussion in the morning, when we all have fresher heads. Del, suffice it to say for now that we've had a couple of run-ins with Glen over the past few years and there's no love lost between us.

Jessie, consider the fact that Del is not her brother's keeper and she knows little about his exploits. We can share our stories in the morning, but I don't have the energy for it tonight."

Del and Jessie turned to look at Widow. Her face showed her fatigue, and Del immediately regretted adding to the strain. They moved immediately away from the table. Jessie hugged her mother good night before heading to her room. Del followed Widow to the guest room, then collapsed onto the bed the moment she was alone.

The house was quiet within ten minutes. Del stared into the darkness of her room. An hour later she remained motionless but continued to stare, the ceiling blank and offering no answers.

CHAPTER EIGHT

Del awoke to the sound of rain against the window and thunder rumbling in the distance, tired after a night of unremembered yet unsettling dreams. The events of the previous evening rushed back over her within seconds, and she dreaded the day ahead, wishing she could just stay in bed. When Sarah was alive, her home was with Sarah, wherever they might be. Since her death, Del's sense of home centered on her furniture, her truck, her things. Now, that home had been invaded and she felt violated on a very personal level. She would fix her door today, but she wondered how long it would take to patch the new hole in her soul. The thought that Glen might be involved only worsened the damage.

Tossing back the covers, she shoved herself to sitting on the edge of the bed and stared gloomily at the streams of rain tracing paths along the window. She tried to pull her emotions together to face the day. The old fears ingrained in her from her family's abuse had arisen again. She wondered if she had ever conquered them at all, or whether she had simply run from them, abandoning Delilah the child here and fleeing to the city where she had assumed the identity of Del. Del was more assertive and had even learned to handle confrontations without showing any sign of the fears that plagued Delilah. But during the previous evening she had become a strange combination of the two.

She shook her head in disgust. *God, now I'm developing multiple personalities!*

Noise in the hallway alerted her that she wasn't the only one awake, so she straightened the bed, then walked down the hallway to the bathroom to clean up. Minutes later, she entered the kitchen, which smelled of freshly brewed coffee.

"Morning Widow."

Widow turned from the stove after sliding a pan of biscuits into the oven. "Oh, good morning Del. Did you sleep well?"

"For the first half hour, I think. After that, I was fighting the boogeyman, I guess." Del chuckled without humor. She sat down at the table across from where Widow stood and continued. "What about you? Were you able to sleep at all? It sounded like last night brought up a lot of bad memories for you and Jessie."

Widow pulled out a chair beside her and placed a hand over Del's on the table as she sat. "Actually, I didn't sleep much at all. Between last night and what I had planned for this morning, I'm afraid I'm pretty keyed up."

The flow of warmth and kindness that passed through Widow's simple touch buoyed Del's spirits more than words ever could. Widow's words puzzled her, however, and she scrunched her eyebrows together. "If you don't mind me asking, what did you have planned this morning?"

"I was going to talk to Jessie first, then Johnnie, and tell them things I should have said years ago." Widow placed both hands over her face, as if to hide from her secrets and the deception she had found necessary in the past.

Del felt the immediate loss of the connection between them. Concerned, she placed a hand on Widow's shoulder. "Are you sure you want to tackle that today? I mean, with everything else that's going on…"

"I don't know, Del. Will there ever be a good time?"

A noise from the hallway brought their attention around to Jessie, who was entering the kitchen scowling. "Everyone else sleep as crappy as I did? Hope the coffee is ready."

She strode over to the coffeepot and poured a cup, then turned to sit down at the table across from the other two women. "Did I interrupt something?" She looked curiously at them.

Widow sighed deeply, then rose. "Del, let me get you some coffee." She busied herself getting a mug from the cabinet, then pouring the hot brew. "Jessie, I think it's safe to say no one slept well last night. Del and I were just discussing that very thing." She set the cup in front of Del. "Cream or sugar?"

"No, thank you." Del sipped the piping-hot coffee, looking from mother to daughter, thinking about her own mother. She doubted any confession from her mother would have much effect on her, if any. Beatrice's willingness to sacrifice Glen and her for their drunken father had created an insurmountable distrust. But she understood Widow's concerns about how Jessie would react and hoped the pair would be able to come to an understanding. She planned to make herself scarce as soon as possible so they could talk in private, if that was what Widow wanted to do.

The timer expired on the stove, signaling the biscuits were done. In near silence, the trio ate them with butter and honey, with no one apparently in a hurry to return to the previous night's discussion of Glen Smith. They cleared the table and put things away, eventually finding no tasks remaining to keep them from the inevitable. With full cups of coffee, they returned to the table and sat quietly for several moments.

Widow finally spoke. "About five years after the house was built, we had a bad storm pass through, and the roof was damaged quite a bit. I had to have it replaced, so I hired a local contractor I had heard of. Glen was working for him, and that's how I met him."

Jessie's expression darkened as Widow spoke, and her brows were pulled down to match the frown on her face. Widow, in contrast, appeared more resigned than angry.

"Glen tried to get me to go out with him on a date several times, and I turned him down. I guess the other guys on the crew heard about it and they were giving him a hard time." Widow sighed. "He caught me behind the shed one afternoon, when no one else was around. He was giving me a bad time about making him look like a fool and shoved me up against the wall. I think he might have tried something more, but Jessie heard us scuffling from inside the shed. She came out with a scoop shovel in her hands and threatened to lay him out."

"Oh God. I'm sorry."

"Del, you have nothing to apologize for. It's not your fault he's your brother," Widow reassured her. She sighed deeply again. "Besides, that's not all."

Oh hell, Del thought. What else?

Jessie broke in now. "I was about ten at the time, and I guess I should have been scared, but I was so mad at him for trying to hurt Mom, I didn't think about being scared. Anyway, he grabbed the shovel from me and threw it aside, all the while keeping one hand on Mom's neck. He was able to grab me and shove me against the wall beside her. Then he threatened to kill us both, or worse. At the time, I didn't know what 'worse' meant." She tried to smile at her innocence but only succeeded minimally.

"I think he heard some of the crew's voices getting closer, because he let us go. He turned his back on us and walked off like nothing ever happened. I grabbed Jessie and sat down on the spot and cried." Widow blinked back tears. "I think that frightened Jessie as much as anything," she admitted. "But I think I was more trusting of people in general back then. I wasn't totally naïve. I mean, I knew there were bad people out there. I guess I just thought if you didn't look for trouble, it wouldn't look for you. That day destroyed any innocence I may have had left."

"Did you tell anyone...the contractor...Gus?" Del asked.

"Not at first. I was too scared. I decided just to be careful to never be alone around him again. And I thought it was all over when the roof was done the next day and the crew left."

"What else?" Del asked in horror. "What else did he do?" A burning feeling rose in her chest, and her mind homed in to the conversation at the table, shutting out all other thoughts and feelings. Her anger was slowly climbing, overpowering her fears.

"Generally, he just harassed us over the next few months, whistling or making rude gestures if I saw him at the gas station or the post office, or anywhere in town. He slowed down and stared if he passed the kids while they were waiting for the school bus, so I started driving them to the end of the lane and waiting with them until the bus came. The last straw came when the kids were walking home one day after school and he tried to force them into his truck. They took off running, and we all hid in the house with the door locked until he left."

Del was sitting stiffly now, picturing the frightened kids hiding with their equally terrified mother, with Del's monster of a brother ranting outside the door. "Tell me you called the cops on him, Widow."

"No, I did better than that. I called Gus. By the time he got here, Glen was gone. The kids were crying, and I told Gus everything that had happened. He tore out of here like a madman. A couple of hours later, he was back. He had a few scratches on his face but acted like it was just another day. He simply said we wouldn't have to worry about our problem anymore." Widow smiled, then added, "I was afraid at first that he'd killed him, but I wasn't going to ask. I saw Glen in town a couple weeks later though. He was still pretty bruised up. He crossed to the other side of the street when he saw us. Whatever Gus did, it worked."

Del nodded, relieved Glen hadn't hurt them. She had seen Gus stand up to Glen when they were kids. Glen was three years older but had been afraid of Gus at least since they were in high school. "Jessie, Widow, I know you may not want me to apologize for my brother's wrongdoings, but, just the same, I am sorry. I'm sorry you moved to this area for a new start and instead had your lives touched in such a negative way by one of my family. I'd believed my opinion of Glen couldn't sink any lower, but I guess I was wrong."

Jessie and Widow reached at the same time for Del's hands, and the three shared what comfort they could. "I'd like to sit down with you and Gus and discuss this further," Del said. "I think something's going to have to be done about Glen, whether he's involved in the rustling or not. But first I think I need to go home and look around a little more, to assess the damage."

"Do you want me to come along?" Widow offered.

"No, but thank you, anyway. I think I'll see where Gus and Jenny are. I imagine they'll want to check the pasture for any sign of who did this. Besides, I know you want to spend some time with Jessie." Del stood and carried her empty coffee cup to the sink. When she turned, Widow and Jessie were standing. Jessie was closer, and Del enclosed her in a hug, seeing not the self-assured young woman but the frightened ten-year-old who had so bravely defended her mother. She hugged Widow after rounding the table, and a protectiveness rose in Del as she held the other woman close. She wanted to hurt her brother for what he had done to this family. She wanted to cause him the same pain and terror he had caused them. This thought stuck in her head as she drove away from the house, waving out the window at the two women watching her.

Del's phone rang as she pulled from Widow's lane onto the county gravel. She glanced at the phone before answering it. "Good morning Gus. How are you today?"

"Morning Del. Are you still at Widow's?" She noted the fatigue in his voice and wondered if he had slept.

"I just left. I'm on my way home now."

"Jenny and I thought we'd come over as soon as you were there. Guess we'll head that way, if it's okay."

"Sure. See you in a few." Del ended the call and shoved the phone in her shirt pocket. She scowled out the window at the passing landscape, the gray, overcast day doing nothing to dispel the remnants of her anger at her brother. As she pulled through her broken gate, a wave of loss washed over her. Loss—now that was something she could identify with, something she had lived with for months now, even before Sarah had died. She had nearly eliminated anger from her life and vowed she would never allow it or violence to control her as it had her parents.

She had maintained a tight control on her emotions for years to ensure it.

She drove slowly down her lane, watching in vain for cattle in the pasture beside her. Thoughts of her brother and the differences between them spun through her head. Glen had learned quickly from their parents and used violence more frequently and more effectively as he grew, until he was bending others to his will as effectively as his father. As he became a young adult, he began to treat their mother much as their father did, and their mother had responded by trying to avoid making either of them angry. Del had always been the scapegoat, responsible for any trouble Glen was in, responsible for any blowups by either Glen or their father, and responsible for all the dysfunction in her family.

She had taken it all quietly, surviving by shoving the hurt, the anger, the abuse, all of it down into a deep corner and suppressing it thoroughly. Only her dream of real love and a real family had sustained her, and she had finally found that dream fulfilled when she met Sarah. But that life was gone now, and her control was damaged. Her emotions whirled recklessly, and the anger, fear and sadness of the past twelve hours spun within her and left her unsettled.

She was giving the contents of her house a quick inventory when Gus and Jenny arrived. Gus sat in the living room while Jenny joined Del as she passed room to room, looking through cabinets, drawers, even her freezer.

"You know, I really don't think anything is missing except my change container from the table inside the front door. None of my electronics are that new, so maybe they figured they weren't worth taking," Del said as she and Jenny returned to sit with Gus.

"It's a good thing you're as far behind on all of that as we are," Gus teased quietly.

"Yeah." Del gave him a small smile. "Gus, you may say it's not my business, but did you have your cattle insured?"

"I don't mind you asking. I had a few of them insured, the registered ones. I figure I lost thirty head, and twenty-three weren't insured."

"Whew." Del whistled through her teeth. "What does that add up to?"

"Some of them were pretty old, but some had calves on them still. I'm figuring maybe thirty-five to forty thousand." Gus's voice filled with tension.

Jenny looked close to tears, and Gus reached out and grabbed her hand, giving it a reassuring squeeze. "We'll make it, honey. Just have to tighten our belts a little tighter, right?" He smiled halfheartedly.

The pounding in her head and the heat suffusing her face were an unfamiliar warning as her anger resurfaced. "Gus, Jenny, you both know I'll help out any way I can. I feel partly responsible anyway." She held up a hand to stop Gus from interrupting. "If I hadn't moved back, your cattle wouldn't have been here, and maybe my brother would have chosen someone else to rob. You can't argue that I'm wrong, Gus, 'cause I'm not." Her directness allowed for no dispute, and neither Gus nor Jenny tried. Del hadn't realized she was capable of the intense determination her anger had fueled. "What I want to know is, do you have any ideas about what we can do?"

"Well Del, I don't know. The sheriff said he'd let us know…"

"To hell with the sheriff, Gus. They haven't caught them yet. What makes you think they will now? Look, this is up to us! I don't plan on letting Glen get away with this."

"Just what exactly do you propose, Del?" Jenny interjected.

"Well, I've been thinking…"

They spent the next forty-five minutes discussing ways to track down Glen. They didn't believe he would have reason to think they suspected him of being involved, so Del concocted a story about a distant relative sending a small inheritance check to be divided between them. If nothing else would bring her brother out of hiding, she knew money would. Time was of the essence, because they knew the rustlers would move the cattle to market quickly.

Del called her last contact number for Glen and left a message with the woman who answered the phone. Initially, the woman didn't sound helpful, but when Del mentioned an inheritance check, her tone changed. She assured Del she could reach Glen immediately. Probably owes her money, Del thought.

"I'll call and let you know what time and where we're meeting," she said as Gus and Jenny rose to leave. "Be careful."

"Don't worry Del. We will. You be careful too." Jenny squeezed her hand.

"Oh, by the way, Gus, Widow told me about your run-in with Glen on her behalf. I wish they made more stand-up guys like you and less like Glen. The world would sure be a better place."

"Widow told you about that?" Gus looked at her, surprised. "Did she tell you everything?"

"I thought she had. Why? Is there something I need to know?"

"Well, you were kind of indirectly involved in that, Del," Jenny interjected. "What all has Widow told you about herself?"

"She told me she's had girlfriends, if that's what you mean. But what does that, and what do I, have to do with Glen attacking Widow and Jessie?"

"The first day the roofers were over to work on her roof, Widow thought they had all left for the day. I don't know if Glen had forgotten something and gone out behind her house again or whether he was spying on her, but Widow had a friend down from the city that day. The kids were in their rooms playing, and she and her friend shared an embrace in the kitchen. A few minutes later, she heard a truck throwing gravel as it sped out of her driveway. She didn't add it all up until a few days later when he caught her behind the barn." Jenny hesitated, shifting her weight restlessly from foot to foot.

Gus picked up the story for her. "I believe his words were, 'You fucking lesbo, you're just as bad as my sister. What you need is a real man to show you what you're missing. I should have fucked her before she turned into a pervert and destroyed our family. I'm gonna fix you before you go fucking up your kids' lives.'"

As she listened to Gus repeat Glen's diatribe, Del felt the color drain from her face, and her knees weakened a little as she imagined his fury. Within seconds, however, her face reddened as her anger found new heights. "She didn't tell me that part," she said quietly.

"When I heard your father died, I was afraid the beating I gave Glen would give him an excuse to take it out on you. That's why I made sure to meet you at the funeral home that evening. I knew he wouldn't try anything while I was there," Gus explained.

Del remembered her father's visitation four years earlier. She had felt some strange sense of obligation to be there. Gus and Jenny had met her in the funeral home parking lot and escorted her inside. She had insisted Sarah remain in the car, not wanting to subject her to the evil that was her family. She had not overlooked Glen's wicked grin when she walked into the room, and she remembered how startled she had been when Glen had suddenly turned and left.

"It all makes sense. Glen disappeared that evening because he saw you. Otherwise, he would have confronted me and maybe even Sarah."

Del imagined Glen following her to the car that day, bringing his brand of anger and violence to the one person in her life she had worked so hard to insulate from the things that had so tainted her childhood. She understood how much she owed Gus for his subtle intervention.

"Gus, I'll call you in a little while. You better get going now. Let's get this bastard caught and locked away before he can do any more damage." Her voice was dismissive but calm and quiet despite the turmoil she felt inside.

They left after a brief goodbye hug, and Del sat in the living room alone, waiting on the phone to ring, waiting on a call from the devil.

* * *

"I didn't know Del had it in her," Gus admitted as he drove slowly toward home. "She never stood up to Glen when we were kids. Hell, she never stood up to anyone. She tried to keep the peace and seemed to almost disappear if someone confronted her, like she did last night when I yelled at her—"

"What?" Jenny asked. "Why did you yell at Del?"

"She was going to apologize to me for Glen being the asshole he is, and I wouldn't let her do it," he explained. "And she did that shrinking-away thing she always did when she was a kid, so I grabbed her and gave her a hug." He smiled without humor. "I bet that's something that never happened when she was a kid."

"Was she okay after that?"

"I think so. I told her she was my sister, not Glen's." He looked over at Jenny for a long second. "And I meant it."

Jenny grabbed his arm in both hands and pulled him toward her as she kissed him on the cheek. "Gus Andrews, you are a wonderful man. I hope you know that."

"I worry about her, Jenny. She's had a tough time since Sarah died and now this. I worry that it'll be too much, that she'll crack under the pressure. And I'm not sure if I can help her."

"I think we're doing everything we can, honey. We just have to keep being here for her."

"I guess you're right. Well, let's get down to business," Gus said, and they both slid from the truck to go into the house.

* * *

"Glen wants to meet at two thirty. You know where the Crossroads Package Store is, down on the county line?" Del's voice was brisk and to the point when Gus answered his cell phone.

"Sure do," he responded.

"There are some old farms back in that area that were deeded to the Department of Conservation for national forest land years ago. Bet they have your cows hidden on one of them."

"Sounds likely. Let me call Tom and we'll meet you there."

"Make sure Glen doesn't spot you."

"Don't worry. See you there."

"Okay, be careful."

Del ended the call, then took a deep breath. She had found a different picture of Sarah in a photo album and placed it in a frame that had survived the break-in. Now she carefully set it onto a shelf. "I wish you were here, Sarah, to keep me strong." Tears came to the corners of her eyes, and she swore, just for an instant, she saw a tear dangling from one of Sarah's eyes in the picture. She blinked and the tears were gone. A steely determination filled her as she gathered her things to go.

At the ATM in town, she withdrew one hundred dollars, enough to lure Glen into her web. She arrived at the meeting place twenty minutes early, parking in a spot not easily seen from either of the roads approaching the business. She went inside and bought a Dr. Pepper and a small bag of chips, then headed outside to wait in her truck. To hell with good eating, she thought. It won't kill me for a day.

She replayed in her mind the things Widow, Gus and Jenny had told her about Glen to strengthen her determination and diminish her fears as she waited. When a stranger drove a dark green, extended-cab truck onto the lot, he parked far enough away that she was visible from where he sat but not so close as to draw attention. The driver went into the store, and the truck appeared empty to her. Only a moment later, the white, diesel dually truck she had seen at the post office days earlier pulled around the store and approached her slowly. She recognized Glen quickly, and he stopped the truck directly in front of her, blocking her in.

"This is it," she said through gritted teeth as she rolled down her window to talk to him. He swaggered up to her door and smiled broadly at her, showing he had lost even more teeth since their last meeting. He spat tobacco on the ground beside her door before bothering to speak.

"Sis, hear you got some money for me." He grinned again, tobacco juice staining the dark stubble on his chin.

"Yeah Glen. I got a letter this morning from Great-Aunt Brenda's daughter. Guess she left us a little something in her will. They sent a check for two hundred this time and said when probate was settled, there'd be about five hundred more to split."

"Well, I guess a little is better than nothing, huh sis?" He leered at her greedily. "Did you bring me my part?"

"Yeah." She handed him an envelope with five twenties in it and waited while he counted.

"Thanks sis. So, how's it been going?"

"I had a bit of bad luck yesterday, Glen."

"Really?" Del was surprised at how innocent Glen's question sounded. Then she remembered he'd had years of practice lying to and cheating people.

"Yeah. While I was gone yesterday evening, someone rustled Gus's cattle from my place and broke into my house. I don't think they took much from the house, just messed it up a little. Gus lost a lot on his cattle though."

"That's too bad, sis. Hate to hear that."

"Yeah. Me too. Sheriff thinks it may be that rustling group that's been active a few counties west of here. I've been hearing about them on the news."

"Damn rustlers need to quit bustin' up gates and stealing livestock." Glen's expression was so serious, Del struggled to maintain the charade.

"Yeah, well, I got somewhere to be. I'm gonna run in and get another soda, then hit the road. I'll call when I get the other check."

"Okay sis. You do that." He leered again and stepped away from her truck, then headed directly toward the store, leaving his truck parked in her path.

She stepped out of the truck and directly into the spit he had left there moments earlier. "Damn Glen. You probably did that on purpose." She spoke under her breath, although he was probably already out of earshot given how fast he was hustling toward the building.

That money must be burning a hole in his pocket, she thought. The stranger was just stepping out the door as Del got to it. He nodded politely to her and held the door as she passed through. Glen was already at the counter buying a large bottle of Jack Daniels. She ambled over to the coolers for a soda and hurried to buy it when she heard him leave.

As she turned toward the door to exit, his truck passed by the front of the store. She tried to look nonchalant as she came outside, in case he looked back. As soon as the green truck blocked the sight of her, she ducked down along the side of it and opened the back door, then slid quickly up into the backseat without raising her head to avoid being seen. She nearly collided with Jenny, who was huddled on the other half of the backseat. As she slammed the door behind her, the stranger started up the truck and took off quickly, tailing Glen from a safe distance.

"What the hell are you doing here?" Del stared, but Jenny's icy glare made her blink. "Gus, why did you bring Jenny? This could be dangerous, you know."

The voice that answered her came from low in the front passenger seat. "You tell her to go home, Del. I'm afraid I'm not man enough to tangle with her." He and the stranger chuckled, then Gus looked over the back of the front seat. She laughed in spite of herself at the curly wig and cowboy hat atop his head. He had smashed the hat on pretty good in an attempt to keep it in place over the wild curls that hung down to his collar.

"Like my disguise, Del? I hid back at the store because I was afraid Glen would look too close, but if he does look back, I think we're far enough behind him he won't recognize me in this getup."

"Gus, I think I might like that look on you. Jenny, what do you think?"

"I think you both should be put away in padded cells, but that's beside the point. Del, don't argue about me coming along. I had to make sure you two didn't play hero and get yourselves hurt." Jenny's tone was final, and Del didn't push her.

"By the way, I'm Deputy Tom Hart, Jenny's second cousin," the stranger said without taking his eyes off his prey in the white truck ahead of them.

"Hello Tom. Nice to meet you. I guess you've already figured out I'm Del Smith and unfortunately, Glen Smith's sister."

"Pleased to meet you. You've done a good job luring Glen away from his hideout. Hopefully, he'll lead us back to the cattle. Then the sheriff's department will take it from there."

"Wouldn't have it any other way," Del responded. "By the way, he knew my gate had been torn up and I didn't tell him, so I think we're definitely on the right trail. Also, I've seen that truck nosing around the area a lot lately, with two other guys in it that I didn't recognize."

They trailed Glen down a gravel road, staying close enough to follow his cloud of dust but out of his eyesight. As they topped a hill in the midst of national forest land, the trail of dust disappeared. Tom slowed as they passed a rutted old logging road that appeared to vanish into the trees. "Looks like that road has had some traffic lately," Tom remarked as he stopped the truck.

He and Gus got out and inspected the tracks while Jenny and Del remained hidden in case anyone was watching from the trees. When they climbed back in, Tom immediately called the sheriff's department while Gus filled them in.

"Looks like something heavy has been down the road recently, like maybe a loaded cattle trailer. Tom is calling for a chopper to check it out, and we're going to move out of the way for now. We'll go back to your truck, Del."

Tom turned around at the end of the road, and as soon as he pulled out of sight of the turnoff, Jenny and Del sat upright.

"No offense, Jenny, but I can't really say I enjoyed our time in the backseat together." Del smiled mischievously at her as she kneaded the spasming muscles in her back.

Jenny chuckled and rubbed her neck. "I would have to agree with you, Del."

Jenny and Tom spent the ride back to Del's truck catching up on their families. The cousins' shared interest in each other was a sharp contrast to Del and Glen, and Del couldn't help but wonder what it would have been like if she had been born to someone else.

When he dropped them off at her truck, Tom thanked Del profusely for her help. Then he returned to the logging road to help in the investigation. Del, Gus and Jenny climbed into her truck and headed home, quietly exuberant, knowing that at least they had a chance of regaining the stolen cattle.

* * *

"Join us for supper," Jenny said when Del pulled into their driveway. "Maybe we'll hear something from Tom soon."

"Let me go by the house and fix my door, then I'll be back," she promised.

Ninety minutes later she'd finished. Although putty filled the hole where the lock had been, the shiny new deadbolt a few inches above it ensured the door could be secured. She had felt energized as she worked on it, pleased at her role in leading the sheriff to Glen instead of letting him get away with walking all over people.

When she entered the Andrews's house, she was glad she had returned. Jim answered Del's knock and tailed behind her as she headed directly to the kitchen, overpowered by the smell of a home-cooked meal.

"Del, Lisa's coming over for lunch again tomorrow. Could you join us?" Jim asked eagerly.

"Jim, I'd be pleased to join you, if that's okay with the cook, that is?" She looked at Jenny expectantly.

Jenny nodded her assent, and Del continued, "How is it going between you and Lisa, Jim? Are things any smoother with your buddies at school?"

Jim reddened slightly and ducked his head. "Yeah. Things are going fine. I told one of the guys off the other day when he got out of line talking about us. I thought I was going to have to line him out, but he finally laid off me. Everyone else has been pretty cool about it since then."

"Good. Sometimes just standing your ground means a lot. That's a lesson I'm learning myself." Del didn't elaborate, and Jenny interrupted them, changing the subject.

"If you two will help me get the food to the table, we can eat," she said.

"Sounds good to me," Del answered. "I'm starving, and everything smells wonderful."

Gus entered the room talking on his cell phone, waving his hand wildly at Jenny and Del. His end of the conversation gave them no clues to whom he was talking, and when he ended the call they looked at him expectantly.

"That was Tom. The chopper spotted a herd of cattle being held in portable corrals on national forest land. The trailers and two trucks were parked at the end of that logging road we traced Glen to. They found a campsite but had to use dogs and choppers to look for the rustlers. Glen and two of his friends were just arrested and are on their way to jail."

Del smiled broadly, unable to contain her delight. "About damned time he got his!"

Jenny rushed over to Gus and leaped into his arms, making him step back for balance.

"The sheriff says after verifying the cattle are mine, I should get them all back safe and sound, thanks to you, Del."

"Don't thank me, Gus. Let's just be glad it's all going to work out. Now, how about let's eat? I'm going crazy smelling all this wonderful food and not being able to eat it." She turned her attention to the meal on the table and filled her plate with fried chicken, corn, mashed potatoes with gravy, and a biscuit.

"Damn, Jenny, are you sure you won't leave Gus and come live with me?" Del joked. "If you'll do the cooking, I'll do everything else."

Jenny raised both eyebrows. "As tempting as your offer may be, Del, I'm afraid I have to turn you down. I've been around these men so long now that I'd be lost without them. They kind of grow on you after a while, you know." Jenny pulled Gary's ball cap off his head as she walked behind him and hung it on the corner of his chair.

"Del, you need to quit making offers like that to my wife, or I'm going to quit inviting you over." Gus tried to sound serious. "She might take you up on it someday, then I'm gonna be really pissed."

Gary and Jim looked up quickly but smiled when they saw the twinkle in their father's eye.

"You two quit fighting over me, or I'll send Gus to stay with you, Del. Then the two of you can take care of each other. Now eat," Jenny said, and they all listened.

Del and Gary cleaned up the kitchen after they ate, then Del made her excuses to leave. She drove home in the gathering darkness, still a little shaken at the sight of her busted gate when she passed through. Her elation at standing up to her brother couldn't overcome the uneasy feeling that settled over her, and she wondered if her troubles weren't over yet.

CHAPTER NINE

The next two weeks were eerily normal, other than a visit to the sheriff's office to verify her statement and to leave her fingerprints. Gus had been busy getting his cattle home. He had temporarily put them in a pasture close to his house until he could make sure none were injured or sick after the ordeal. He moved a smaller herd over to Del's pasture after she fixed her gate, and she found it comforting to look out her window and see them milling around, looking for their favorite clumps of grass.

As the days passed, the return to her normal daily routine lulled her into a sense of complacency. When Widow called her on a Saturday afternoon and invited her over for dinner that evening, Del quickly accepted. She welcomed the excuse to put her yardwork on hold until another day, and though she had trouble admitting it to herself, she wanted to see Widow again.

Del presented Widow with a bottle of wine from a local winery when she arrived that evening.

"Thought we should celebrate," Del said. "Hope you like wine."

"As a matter of fact, I do. And this just happens to be one of my favorites," Widow said. "So, what exactly are we celebrating?" She arched her eyebrows as she glanced over her shoulder at Del, who was following her down the hall to the kitchen.

"Glen getting what he deserves. How about that?" Del smiled broadly. "I hear he hasn't been able to make bail and several other counties are looking at him for rustling too. He might be busy for a while."

"Good for him." Widow smiled back, then handed her a corkscrew and the unopened bottle. "Would you do the honors? I personally hate corkscrews. I'm not sure why."

Del went to work opening the bottle. "Must have had a traumatic run-in with one sometime, huh? Break a bottle? Or just destroy a cork?" She smiled mischievously at Widow as the cork slid out of the bottle with a muted pop.

"I don't know. It just seems to take me an awful lot of time and effort to get them to work. By the time I get the cork out of the way, I'm aggravated."

Del chuckled and tossed Widow the cork.

"So how have you been, Widow? Last I knew, you were getting ready to have a heart-to-heart with your kids." Del filled the two wineglasses Widow had placed on the counter, then handed one to her.

"I've already set dinner out in the dining room. Why don't we talk as we eat?" Widow motioned for Del to follow her.

The dining room table was set comfortably for two, and several steaming dishes were gathered there. The tempting aroma emanating from them made Del's stomach growl.

"Who's going to help us eat all of this, Widow?" she teased good-naturedly.

Widow colored slightly. "I wasn't sure what you'd like, so I fixed several things."

"Everything here looks so good, I'll have to try it all. You may have to roll me away from the table when we're done. I'm not sure I'll still be able to waddle." Del's lighthearted laugh brought a smile to Widow's face.

After filling her plate with pot roast, mashed potatoes, gravy, carrots, corn and a large, homemade yeast roll, Del got down to the business of enjoying her dinner. She had never been shy about food, and Sarah had often told her she ate like a lumberjack. After months of eating mostly her own cooking or not eating at all, she truly enjoyed a real meal. A few bites later, she remembered her unanswered question.

"So, how did the talk go?"

Widow took a sip of wine before responding. "Johnnie was fine. He seemed a little surprised, but only for a few minutes." She paused for several seconds.

"And...?"

"And Jessie...Jessie was pretty upset. First, she was mad at me for not telling her. Then she was mad at her grandparents for threatening to take her away from me. And she was mad that Gus and Jenny knew and hadn't told her."

"So, how is she now?" Del asked quietly.

"I think she's over the mad part. Maybe *disappointed* would be a better word for it now." Widow smiled, but her eyes looked sad. "You know how you put your parents on a pedestal, then when you find out they're only human, you're disappointed?"

"No, I really don't. My parents never came close to a pedestal," Del said sadly.

Widow put her hand over Del's on the table. "I'm sorry, Del. I guess that wasn't a good example to choose."

"No, that's okay. Most people don't have parents as bad as mine. I realize that. But it's all in the past now. That part of my life is over and done with. Now that Glen is in jail, it puts it all a little further behind me. By the way, Gus and Jenny told me about what Glen said to you when he assaulted you, including the part about me."

"Well, I couldn't tell you in front of Jessie the other morning, not until after I talked to her."

"Let's toast to Glen leading a long and confining life in jail." Del lifted her wineglass and smiled as Widow lightly clinked hers against it.

"Here, here," she agreed.

"This food is delicious, Widow." Del returned to eating and remarked after several more bites. "Thank you for having me over this evening."

"I've been meaning to invite you sooner, but we were pretty busy around here the past several days. Johnnie went out with friends tonight, and I found myself with time on my hands, so I decided to risk it and give you a call. I'm glad you could come."

Del mulled over Widow's words about Jessie while she finished her meal. "So, I don't get it," she finally said in confusion. "You said Jessie is disappointed in you. Surely it's not because you're gay?"

"No, no. Nothing like that. She's upset because I was afraid to be open about it, especially with her and Johnnie. I don't know if anyone who hasn't had children would understand the panic you feel when you're threatened with losing them. My in-laws would have fought for custody and probably would have won. Things are different now. Today I'd have a better chance. Jessie just doesn't realize how it was back then."

"Maybe I could talk to her," Del suggested.

"Thanks for offering. For now, I think it's best to just give her some time. If she's still giving me the cold shoulder in a couple of weeks, I'll ask Jenny to talk to her. She'll listen to her."

Widow stood and began clearing the table. Del helped her put away the remains of the meal and load the dishwasher. Widow poured the last of the wine into their empty glasses before discarding the bottle. When she headed up the hall toward the living room, Del followed wordlessly behind.

"You know, I seldom drink," Widow broke the silence. "I've had a bottle of this same wine in the cabinet for about a month. I don't even remember why I bought it."

"I know what you mean. The only alcohol I have in the house is that bottle of whiskey up over my refrigerator, and I bought it the first weekend I was in the house. At the rate I'm going, I'll get it finished in another three months." The wine was beginning to fill her with a warm glow, and she was glad to be sitting in Widow's modern home with central air-conditioning instead of her own house with pockets of hot and cold depending how far you were from the window unit.

"So…" they both started at the same time. Widow broke into giggles, and Del grinned and waited for her to speak.

"So, I was thinking, Del, that we should listen to some music." Widow set her empty wineglass down and walked over to the stereo. "Do you have any preferences?"

"What do we have to choose from?" Del joined her, and eventually they decided on playing several old vinyl records on Widow's phonograph.

"I need to get a phonograph," Del remarked. It had been years since she had listened to a vinyl record and was surprised to realize how much she liked the warm sound, including the occasional pops and crackles.

"I think I want to open that other bottle of wine," Widow responded. Del followed her back to the kitchen and deftly uncorked a second bottle, then filled their glasses again.

"Sorry it's not chilled," Widow commented, but it didn't seem to matter to her because she tilted up her glass again.

"Not a problem." Del smiled. She hadn't allowed herself to unwind in a long time. And Widow was a friend she could trust, someone she could let her guard down around and just have a nice, relaxing evening. She tipped her own glass, letting the warm wine soothe her soul. As they headed back to the living room, Del grabbed the wine bottle from the counter and brought it along. *What the heck?*

They enjoyed the wine, the music and each other's company. Del was amused by the slight weave in her path when Widow arose to change the record. As Patsy Cline began to sing, Widow reached a hand out to Del. "Dance?"

Del wondered if she would be able to dance, considering she was also feeling the effects of the wine, but she grasped Widow's hand and pulled herself upright. Thoughts of Sarah emerged briefly, but a sense of peace quickly followed them. Del wasn't sure if the wine had numbed her or if Sarah was finding a way to tell her it was okay. But Widow didn't seem to notice the turn her thoughts had taken, and Del pulled her close, marveling at the sensuous feel of her in her arms.

Widow placed her head on Del's shoulder. "Why does Cindy call you Dee?"

Del chuckled. "She called me Del at first until she found out what my full name was."

"What's that?" Widow asked, her tone curious.

"Delilah. But please don't. I hate that name. My mother used to say it in an awful, mocking voice."

"Don't worry, I won't," Widow assured her. "But where did Dee come from?"

"Cindy can be such a pain sometimes," Del explained. "She started calling me Delilah, really drawing out the beginning of it, and I took it for about a week. Finally, one day I was really having a bad day. When she started in, I popped off some rude comment, then I didn't speak to her for about a week. She tried to stop but couldn't seem to switch to Del after saying it the other way so many times. So I convinced her to shorten it to just Dee."

Widow laughed quietly. "Even though I barely know Cindy, somehow, that makes sense."

The song ended, and they stopped moving, each waiting for the other to step away.

"Del…or Dee…or whoever you are, can I kiss you?" Widow asked, her eyes asking the question along with her words as she gazed at Del. She was nearly able to conceal the remnants of apprehension the wine had failed to chase away.

The warning bells in Del's head were silenced by an overwhelming feeling of rightness, and she dipped her head down until their lips touched. The kiss was soft at first, gentle, questioning. Feelings long dormant exploded in Del, and she deepened the kiss, tentatively questing with her tongue, then tasting the softness of Widow's mouth. She groaned in pleasure, then eased her lips away. Widow's blue eyes were nearly concealed by heavy lids, her face was flushed and she had a hint of a smile. Del kissed the upturned corners of her lips before tracing along them lightly with her tongue.

Widow sought her lips again as she ran her hands through Del's short hair. Del was quickly losing herself and wasn't ready when Widow backed away. Del chased her lips briefly, not wanting the exquisite contact to end, but Widow put a finger to Del's lips and stopped her forward movement. Del tried to capture it with her tongue and teeth, but Widow won the game of cat and mouse. She lingered a moment at the tip of Del's chin before dropping her hand to the center of Del's chest, keeping a few inches of space between their breasts, although their hips remained snugged together.

"Thank you," Widow said, smiling at Del with her blue eyes now open wide and sparkling.

"Thank you," Del replied, captured in her gaze. Simultaneously, their attention wavered, and the spell was broken as they noticed the music—short bursts of "crazy" over and over again as the needle jumped across the scratch on the old record repeatedly. Their laughter began as a low chuckle and grew as Patsy Cline expressed her opinion of them in the background.

Johnnie stepped through the front door in the midst of their laughter, and the odd expression on his face only added to their hysteria. He stared at them a few seconds, then his gaze alit on the empty wine bottle. Nodding in apparent understanding, he turned without a word and walked down the hall to his room.

Del managed to control herself enough to walk over and stop the record. "Now I remember what I didn't like about these things."

Widow wiped the tears from her eyes. "Guess I better go check on Johnnie. Would you mind waiting a few minutes?"

Del held out a hand to her and squeezed her fingers briefly before letting them go. "Of course."

Del tried to concentrate on looking through the stack of old records while Widow walked after her son.

After a couple of minutes, she returned, smiling broadly. "He's okay. He thinks we're both a little insane but forgives us because we are *old*...or something like that."

"I've had a wonderful evening." Del slipped her arms around Widow's waist and pulled her close. It felt so right to kiss her again, and she did—a sweet, nurturing kiss.

When Del released Widow at last, she knew she had to go home. As much as she desired this woman, as much as she wanted to let go and love again, she knew she wasn't there yet. The short time it had taken for Widow to talk to Johnnie had given her a chance to examine the walls she had erected around her heart. Although one may have fallen, she convinced herself that her heart was still steeply guarded and that it was a good thing. She only hoped she could explain without hurting Widow's feelings.

She knew her eyes must reveal her struggle, and she alternated between expressions of longing, fear and guilt as she tried to find words. Widow placed a finger over Del's lips and stopped her from speaking. "Shhh," she whispered. "It's okay. Let the evening just be what it was."

Del nodded slowly.

"I had a wonderful time. Thank you for having dinner with me. Can we try it again sometime?" Widow asked softly.

Del smiled. "Yes. I'd like that."

Widow walked with her outside. "Are you okay to drive? The wine…"

"I wouldn't chance it out on the highway, but I can take the gravel roads home. This time of night, I won't meet anyone," Del reassured her. She reached for Widow's hands and squeezed them gently. "Thank you for dinner and dancing. I do want to try it again." She smiled and shrugged. "One day at a time, okay?"

"One day at a time. Good night Del. Sweet dreams." Widow kissed her quickly.

"Good night Widow. Sweet dreams to you also." Del climbed into her truck and started it before she could change her mind. She shifted to reverse and backed out with her eyes locked on Widow. When she changed gears, she dragged her gaze away to focus on the drive home.

Del made her way home slowly and carefully, knowing she shouldn't be behind the wheel but willing to take the risk. She pulled into her drive and turned off the engine, then sat quietly in the dark.

"Sarah," she whispered, "I don't know if you can hear me, but I can't help but think you're watching. You know I will always love you. You were my life."

She blinked rapidly, willing herself not to cry, afraid the tears might not stop. "Sarah, if I can find the courage, is it okay, you know...okay to love? No one will ever be you, because you were my everything. But maybe I can be...not so alone, you know?" She choked out the last words, unable to force more past the growing lump in her throat.

The moonlight was dim through the thin clouds in the night sky, and strange shadows lurked around the old farmhouse and the yard surrounding it. With effort, Del made out the latticed arch centered between her porch and the driveway. She had been watching her moonflower vine slowly grow over the past few weeks, and, earlier in the day, she had noticed the shiny, green leaves had covered the trellis. As she gazed now at its dark silhouette, the clouds cleared momentarily and the moonlight peeked through, illuminating the verdant profusion like a spotlight.

Del looked up at the sky in wonder. "Thank you Sarah."

CHAPTER TEN

Sunday found Del whistling while she worked around her house and yard. When Cindy called late in the afternoon, she commented on her friend's positive mood, but Del denied she was feeling anything special. For the first time in months, she even found herself looking forward to returning to work the next day, and she wouldn't allow herself to consider what that might mean.

On Monday, none of her co-workers seemed to notice the extra spring in her step. One of her more observant patients did, however, and gave her a knowing smile and a wink when Del assured her that her weekend had been nothing special.

She decided to visit her mother on the other side of town on her way home. Del had shopped for new socks for her one evening the previous week, and, after several minutes of searching, had found the specific brand and style her mother requested. The nursing facility would shop for residents if they asked, and she wondered why she bothered spending the time and money to meet her mother's demands. But her mother always asked Del to run personal errands for her, and, through some twisted sense of duty, Del felt obliged to meet her frequent requests.

When she arrived at the facility, the visitors' parking lot was empty. She immediately felt guilty for questioning whether she should run errands for her mother, thinking of all the long-term care residents she had known throughout her years of work who never had a visitor, whose family had deserted them the second the nursing home door closed behind them. Maybe that was the reason she had felt obligated to visit at least twice a month since she had returned to the area. It certainly wasn't because she enjoyed her mother's company. A wry smile played across her lips as she entertained this thought.

She turned from the hallway into the door of her mother's room, the bag of socks swinging in one hand while she tapped on the door to signal her presence.

Her mother had gained weight since she had entered the nursing home. Her flower print dress was gathered high on her legs, showing the small indentations her wheelchair had made into them and the discoloration and weeping of her lower legs. Del made a mental note to speak to her mother's nurse about finding her a wider wheelchair and treating her cellulitis. As soon as Vanna displayed the letters on the letter board on *Wheel of Fortune,* her mother turned to find the source of the knock. Her expression changed as soon as she recognized Del. The color drained from her face, and her eyes fixed on Del in a steely stare.

"You! I can't believe you would show your face here!" That's how it started.

Del was taken aback at her mother's words.

Beatrice's cheeks became redder with each word she spoke. "Do you know what you've done to your poor brother? He's stuck in a jail cell because of you, for something that isn't even his fault. He wasn't involved in any rustling, and they can't prove he was. He was just trying to help out some guys he knew. He didn't know those cattle were stolen. And you didn't even bother to tell me Glen was in jail."

"Now wait a minute, Mom. I don't know what he's been telling you but..." Del trailed off as the all-too-familiar rush of anxiety at her mother's onslaught thrust her instantaneously back into her childhood. A little voice in the back of her head tried to snap her back to the present, tried to remind her she was stronger now.

"And another thing. He told me you've been buddying up with that Widow woman and that Gus Andrews. That no-good Andrews kid was always so mean to your brother when you were kids. That whole family was always a worthless bunch. Glen loves you, Delilah. He always wanted the best for you, and you've done nothing but try to ruin him. I hope he'll forgive you after this. I know I wouldn't."

Del raised her hands as if to protect herself, to no avail. She desperately tried to think, knowing the guilt and shame she was feeling weren't right but unable to force her thoughts back on track. "Mom. Listen—"

"I'm going to pay his bail. I talked to the banker today. He'll let me borrow against the house. My poor son, locked up in jail like some criminal. You really disappoint me, Delilah. I never thought you would turn on your own flesh and blood. After everything we've done for you, you would throw us to the wolves. And look how you've upset me. My blood pressure is probably through the roof. Go get my nurse. I'm feeling kind of weak..." She sank into her wheelchair slightly.

Del was still trying to reconcile her thoughts, and she wasn't initially alarmed by the way her mother slumped in the chair. The increasing extension of her mother's arms and legs followed by a gentle tremoring of her head and neck caught her attention though. As her mother stiffened further, she nearly slid from the chair, and what had begun as a gentle tremor rapidly progressed to a violent shaking of her entire body. Del dropped the bag of socks and stepped quickly forward. She braced her knees against her mother's legs to prevent her from sliding to the floor while trying to hold her body up.

"Help! Nurse! I need a nurse!" Del yelled. She tried not to panic, tried to tell herself she was trained to deal with this. But somehow her training seemed less than enough to prepare her for holding her mother, a woman she had tried to hate most of her life but who had maintained some strange hold over her in spite of everything, while Beatrice's mind was ravaged by a grand mal seizure.

A nurse ran into the room, and she and Del lifted the convulsing woman onto her bed and rolled her to her side. Del ran to the nearby nurses' station for more help, and two additional nurses hurried back to the room with her. Del stood at the doorway, feeling as though she was watching a bad movie. The charge nurse walked past her briskly, leaving the others to tend to her mother. Del didn't ask, but her assumption that someone had summoned an ambulance was proven when, a few minutes later, two men wearing multipocketed black pants and gray shirts with emblems on the shoulders rushed a gurney down the hall toward her.

The medics ordered everyone but the charge nurse out of the room, then one began setting up their equipment while the other, who Del assumed must be the paramedic, began assessing her mother, who was still seizing on the bed. Del, stunned, continued to stand near the door until a young woman dressed in scrubs gently laid a hand on her arm. She turned her attention to the short redhead, who looked up at her with genuine concern in her eyes.

"Why don't you step out with me for a few minutes?" she asked, her voice sounding distant to Del's ears.

Del shook her head and looked back toward her mother, who was hidden by medical staff on the other side of the room. The hand on her arm became more insistent, and she turned to look at the young woman again.

"Miss Smith, really. I think you need to sit down. They'll let you know if anything changes." She tugged on Del's arm, and Del allowed herself to be turned away from the nightmarish scene unfolding in the room. She walked a few steps down the hall and sat in a chair by the nurses' station, silent, waiting...for something. Del was barely aware of the Styrofoam cup of coffee that had been placed in her hand, but she stared into the depths of its blackness regardless.

After an immeasurable time had passed, the charge nurse was beside her, talking to her in a calm tone as if nothing out of the ordinary had happened. "They're getting ready to take her to the hospital now."

"Is she still…is she still seizing?" Del asked, knowing the length of the seizure did not bode well for her mother.

"No. But she isn't responsive either. They'll know more when they get her to the hospital." The charge nurse delivered her status professionally but with an emotional detachment that Del recognized immediately. After dealing with death and dying on a frequent basis, you learned to keep the core of yourself shielded from the pain. After losing Sarah, Del had been unable to reestablish that distance, and, in the few instances since then when a patient she had worked with closely had died, she had been flooded by the pain again.

Now, she nodded to the charge nurse in understanding. Del stood and walked up the hall, following the gurney carrying her mother out the front of the building. She sat in the front seat of her truck and watched the ambulance crew lift the gurney into their rig. It occurred to her that she should call someone, then she realized she didn't know who she should call. Oddly, her dry chuckle sounded much more like a sob than a laugh.

Who to call? Cindy was more than two hours away. Widow's history with her brother ruled her out. She pulled out her cell phone and scrolled to the Andrews's number.

"Jenny? This is Del," she said when Jenny answered. "Listen, I'm at The Pines. I stopped by here to see my mom on my way home. She…she's had a bad seizure, she's unresponsive…" Del stopped as a sob escaped.

"Del, you stay right there."

Del could hear muted voices over the phone and assumed Jenny was talking to Gus.

"Don't go anywhere until we get there, Del. We'll be there in fifteen minutes. Del, do you hear me?"

"Yeah Jenny. They're taking her to the hospital. I was going to follow the ambulance." Del's voice sounded almost childlike in her own ears.

"Can you wait for us to drive you? Are you sure you're thinking well enough to drive?" Jenny asked, her concern making her voice almost sharp.

"I think I'll be okay. I just thought I should call and let someone know."

"Okay, but be careful. And if you need to pull over, call my cell and we'll come to you. Otherwise, we'll meet you at the hospital."

"You guys don't have to come—"

"Nonsense. We'll be there as soon as we can. We're leaving right now. And, Del…be careful."

"Yeah, sure. Bye." Del slipped the phone into the cup holder on the console. She took a deep breath and shook her head, trying to clear the cacophony of thoughts and images racing through it. She focused on the windows of the ambulance doors and the movements of the medics inside. Del started her truck as the rig began moving, and lights and siren filled the evening.

"Keep your eyes on the flashing red lights," she said quietly, determined to focus on the task at hand. She saw nothing but the flashing lights of the emergency vehicle in front of her as they rushed the few miles to the hospital, and Del parked in the emergency room parking lot while the ambulance disappeared into a hidden back entrance. She took another deep breath and removed her keys. Bracing herself for what might be ahead, she stepped out and went inside.

The waiting room was nearly empty at seven o'clock on a Monday evening. The attendant at the reception desk looked bored as she informed Del that she should have a seat and someone would contact her as soon as they knew something about her mother's condition. She sat numbly in front of a TV bolted to the waiting room wall. A home remodeling show was on, and Del wondered inanely who decided what the people sitting there should watch. Why not sports, or news, or sitcoms?

Del startled when Jenny sat beside her and threw an arm over her shoulder.

"Have you heard anything yet?" Jenny asked.

"No. Nothing."

Gus turned immediately and strode up to the desk. The attendant looked up as if annoyed, then sat back in her chair when he set his hands down heavily in front of her and demanded information. She arose slowly and walked through a door behind her into another room. Shortly thereafter, she returned. Gus remained with his hands flat on her desk. His intense scrutiny obviously made her uncomfortable, and she avoided looking directly at him as she spoke hesitantly.

"Sir, the doctors are working with Mrs. Smith right now. They are doing everything they can. The nurse promised someone would be out to talk to the family as soon as possible." She spoke in a soft, comforting tone, designed to soothe agitated loved ones. Del heard the woman clearly from where she sat and thought she sounded ridiculous.

How do you make it easier? she wondered. If you say it quieter, or with a certain tone, or if you touch their arm, or look sad or professional...does it really change anything?

"Tell me what happened," Jenny interrupted her thoughts.

"I went by to see her, to take her some socks she wanted," Del began slowly. "She...she was really mad and she started yelling."

"Mad? Why was she mad?" Jenny asked.

"Over Glen. I guess he must have called her. She started yelling at me, then she got really red in the face, then...oh God. Then she slumped down in the chair and started seizing. Next thing you know, the ambulance crew was there and they were taking her out, bringing her here."

"And what about you?" she asked. "Are you okay, Del?" She reached for Del's chin and turned her head so she could look into her eyes.

"Yeah, I guess." Del sounded anything but confident.

Gus sat down on Del's other side and placed an arm along the back of her chair. "Well, we're going to sit here with you as long as it takes. Okay?"

"I guess, if that's what you want. But you really don't have to, you know."

"I know, Del. We want to," Gus answered simply.

They didn't have to wait long. Less than ten minutes later, a white-coated man with a stethoscope around his neck emerged from the double doors separating the lobby from the treatment area. He walked across the empty room toward them.

"Are you the Smith family?" he asked.

Del stood immediately. "I'm Del Smith. You have my mother…" She stopped speaking when his eyes darted quickly away from her, then looked at the floor briefly before returning to meet her gaze.

"Mrs. Smith suffered a significant cerebral infarction, eh, stroke. I regret to say, she was unable to survive the damage to her brain caused by this event. We tried to revive her, but our efforts were not successful. I'm sorry." He delivered his words in a direct manner, not unsympathetic, but with no real attempt to soften the impact.

Before Del was able to stop it, a small sob escaped. She breathed in deeply and switched to autopilot, doing and saying what she thought was appropriate, shutting off her feelings. She shook the doctor's hand. "Thank you for trying."

He held her hand for a few seconds, then released it. Del wondered briefly if he was relieved at her controlled response.

"We will contact the nursing home for information about arrangements, so you won't have to attend to any of that tonight, ma'am." He looked at her expectantly.

Del just nodded. She looked blankly at Gus and Jenny as the doctor walked away, and Jenny shuddered.

"Come on Del. Let me drive you back to our place. Gus can take our truck," Jenny said, taking her hand.

"No. I think I'd rather go home."

"Okay. I'll take you home. Gus can follow us."

Del nodded, suddenly overcome with exhaustion and unable to argue.

Jenny walked beside her to Del's truck, and Gus opened the door for her to climb inside. He followed Jenny to the driver's side and spoke quietly to her before she opened the door and stepped up.

"Gus will be a few minutes behind us. He needs to stop and fill up with gas," Jenny explained. Del didn't respond, and Jenny started the truck and backed out of the parking lot.

Del was silent most of the way home, answering in a word or two only when Jenny asked her something directly. They were pulling into the driveway when Del realized she should call Glen. She found the phone book as soon as she was inside and dialed the county jail. Although she had been unsure whether she could get a message delivered to her brother, the deputy who answered the phone assured her that he would notify Glen of their mother's passing.

As she placed the cordless phone back into its base, Jenny appeared in front of her with a small tumbler of honey whiskey over ice. Del reached for it wordlessly, her mind numb. Jenny sat on the front edge of the couch while Del sank into her nearby recliner.

"Did your mother have any funeral prearrangements made?" Jenny asked.

"Hmm?" Del had to concentrate to focus her attention on the question. "Oh yeah. She had a plan set up with Ray Brothers' Mortuary in town. The home has all the information."

"You'll need to go there tomorrow sometime to take care of a few details, I'm sure," Jenny said. "Gus and I can come along if you'd like."

Del knew what Jenny and Gus thought of her mother and could honestly find no fault with their opinions of her. It didn't seem right to take them away from work and their lives to set up a funeral for someone they despised. Still, she hated the thought of doing it on her own.

She barely remembered the days following Sarah's passing. Cindy had led her through it all, much like a puppet master. It had seemed like weeks before she was able to snap out of the fog that had shrouded her mind.

This time was different. It was more as if she were in the center of a roulette wheel, her emotions spinning around her as a crazy little ball bounced here and there, trying to decide which one to land on next. She imagined stopping briefly at sadness at the loss of the only woman she had ever called mother, at frustration for not being able to control her emotions better, at guilt for never being the daughter her mother wanted and at anger at her mother for never being the parent she should have been.

"Jenny," she started, trying to halt the whirling in her mind and focus on what needed to be done. "Thank you for wanting to help. I appreciate it. Don't put yourself and Gus through this. I know you don't want any part of dealing with my mother. I can handle it. I'll just drive there tomorrow and get everything taken care of, then I'll go by the home and collect her things. I can handle it." Her voice became more determined as she spoke.

"Okay," Jenny agreed reluctantly. "On one condition. You call me if you need me for anything...you hear? Anything."

Del held up one hand in surrender. "Okay, agreed. I'll call. I promise."

They both heard the sound of a truck moving slowly down the hill toward her house, and Jenny stood and moved toward the door. She paused with a foot on either side of the threshold and looked back at Del, who sat motionless in the recliner. "Don't forget, Del. You're not in this alone. Widow, Gus and I are all your friends. We're all here for you if you need us. Don't shut us out, Del."

Del's smile fell short of her intent to reassure. "Don't worry, Jenny. It's all okay."

Del sat sipping her whiskey until it was gone, then sat longer holding the empty glass in her hand, staring at the blank TV screen in front of her. Finally she stood and set the glass on the top of the entertainment center. One flip of the light switch turned her outside world as dark as she had become inside. She made her way by memory down the short hallway to fall onto her bed, fully clothed, where she sank into a troubled sleep.

* * *

At six a.m., Del stepped out of the shower and grabbed the nearby towel from the rack. She rubbed her short hair vigorously to dry it, then stared at her reflection in the medicine cabinet mirror. The stranger looking back at her had dark circles around her eyes, and her face looked calm but dispassionate.

After the nightmare had dragged her from the deep blackness she had fallen into, she had found it impossible to still her thoughts long enough to sleep again. Childhood memories had twisted in her mind, and the few moments of happiness she had experienced seemed like the norm rather than the years of abuse. Sometime between two and six o'clock, she had made a decision she felt was necessary even if wasn't going to be popular with her friends. She *wanted*, no, she *had* to bail out her brother for the funeral. It wouldn't be fair if he couldn't say a proper goodbye. After all, it was her fault he was in jail in the first place.

She dressed and made coffee, then called her supervisor to ask for a few days of bereavement leave. It would leave them shorthanded, she knew, but over the next few days she would be busy getting the funeral taken care of and getting her mother's affairs in order.

"Breakfast," she said quietly. She might not have a chance to eat lunch, and it was too early to start running her other errands, but she didn't feel like fixing anything. She made up her mind quickly and grabbed her keys. On her way out of the kitchen, she grabbed her cell phone from the charger and jammed it into her shirt pocket.

Biscuits and gravy at the diner up the road seemed like comfort food. Still, she didn't get the same satisfaction from it as she did weeks earlier when she took Cindy there for breakfast. The food stuck in her throat, and it took several gulps of coffee to get it to go down. But she swallowed hard, knowing she would be sorry later if she didn't.

The next stop was her mother's house. She had a key so she could check on it from time to time. This morning, it looked no different than on any other morning. Nothing indicated it was now abandoned, all its former residents dead or moved on. The old wooden porch sagged a little, as it had for years. The lock always stuck, and she struggled to turn the key completely. When the lock finally released, she shoved open the door in frustration. The musty smell of a shut-up house nearly overwhelmed her, and she left the front door standing open as she went inside.

All her life, her mother had used the same metal lockbox to store her important papers. Del walked to her parents' bedroom and opened the top dresser drawer. She pulled the box out and dropped it onto the bed, shaking her head at the small puff of dust that arose from the bedspread where it landed. She worried the house had been slowly going to ruin sitting empty, but her mother had refused to rent it. Del believed she was waiting for Glen to ask for it, but he was too lazy to deal with the responsibility and the expense of a home. Sleeping on someone else's couch, eating someone else's food, taking someone else's wife to bed while they were away working to meet the expenses, that was Glen's style.

Del retrieved the key to the lockbox from beneath a false bottom in an empty jewelry box on the dresser. The dull click of the lock sounded loud in the empty house, and Del opened the box after a nervous look over her shoulder. Loose papers spilled out over the top as soon as the lid rose. The first thing she recovered was the paperwork for her mother's preplanned funeral. She set it to the side, then rummaged through further, looking for a will. When she found the envelope she sought, she placed it beside the box on the dusty bed. She quickly stuffed the remaining papers back into the box and shoved it closed. She started to place it back into the dresser drawer but changed her mind at the last second. Instead, she slid the small key into her pocket and tucked the box under one arm. With her free hand, she grabbed the will and the documents from the funeral home and walked quickly through the open front door, determination leading her steps. The door shut easily, and she wondered if it was some kind of sign, that she had faced such resistance on entering yet made an unimpeded exit.

No one at the nursing home complained when she showed up before the end of breakfast. Most of the staff were busy picking up breakfast trays and assisting residents to return to their rooms, but she was able to find the social worker and a housekeeper to help her go through her mother's things. She donated her mother's clothes to the facility for those residents who might need them. Although she didn't want any of her mother's personal items, she thought Glen might, so she gathered the knickknacks and books into a box. She left her mother's walker and wheelchair for the facility to use and walked away carrying only the one box held against her hip with one hand. It bothered her to think the sum of her mother's last year of life could be packed away so simply. One last look into the room on her way out had done nothing to ease her mind, seeing all traces of her mother vanish as if they had never existed.

The social worker assured Del her mother's body had been taken from the hospital to the mortuary, and they were expecting her to meet with them today to finalize the arrangements. The disapproving look from one elderly lady sitting in the hallway in a wheelchair did not escape Del's notice as she left the social worker's office. She was puzzled at first, then a wave of shame swept over her as she overheard the woman speaking to a nearby nurse's aide. "I heard she's the reason her mother had a stroke. Got her so upset she killed her, she did."

She didn't pause, only stepped toward the door a little quicker. Was that what they all thought? Del wondered. She hadn't noticed the social worker treating her any differently than she had on any other day. They had to know what kind of woman her mother was, didn't they? Or maybe she was different in here and they all thought she was just a sweet little old lady? It didn't matter, she supposed. It was over and done, and maybe they were right. Maybe she did kill her mother—not intentionally of course, but dead was still dead.

She set the box in the passenger seat of her truck. The sight of the lockbox and papers on the center console reminded her of what she still had to do, and she shoved any shame or doubt aside. There simply wasn't time to get emotional.

The trip to Ray Brothers' Mortuary took only a few minutes, and Del was relieved to discover she had only a few decisions to make concerning the services. In less than an hour they had established that a one-hour visitation followed immediately by the funeral would be held at the mortuary starting at ten a.m.

on Thursday morning. She would return to the mortuary on Wednesday with a new dress for her mother to be laid out in. The thought made her a little queasy—the mortician attempting to gracefully arrange a dress designed for the living onto a cold, unmoving corpse, to give loved ones an impression of normalcy when they viewed her at the visitation and funeral. It suddenly seemed grotesque to her.

"Now for the hard part," Del said under her breath as she climbed back into her truck. She looked at the lawyer's address on the envelope containing the will and pulled her truck out onto the road.

At the lawyer's office, Del met with her first resistance of the day. Although she explained her mother's death to the secretary, the stern, professional-looking woman was adamant that Del would be unable to meet with an attorney until late the following day. That would be too late for what Del needed, and she was trying to explain the urgency to the woman, aware of her increasing frustration at Del, when the office door behind the secretary opened and a slender, fortyish-looking man walked out with a briefcase in his hand. He looked at Del with a hint of recognition in his eyes. "David Fincher. Can I help you?" he asked pleasantly. "I know," his voice warmed. "You're the therapist, aren't you? You took care of my mother-in-law last month, Hildegard Meyer."

"Right." Del shook his hand as he extended it in greeting. "I'm Del Smith. How is Hilda doing at home?"

"She's doing well, very well. Thank you for asking. Is there something I can help you with?" He looked curiously at the envelope in her hand that bore the name of his firm.

"I was just trying to explain, see…my mother passed away—"

"Oh, I am so sorry. Was she a client of ours?"

"Yes, I mean I guess so. You helped her with her will." Del held the envelope out to him.

Mr. Fincher took it from her and looked at his secretary questioningly. "Do I have a few minutes, Cathy?"

"Fifteen minutes, if traffic doesn't hold you up," she said tersely.

"Del, come back into my office with me, and I'll see if I can answer your questions." He turned away and ushered her through his office door.

Del settled into the hard leather chair in front of his desk and tried to organize her thoughts. She wasn't certain if there was an answer to her problem, but she knew she had to find out.

"Now, how can I help you?" Mr. Fincher asked.

"As I said, my mother passed away yesterday. I'm interested in finding out if I can use any inheritance my brother may receive from her estate as collateral to bail him out of jail for the funeral." Del saw the look that crossed the lawyer's face before he was able to mask it—*another greedy person, can't wait to get her hands on her mother's money and, with a new twist, wants to use it to bail out her brother.*

"Ms. Smith," he began, in a tone that Del assumed would be followed with a request to make an appointment to come back another time.

"Mr. Fincher," she broke in, "I'm not asking for myself. My brother is in jail for stealing cattle from a good friend of mine, from my pastures. I was actually involved in helping the police catch him. I just…I just feel bad that he can't tell our mother goodbye. I just thought if I could bail him out…I don't know, maybe…" She was unwilling to admit she was thinking maybe her deceased mother would forgive her for putting him in jail in the first place.

With a nod of understanding, he looked at the papers contained in the envelope. "Do you know you are the executor of her will?"

Del nodded. Her mother had told her this when she had moved into the long-term care facility. But, although she had known the will was in the lockbox, she had never looked at it. She wanted nothing from her mother and wasn't concerned about what it said.

Mr. Fincher scanned through the few pages quickly, then looked at her seriously. "Have you read this?"

"No."

"Well, it seems that although you are the executor, your mother left her house and her estate to your brother, of course after any debts are settled."

Del smiled wryly. "I'm not surprised. You could say we were a dysfunctional family and I wasn't what she considered a perfect daughter."

"Even though it will take some time before her estate is formally settled, you may be able to find a bondsman who will draw up a contract for him based on this planned inheritance. I know of a couple who have been known to take some chances if they feel like it's a good risk."

"That sounds great. Should I schedule an appointment with you for another date to figure out what to do as executor?" she asked in relief.

"Sure." He handed her his card after jotting down a couple of names and numbers on the back. He rose and picked up his briefcase, then held out his hand to her again. "Just ask Cathy to schedule you an appointment on your way out. Good luck Del. Are you sure you want to bail him out though?"

Del paused before answering, then nodded emphatically. "I'm sure."

The first bondsman Del called sounded hesitant as she described her circumstances, but when she mentioned her brother's name, his hesitancy quickly changed to a resonant "not interested."

"Oh great," Del said as she punched in the second number. "Wonder how many bridges Glen has burned?"

She had an immediate dislike for the man who answered the phone at the second bondsman's office. His cocky and overbearing tone left a bad taste in her mouth after just a few minutes, and she would have probably ended the call if she had any alternatives. But, she thought, maybe the best one to help her jackass of a brother was another jackass.

While she didn't look forward to doing business with him, he assured her that he was interested in helping her brother post bail. She made plans to meet with him at eleven, then ended the call with a sigh of relief. "He had better appreciate this," she muttered, knowing Glen wouldn't.

She had twenty minutes before her meeting with Joe Bond of Bond's Unlimited, and she didn't want to spend any more time in Joe's presence than she had to. She was surprised none of her friends had checked on her yet and decided she would head off their calls with a text. First, to Gus's and Jenny's phones— "*Doing okay. Getting business taken care of. Visitation and funeral Thursday am. Will call you this evening.*"

Del assumed Jenny had called Widow, but just in case, she decided to send a different message to her. "*My mother passed away last night. I am okay. Funeral Thur. morning. Don't come. Glen may be there.*"

Now for the one who knew her best, Cindy. She thought about what to text and finally decided to leave her a voice message instead. She knew Cindy seldom answered her phone at work, leaving it at her desk and checking it at lunch and after work. She also knew if she didn't call and let her know what was going on, Cindy would probably be there kicking her in the butt before she could say "uncle." And right now she wasn't sure she had the energy to stop her.

She waited for the third ring to switch her to voice mail but was surprised when Cindy's exuberant voice came over the phone. "Dee, how are you? And what are you doing calling me on a Tuesday morning when we both should be working?"

Del smiled in spite of herself. "Hey Cindy. Sorry to bother you at work. I wasn't expecting you to answer. I figured I'd just leave you a message."

"I just happened to be walking past my desk when you rang. What's up?"

"I thought I ought to let you know that my mother died last night."

"Oh Dee. I'm sorry to hear that. Are you okay?"

"Yeah, I'm making it. Just getting the arrangements made, taking care of some business, you know. I've taken three days off, but I plan on going back to work Friday." Del tried to sound confident. All she needed was her friends second-guessing her and making her question her decisions. Better if they just all stayed home and pretended nothing had even happened.

"I have some time I can take off, Dee. I can be there tonight if you want me. Heck, even if you don't want me."

"Cindy, you don't really need to bother. I think I've got it under control. I should be getting good at it by now." Del tried to joke, but her tone was still too somber and didn't match her words.

"Why don't I go ahead and plan to take a couple days off—?"

"No Cindy. Really. I'm fine. Why would you want to come to a funeral for someone you've never met?" Del asked, exasperated.

"Maybe because my best friend is going to be there and she might just need a shoulder to lean on," Cindy said, her tone frustrated. "Look," she started in a softer tone, "I worry about you, Dee. You know I'll always be there if you need me, and whether you realize it or not, you might just need me before this is all over."

Del sighed deeply and rubbed her forehead with the heel of her free hand. She quickly thought of her options and realized she would probably have to let at least one of her friends go to the funeral with her, or they would all gang up on her and go. Cindy would be the best choice. At least she didn't have a history with Glen like Widow and Gus did.

"Okay, but I don't want you to take off more than one day. Thursday is the funeral. How about you leave Wednesday after work and stay the night, then you can head back right after the service?" Del hoped the combination of her outspoken friend and her jackass brother wouldn't blow up in her face but wasn't sure she had any better alternatives.

"Sounds like a plan," Cindy agreed. "Dee, I want you to call me if you need me for anything, you hear? I mean it."

"Yeah, I hear you, Cindy. Look, I've got an appointment to make, so I'll see you Wednesday night."

"'Til Wednesday. Bye."

"Later Cindy."

Del looked at her watch. Ten minutes 'til eleven and about seven blocks to drive, she thought as she started her truck. She turned out of the parking lot beside the lawyer's office and was at the bondsman's with two minutes to spare. Del took a deep, fortifying breath before getting out of the truck. "You better get used to it," she said to herself, thinking of the unpleasant conversation she had earlier with the owner of the bond company. "You'll be dealing with Glen soon enough."

* * *

"Now that wasn't so bad," Del said sarcastically as she walked out of the office thirty minutes later. After being in the company of Joe Bond for half an hour, she felt as though she should go home and take a shower, or at least wash her hands. He had leered at her from the second she had walked through his door, scanning her repeatedly from head to toe, with no attempt to disguise his interest in seeing what was beneath her clothes. His condescension was even worse. He questioned everything she presented to him and ultimately instructed her to have Glen or his attorney call to talk to him about the bond.

The next stop was the one she had been dreading—the jail and Glen. She steeled herself for a confrontation before she entered the tall, red brick, square building. Glen sat in the chair opposite her, a glass wall between them, and stared at her sullenly when she picked up the phone to speak to him. He finally relented and lifted the receiver to his ear after she mouthed "please."

"What do you want?" He sounded impatient, as though she was keeping him from something.

"I...I've been trying to arrange it so you can come to Mom's funeral—"

"Forget it. They're not going to let me out of here unless I can post my bond. Unless you're going to bail me out, sis." He said the final words so sarcastically that she felt a little quiver of shame for her part in his incarceration.

"I talked to Joe Bond at Bond's Unlimited, and he sounds like he'll be willing to help you," Del said, feeling a little reprieve from her brother's disappointment in her when she saw a glint of interest in his eyes.

"Now why would Joe Bond want to bail me out?" Glen asked. "What's in it for him? It's not like I can pay him back."

Del lifted her eyebrows and held up the envelope with the law firm's logo. "That's just it, Glen. You can pay him back, or at least you'll be able to when Mom's estate is settled."

"What's that, her will?"

"Yes. And she left it all to you, Glen." Del tried to sound as though it didn't disappoint her, but Glen looked at her closely when she made this admission, and she worried he had seen something in her face she wouldn't admit to herself.

He sat back in his chair and appeared to think about what she had said. Finally, he answered with a simple "huh." Del waited for him to go on, and after a few seconds, he continued, "So, she left everything to me. So, why are you here helping me out, Del? What's in it for you?"

"Nothing Glen. In case you'd forgotten, our mother just died. I thought it would be the right thing to do, to try to find a way for you to get to her funeral, that's all." She thought her explanation sounded a little unlikely even to her own ears, but she wouldn't let him know about the depths of her guilt.

"Huh," Glen said again. "Don't guess it matters. So, what've I got to do to get outta here?"

"Joe Bond said for you or your lawyer to call him and he would make the arrangements. I thought I could take this will to your lawyer for you. He should be able to take it from there, shouldn't he?"

"Doubtful. But worth a try. Bob Parsons is my lawyer. His office is about a block down from the courthouse."

"Mom had already prearranged her funeral, so all I had to do was set the day and time. Thursday at ten is when the visitation starts, and the funeral is at eleven. I figured that would give you a day or two to get everything together to get out of here."

"Oh, okay, yeah. Where at?" Glen asked distractedly, as if he was bored with the conversation and wanted her to leave.

"Ray Brothers' Mortuary."

"Those crooks?"

"Mom already had it set up, Glen. I told you that."

"Yeah. They're still crooks. Wonder how much they took her for?" Del wondered how Glen could take offense at someone cheating their mother when he seemed to have no concern about stealing from others.

"I've got to go, Glen. I'll take this out to Parsons for you, then I'll see you at the funeral home, right?" Del asked, suddenly concerned he might not show up.

"Of course, little sister." Glen grinned at her as she hung up the phone, lifting one hand to wave a little to her before he left the room.

Del drove to Parsons's office immediately and explained the situation to the secretary. The secretary made a copy of the will, then handed the original back to her. She assured Del that Mr. Parsons would look into Glen's release as soon as possible and pressed his business card into her hand before dismissing her with a look toward the door. Del gladly turned and walked out of the office, relieved to hand the responsibility over to someone else.

Del leaned back in her truck seat, exhausted now she was done with her errands. "Home," she said. She looked over at the box sitting on her console, saw the papers from the funeral home and remembered. "Crap. I forgot. I gotta shop for a dress for Mom."

Instead of turning her truck south out of town toward home, Del headed for a Kohl's on the north side of town. She pulled into the parking lot and stared at the front of the building. "Damn, I hate to shop." The elderly lady stepping into the car beside her looked up sharply when Del spoke.

Thirty minutes and a splitting headache later, she returned to her truck with her bank account considerably lighter and with a dress in a bag in her hand. She glanced at her watch. "One o'clock," she muttered.

Del buckled her seat belt and headed home, glad she could rest knowing all her errands were finished. But rest wasn't as easy as she had hoped when she finally sank down into her recliner in her living room. "Just a few minutes," she said as she kicked it back and closed her eyes. Instead of the darkness her eyelids should have created, Del's mind flipped through images of her trying to explain to Gus, Jenny and Widow why and how Glen was going to be at the funeral. Maybe it would be easier if she didn't show up for it either. But she knew she couldn't do that. Her damn sense of responsibility to her family just wasn't that easy to turn off. They had done nothing to earn the loyalty she felt toward them, but, somehow, that didn't seem to matter. Her friends, she knew, wouldn't understand that unbreakable tie.

After abandoning an unsuccessful attempt at rest, Del decided to clean her house, even though she had cleaned thoroughly just two days earlier. She was trying to decide between cleaning the glass on the front door and throwing some rugs into the washing machine when she thought she heard a motor running outside. Widow's truck pulled up into her driveway just as Del reached the door to look out.

"The fun begins," she muttered under her breath, then pushed open the door for Widow. She hadn't spoken to her since Saturday evening when they had enjoyed dinner, wine and dancing at Widow's house. The brief text she had sent earlier that morning had gone unanswered. Del wasn't certain what to say, so she started with a question.

"Shouldn't you be at work?" Her words came out sharper than she had intended.

"Good afternoon to you too. I had the afternoon off. Mind if I sit a spell?" Widow's voice was steady and calm.

Del was immediately contrite. "I'm sorry. Good afternoon. Please, have a seat. Can I get you anything to drink?"

"No thanks. I'm good," Widow responded. "How are you doing? I got your message, and Jenny called early this morning too. Are you okay?" Widow frowned as she studied Del closely.

"I guess so. It was a surprise, and I've had a lot of business to take care of, but I had a really productive morning. I even bought a dress today," Del tried to joke.

Widow's eyebrows shot up at this admission. Del had been unable to suppress a grin, giving away the truth. "For your mother, I suppose?" Widow asked.

"Of course," Del admitted. "I haven't worn a dress in twenty years, and I don't care how obligated I may feel toward someone, I don't think it will ever be enough to make me wear one again."

Widow smiled and shook her head. "Is that how you're feeling about all of this, Del? Obligated?"

"Yeah. Well, maybe. I don't know. Did you ever meet my mother?" Del asked, realizing she'd never thought to ask despite Widow's past problems with Glen.

"Yes. Believe it or not, Glen introduced us. There was a fundraiser for the volunteer fire department in town a couple of weeks after Glen attacked me behind my shed. I was there with the kids and didn't even see him until I turned and he was standing right behind me. Your mother was with him, and he introduced us like I was an old friend. I was so shocked that I couldn't even respond. I just nodded, grabbed the kids and left. She probably thought I was either rude or crazy. No telling what Glen told her about me."

"I'm sure whatever it was, it included a bunch of lies to make him look good and to paint you as the bad guy," Del said, her mother's pronouncement of *that no-good Widow woman* echoing in the back of her mind.

"Probably. I saw her occasionally over the next few years, at the grocery store or the bank, you know, around town. She usually scowled at me, so I never felt like I needed to acknowledge her," Widow admitted.

"I guess she wasn't all bad, but she wasn't exactly the nicest person in the world either. She was pretty rough on Glen and me growing up…well, especially on me. Dad yelled at her, she yelled at us. Dad slapped her, she slapped us. Guess she just passed along all the crap she took, instead of trying to get herself and us out of a bad situation."

"How long has your dad been gone?" Widow asked.

"I guess it's been about four years," Del said.

"Did she treat you any different when he wasn't at home, slapping her around?"

"No." Del dropped her head down and looked at the tops of her shoes. "Guess you're wondering why I bothered looking out for her in the nursing home and taking care of all her business, huh?"

"Not really Del." Widow's tone was softer. "People often do some pretty incredible things for loved ones who don't deserve it. Severely abused children beg to go back to their abusive parent. A parent who has been a model citizen all of their life will go against everything they believe to hide their son or daughter who is running from the law. Don't be so hard on yourself, Del. You *are* human, you know." She smiled as she said the final part and rested her hand on Del's arm.

"Thanks Widow. I've been having a lot of second thoughts, and it helps to think I might be acting normal." Del grinned at her and felt lighter than she had since before going to the nursing home the previous evening.

"So, are there still any errands left today, or are you finished for now?" Widow asked.

"Thankfully, I'm done for today. I have to run the dress to Ray Brothers' Mortuary tomorrow. The funeral is Thursday morning, and I have to meet with her lawyer next week. She made me executor of her estate, even though she left what she had to Glen."

"Why am I not surprised?" Widow shook her head in wonder. "She expected you to deal with all the headaches of it for nothing. Can you refuse to do it?"

"I don't know. I guess so. I just thought I'd do it and get it over with. Then it'll be done and I can get on with my life. Put it all behind me," Del explained.

"Obligated again?"

Del grinned sheepishly. "Yeah, I guess so."

"Well, if you're not busy right now, how about coming over to my place for a while? You can help me make dinner," Widow suggested.

"I don't think I'd be good company. I didn't sleep much last night, and I've still got a lot running through my head," Del admitted. "Maybe another time?"

"Del, if there's one thing I'm sure about, it's that you'll have plenty of time over the next two days to think. And if I'm right about how you do things, you'll be thinking yourself sick. Come on over, and maybe I can take your mind off all of this for a few hours. You can even crash in my recliner while I cook, if you'd like."

Widow's eyes were so entreating that Del had a hard time refusing her. She admitted to herself that she really didn't want to refuse Widow either. Last time she had been there, the wine had relaxed her and she had let Widow get closer than she had ever intended. This time she was just plain tired and was already having trouble controlling the whirlwind of emotions stirred up since her mother's death. Adding her growing feelings for Widow to the mix might just overwhelm her.

"I should probably say no, but..." Del said. "I might take you up on that nap in the recliner part." She grinned, trying to banish her fears, as Widow smiled in delight.

Widow stood and grabbed Del's hand. "Let's go."

Del allowed herself to be propelled out the door, with Widow pausing long enough to allow Del to lock it behind her before pulling her along, laughing, to the passenger door of her truck.

"Wait, why can't I take my truck?" Del asked.

"I'll bring you home later," Widow said. "Promise."

Widow was as good as her word. She settled Del into a recliner in her living room, turned on the local news and went to the kitchen to prepare a meal. Johnnie wouldn't be home for supper. He was working at a job just a few miles from J.T.'s apartment and stayed with her two or three nights a week to save gas money.

Del wasn't aware of Widow slipping quietly down the hall to check on her after she had slipped a casserole into the oven for their dinner. Del slept soundly in what she had quickly declared to Widow to be the most comfortable recliner she'd ever sat in. Nor was she aware that Widow turned the oven temperature down, delaying their meal so Del would have more time to sleep. Widow was careful not to awaken her when she retrieved the phone from the living room, then returned to the kitchen before she called Jenny.

"Jenny, this is Widow," she said when Jenny picked up. "I just wanted to let you know I talked Del into coming over for dinner. She's here now. I figured you would try to call her tonight and would be worried if you couldn't track her down."

"Good. How is she doing?" Jenny asked.

"As good as can be expected, I guess. She said she didn't sleep much last night. I believe it. She's napping in my recliner right now." Widow chuckled.

"Sounds like you're taking good care of her," Jenny said.

"Trying to. She doesn't make it very easy, you know."

"I've noticed that about her." Jenny laughed. "Kind of self-sufficient, isn't she? Tries not to need anyone for anything."

"I guess you could say that. She makes it hard to get close."

"Just hang in there, Widow. If anyone can do it, it'll be you," Jenny assured her.

"I hope you're right. By the way, she texted me earlier today and told me I probably wouldn't want to go to the funeral Thursday because Glen would likely be there. Do you know anything about that?" Widow asked.

"No. But she discouraged us from going too. Maybe Glen found someone to post bail. I don't feel very good about Del being around Glen without friends around to back her up."

"I don't either. Jenny, you don't think Del would bail him out, do you?" Widow asked.

"No. I think she knows if she did he would never show up for court and she would lose everything." Jenny sounded certain, but Widow wasn't convinced.

"Well, I hope you're right. She's got this strong sense of obligation, you know. Look, I'd better go. I'll talk to Del about it later and see what I can find out. I'll call you tomorrow."

"Okay Widow. Sounds like a plan. Talk to you tomorrow."

Widow hung up and walked quietly down the hall to the living room and sat on the couch opposite Del while she watched the news. She stole a glance at Del every few minutes, but she seemed to be sleeping soundly. The deeply etched worry lines had nearly faded from her forehead, but she frowned slightly even in her sleep. The pain Widow had seen in Del's eyes earlier when she spoke of her mother had hinted of a much bigger scar than her words had indicated. Now, flinches and Del's entire body jerking at times suggested her memories were less than peaceful.

Widow's attention repeatedly returned to the troubled sleep of her friend, and her concern for Del grew as the minutes passed. The stove timer going off sounded unusually loud, but Del didn't wake. Widow hurried to the kitchen to turn off the annoying beeping. She slid the casserole from the oven onto the stovetop. "All done," she said quietly. "Now to rescue Del from her dreams."

"Del," she said softly from the living room doorway. She walked closer to the chair and placed a hand on Del's forearm where it rested on the arm of the recliner. "Del, it's time to eat."

Del startled awake despite Widow's attempts to be gentle. "What?" she cried as she nearly leaped to her feet.

"Easy Del," Widow said, moving her hand quickly to Del's shoulder. "You fell asleep waiting on supper. I was just waking you to let you know the casserole is done. Are you ready to eat?"

"Oh," Del said with a sheepish grin. "Sorry. I didn't mean to fall asleep. Is there anything I can do—set the table, pour drinks, you know, make myself less of a bum?" She smiled wider when Widow chuckled.

"Come on to the kitchen. I'll let you fix our glasses so you can say you weren't a bum." Del stood, and Widow took her by the hand and led her to the kitchen cabinet where the glasses were kept. "There's sweet tea in the refrigerator, or soda, or water if you would like. Ice is in the freezer. I'd like a glass of tea, please."

"Okay. I asked for it," Del said as she dropped ice into both glasses. She filled both with tea, then turned and handed one to Widow. "M'lady, your tea."

"'M'lady'? Where did that come from?" Widow shook her head. "Do me a favor. Take our glasses in to the table, and I'll bring plates and the casserole. Hope you weren't expecting a four-course meal."

"All I was hoping for was more of your home cooking, in whatever form you'd like to create it," Del said seriously. "I can and I do cook, but it's not even in the same league as what you do. That casserole smells great."

Del expressed her delight when she tasted it, and insisted it was even better than it smelled. After two large helpings, Del pushed back from the table with a groan. "Any more and I won't be able to walk."

"I'm glad you enjoyed it," Widow responded. "I'm glad you came over too. I hate to eat alone, and after cooking for the kids all these years, I don't know what to do with myself when there's no one here to feed."

"You may have to let me know when Johnnie isn't going to be here and I'll see if I can help you out then." Del smiled. "Shoot, I'll even buy groceries."

Widow wondered if Del realized the warmth glowing in her eyes as she spoke. She noticed Del's sudden uneasiness when she wrinkled her forehead and changed the subject. "So, can I do dishes?"

"No," Widow answered immediately. "But you can help me load the dishwasher." She handed their empty plates to Del to carry into the kitchen. Del led the way with Widow following closely with the remains of the casserole. "Can I send some of this home with you for lunch tomorrow?" She held out the half-empty dish toward Del.

"You don't need to do that, Widow. Won't you and Johnnie have it for supper tomorrow?" Del was eyeing the dish greedily, her eyes saying yes despite the words coming from her mouth.

Widow reached into the cabinet with her free hand to retrieve a plastic dish, which she quickly slid the remaining casserole into. "No, Johnnie won't eat it. I don't know how I managed to raise such a picky child, but I swear he has more dislikes than likes when it comes to food. He sure didn't get it from me." She smiled as she rubbed her stomach.

"What? Are you trying to imply you have extra pounds there to rub, Widow?" Del set the empty plates onto the dishwasher rack and turned to look closely at her. "Because I can tell you that I don't see anything to spare."

"I just hide it well," Widow said. "Trust me, there's extra. You should see me naked, then you wouldn't doubt me."

Widow's words were teasing, but she could see their immediate effect on Del as her eyes widened and her breath caught. She recovered quickly, though, and arched her eyebrows playfully at Widow, then winked as she responded, "Hmmm. I might have to do that sometime, just so I could prove you wrong, of course."

Widow felt herself blush and turned to finish loading the dishwasher. After spending an unusual amount of time getting it started, she brushed past Del without making eye contact, walking briskly down the hall toward the living room. "Come on. You are impossible, you know."

Del laughed as she followed her. "So, what do you usually do home alone on a Tuesday night?"

"Nothing much. Watch TV or read, usually. Did you have something in particular in mind?"

"No, television or reading sounds good to me. By the way, how long do you plan to keep me?"

Widow looked at her watch before answering. "It depends on how tired you are. I thought maybe we could keep each other company for a couple of hours. I can take you home anytime you want though."

"Actually I'm really not in any hurry to get back. You were right, I've got too much time to think right now, and that's probably what I would do if I went home now—just sit and think about Mom and growing up." Del looked around the living room, and her gaze landed on a stack of games in the corner on a desk. "How about a game?" she suggested, gesturing toward it.

"Sure," Widow said. "Do you have any preferences?"

Del rose to look over the choices. "How about Monopoly?"

"Are you sure?" Widow asked. "I should warn you, I have a reputation for being ruthless when I play Monopoly. The kids won't even play it with me anymore."

"Ooh, sounds serious. Maybe I'll reconsider." The Wii console next to the TV caught Del's attention. "I know," she said. "Let's bowl."

"Smart choice." Widow laughed. "I suck at bowling."

Del was ahead three games to one when Widow finally begged for a reprieve. "Please, no more. I don't think my ego could take it. I'm usually quite competitive, but I've never done well with bowling. How about baseball or tennis?"

Del was the one to look at her watch this time. "Can I take a rain check on that? I promise, next time we'll start with anything but bowling."

"I'm holding you to that, Del Smith."

"I guess I'm starting to feel my early morning. The nap in your recliner helped, but I'm fading fast. Would you mind if we called it a night?"

Widow stepped up and placed her hands lightly on Del's arms just above her elbows. "Thank you for coming over, Del. Of course we can call it a night. Come on, I'll take you home." Before she released Del, Widow leaned closer and kissed her lightly on her cheek.

"Thank you," Del said quietly.

The effort it took for her to keep her voice from quavering was obvious. Widow took Del by the hand and led her toward the door. "Stay here and I'll get your casserole," she said.

Minutes later, they were in the truck. They didn't speak on the short drive to Del's house. Del didn't move her hand from the seat between them when Widow reached over and rested her hand on top of it, gently interlinking their fingers. When Widow moved her hand to shut off the truck, she was surprised when Del chased after it briefly.

Widow got out of the truck and met Del at the passenger side. She grabbed Del's hand, then walked beside her up the steps and across the porch to the door, gently swinging their linked hands between them. Del unlocked the door and flipped on the light switch. "Would you like to come in?" Del gestured toward the door with her other hand.

"I think I'll leave you here tonight," Widow said. She smiled impishly. "Might be safer for you."

Del's cheeks flushed and she smiled back. "Might be," she said quietly.

Widow moved in front of her, slowly winding her arms around Del's neck, pulling their faces closer together. "Thank you for a wonderful evening," she whispered.

"No. Thank you for a wonderful meal and for a chance to beat you at bowling," Del whispered in return, smiling slightly before she leaned forward to touch their lips together.

Widow was nearly overwhelmed by the melting, wet heat. Only her concern for Del's roiling emotions prevented her from getting lost in Del's kisses. When she knew her control was slipping, she drew her lips away. Del's sudden look of loss was heartbreaking, and she held Del close, allowing her warm breath to caress Del's cheek, letting her know she was not alone.

"Good night Del. Call me for anything and I'll be here." Widow put her hand on Del's chest and gently but firmly pushed her away.

Del took a breath and stepped back, a gentle breeze flowed between them. "Good night Widow." Del stood in the light of the open door and watched as Widow turned away, put her hands in her jeans pockets and walked back to her truck. Widow could see her, standing in the porchlight, with one hand lifted and waving as she backed out of the driveway and started up the hill.

CHAPTER ELEVEN

The bedframe creaked and groaned as Del tossed and turned, keeping with the revolution of the thoughts in her head. Sleep was elusive, and initially her mind shifted from Widow to the much more troubling thoughts of her mother and the nagging belief Del was responsible for her death. She tried relaxation drills, and when that failed, considered drinking enough whiskey to render herself unconscious.

Visions of her brother in an orange jumpsuit flitted through her thoughts, mixing with the images of Widow telling her good night at the door and the gruesome sight of Beatrice stiffening in her wheelchair as the seizure overtook her. In the half-asleep state she had finally sunk into, they twisted together into a horrific blending of love, hate, fear and guilt.

At some point, she must have drifted deeper, because the demons that tormented her were quiet when she awoke at four a.m. The world was silent around her, and she couldn't tell what had awakened her. What was all too clear was that sleep had abandoned her again and there was no going back.

"I'm not going to sit in this house all morning and go crazy," Del said. She threw the covers back and started her day.

* * *

An hour later Del was finishing a warm-up on the treadmill in the nearly empty recreation center. She watched the morning staff trickling into the building as she walked, and she wasn't surprised when she saw Jessie winding her way around the equipment toward her.

"Morning!" Del said brightly.

Jessie grinned and echoed, "Morning. Surprised to see you here this early. Skipping work today?"

"Naw, got the day off," Del replied, hoping she could avoid going into more detail.

"I don't get it. You've got the day off, so you come to the gym at the butt crack of dawn to work out? That doesn't make much sense, Del."

Del shrugged and grinned. "Who said I have to make sense?"

"Good point. Is everything okay though?" Jessie's voice became more serious.

"Yeah." Del could see from the way Jessie tilted her head that she probably wasn't going to settle for her one-word answer. "Just got a lot on my mind. I couldn't sleep any longer, so I gave up and decided I might as well do something productive."

Jessie nodded in understanding. "Now that makes more sense. Been there, done that."

Del looked at the younger woman and smiled. *I wonder what she'd think if she could see all the crap floating around inside my skull. Probably call 911 to take me to a psych ward.*

She stepped down from the treadmill and walked toward the nearest row of weight equipment. Jessie followed and waited until Del was settled in place before speaking. "Well, if you need anything, give me a yell. Even if you just need to talk."

"Thanks Jessie. I will."

Del took her time making her rounds through the exercise equipment, then showered at the gym instead of returning home to shower and change as she usually did. When she fastened her watch around her wrist, she looked at the time. "Only six," she said under her breath. "I was hoping to kill more time than that."

She decided to look for Jessie again before she left and found her near the pool. "Hey," she said, lifting her hand in a small wave. "Got time for a cup of coffee?"

"Sure." Jessie smiled. "Just give me a minute to get everything squared away here."

Del watched as Jessie set out the items needed for the aquatics class that would begin shortly, then Jessie strode over to her. "Follow me. I know the way to the best coffee in the building." She turned and walked away with Del a half step behind.

"Jessie, you're right. This is pretty good coffee." Del leaned back in a chair in Jessie's small office, a large cup of black coffee in her hand.

Jessie took a sip from her own cup and smiled her agreement. "So Del. What's up? And don't say 'nothing,' because I know there's something keeping you from sleeping nights."

Del grinned and ducked her head. She knew the question would come and she wasn't surprised when Jessie got right to it. "I've got a few days off for bereavement leave because my mother died. I don't quite know what to do with myself, so I came in to work out."

Jessie whistled softly between her teeth. "Wow. That so wasn't what I was expecting you to say. Sorry to hear about your mother. Are you okay?"

Del nodded and met her concerned gaze. "Yeah. I'm doing fine. We weren't close like you and your mom are." She hesitated a moment, then continued, "I mean, I loved her 'cause she was my mom. I even looked after her this last year when she was at the nursing home, but...let's just say we had a lot of differences when I was growing up."

Del knew her words were inadequate to describe the jumble of emotions she'd discovered she had toward her mother. For many years, she thought the word *hate* summed up her feelings very well. But when her mother needed her, Del felt obligated, needed, even responsible for her. It wasn't until her death that Del found these other feelings she'd buried as a child. Now she was uncertain how to express everything she felt, maybe even uncertain how to feel all of it at the same time. Trying to explain it to someone else was impossible.

To her relief, Jessie didn't ask for a better explanation. She just nodded and sipped her coffee again. Del wanted to avoid more questions about her mother, so she quickly changed the subject. "So Jessie. How have you been?"

"Good. Good. You know, I like my job. And, don't tell Mom, but I've gone out a few times with this cute redhead named Kelly."

Del's eyebrows raised at this admission. "Oh. So is this Kelly thing serious?"

"I don't know. I don't do serious. Or at least I never have before. But I can't seem to get her out of my head."

"Uh-oh." Del smiled as she remembered when she first met Sarah. She had fallen hard and fast for her. "Sounds like you've got it bad."

"Yeah, maybe," Jessie agreed, grinning back at her. "So what about you, Del?"

"What do you mean?" Del asked, quickly remembering she was speaking to Widow's daughter.

"Johnnie seems to think you and Mom might be seeing each other," Jessie announced. "What a change, huh? It wasn't that long ago that I asked you out on a date. Then I find out that all of these years, Mom has been hiding the fact she's a lesbian from me. I suspected it all along, you know. I thought maybe she was in denial. I didn't realize she was just so deep in the closet she was afraid to come out. Then my brother tells me our mother has been drinking wine and dancing with our eligible lesbian neighbor…you!" Jessie spoke more rapidly as she went on, her tone becoming more frustrated.

Del breathed a sigh of relief when Jessie stopped before yelling at her. "Okay," she said calmly. "Well, truthfully, I wasn't really planning on dating anyone. Besides, your mother and I are just…just friends."

Jessie snorted in disbelief.

"Really Jessie. At this point we are friends. I think…maybe… in the future…maybe…we might see what develops." Del knew Jessie probably wouldn't believe her. She wasn't sure she even believed herself.

"I think you and Mom need to quit lying to yourselves and to everyone around you," Jessie said point-blank.

Del looked at her sadly. "Sometimes things aren't that easy. Give your mother a break, at least. She kept secrets to protect you and your brother, because she was afraid of losing you both."

"I know she was afraid, Del," Jessie said, her tone softening a little. "But I still think she should have been honest and fought instead of lying and avoiding a fight."

"And what would it have done to her if she would have lost that fight, Jessie?" Del pointed out. "You'll never know what you might have done in her place. Times were different then."

"Maybe. But back to you and Mom and your, um, friendship. I'm okay with it if you two are dating, as long as you aren't just playing with her. You keep saying you're just friends. How would she describe it? Do you mean more to her than just a friend? Is this one-sided, Del?" Jessie peppered her with questions faster than she could think of answers.

Del had asked herself the same things and had never even answered them to herself. Her fear of what the answers might be kept her from looking too deep. Either direction scared her. She was either a callous user or she was opening herself up again to the pain of loss she felt with Sarah's death. Now she sat staring at Jessie, who was waiting for an honest answer.

"I don't think it's one-sided, Jessie," Del admitted. "I'm just not sure I have the courage to do this again."

"I think you need to find out, and fast, before you pull Mom in any deeper. The longer it takes you to make up your mind, the more you're going to hurt her," Jessie warned.

Del nodded and rubbed her forehead with the heel of her hand, wondering when it had begun to pound. "You're right, of course. There's one thing I am sure of. I know I don't want to hurt her. I'm trying to take it very slowly, Jessie. Believe me."

Del knew she was unable to disguise her look of worry, and every word she had spoken was sincere. Jessie nodded and replaced her frown with a small smile of apparent acceptance.

Del stood. "I probably ought to let you get back to work."

Jessie looked at her watch. "You're right. I have a class in ten minutes, so I need to get ready." She stood and walked around her desk to stand beside Del. When Del turned toward the door, Jessie stopped her with a hand on her shoulder before she could take that first step away. "Del, thanks for being honest with me…about everything."

"Thanks for looking out for your mother," Del responded. She wrapped one arm around Jessie's shoulders and gave her a quick squeeze, then walked out the door, swinging her gym bag in her hand as she made her way to the front of the building.

Del stopped at the grocery store and forced herself to go up and down every aisle. She spent an unusual amount of time going over the list of ingredients on several items and checking prices against each other. Unfortunately, her shopping list was short, so there was a limit to how long she could stretch her time in the store. She stashed the frozen and cold items in a cooler in the back of her truck and threw the other items on the passenger seat and floorboard after moving the bag with her mother's dress up onto the center console.

On the way home, she took a chance that the mortuary would be open early. When she tried the front door of the stately brick building, it was still locked. She hadn't even made it to the sidewalk, however, when the doors opened and a short, thin man in a dark suit summoned her into the building. He wasn't the same man she had dealt with the previous day, so she introduced herself and showed him the dress she had chosen for her mother.

He approved of it, and Del wondered if it would be prudent in his business to ever disapprove of a family's choice of attire for their loved one.

"Before you leave, Ms. Smith," James, the thin, agreeable funeral director said, "can we review her obituary, please? I believe there was an oversight when your mother gave us her information several years ago when she purchased this plan."

Del was puzzled. "Sure. What do you need to know?"

"Were there two children, then? You and your brother, Glen?"

"That's certainly all I ever knew about. Why? Did she claim to have more?"

"No. Um, actually, she only listed your brother, Glen. I'm sorry if I've upset you," he said quickly as a rapid blush colored her cheeks.

"That's okay. She...she and I didn't always see eye-to-eye. It must have been during one of those times when she filled it out."

"Is there anyone I need to list with you?" He looked at her expectantly, and when she didn't answer, he continued, "You know, are you or your brother married or have significant others you would like to have listed as surviving family?"

"No. There's no one else." Del had a moment's thought of listing Sarah as a daughter-in-law preceding her in death but didn't want to even think about her mother being that close to Sarah, even in black-and-white print. She had separated the two of them in her mind just as she had divided her life into two parts, seldom allowing the pain of her childhood to taint the love and peace of her years with Sarah.

The ride home gave her time to think again, and she was certainly tired of thinking. Jessie had stirred up a mess in her mind that morning, and while going to the gym had been good for Del's body and had certainly killed some time, it hadn't brought her any peace as she had hoped. Cindy wouldn't arrive until late that evening, and Del wasn't sure what to do until then.

She wasn't home fifteen minutes before her cell phone rang. She answered it with a sigh of relief, glad to have someone to talk to. "Hello, this is Del."

"Hi Del. This is Jenny. How are you today?"

"Oh good. Doing fine. I thought you'd be at work. How did you find time to get to a phone?"

"Actually, I'm home today. I had some comp time built up at work and decided to take a couple days off," Jenny explained.

"You aren't using your time off to check up on me, are you?" Del asked, immediately suspicious, especially after Widow's sudden appearance the previous afternoon.

"It's like I said, I had comp time built up that I needed to use. Now, if I decide to use it because I think my friend might need some company after her mother died, well that's my right, isn't it?"

Del could tell from her tone there was no use quarreling with her. She was actually surprised to find she was glad Jenny had thought of her. "Okay. I won't argue with you, Jenny. You'll just win anyway." Del laughed.

"Good. I'm glad you figured that out quick and decided not to waste your time." Jenny was laughing too but still managed to sound confident in her ability to come out ahead in any match. "So, what do you have planned for today?"

"I'm done with everything I have planned. Got nothing to do until Cindy gets here this evening."

"Cindy is coming for the funeral?" Jenny asked.

"Yeah. She wouldn't take no for an answer." Del didn't mention her hope that if Cindy went to the funeral, maybe Gus, Jenny and Widow wouldn't.

"I thought I would see if you wanted to do some shopping with me today," Jenny said.

Del fought to keep the relief out of her voice at the change of subject. "What kind of shopping?"

"I really need to make some changes to my wardrobe," Jenny said. "Are you up for a round or two of racks and racks of the latest fashions and fitting rooms?"

Del groaned, which drew a laugh from Jenny. "You have caught me at a desperate time, or I would find a way to beg off. I guess I'm up for it, even though I might not be the best company for clothes shopping."

"You've got to be better than Gus or the boys. You'd think I was torturing them to even suggest they go along."

"I hope you're right, Jenny, but no promises."

"I'll take my chances. How about I come over and pick you up in about thirty minutes?"

"Sounds good. See you then."

* * *

It was lunch before Jenny finally allowed her to stop and rest. "As far as I know, Ray Brothers' doesn't give a two-for-one discount on funerals, so you don't need to shop me to death," Del complained to Jenny, who feigned innocence with widened eyes.

They had agreed on Mexican food, and Del watched with interest as Jenny mixed salsa with cheese dip before dipping a tortilla chip into the swirly combination and eating it with apparent enjoyment. Jenny noticed Del's focus on her creation and shrugged. "What? Don't tell me you're going to harass me about my cheesy salsa. You're as bad as Gus."

"I didn't say anything," Del protested. "Not a word."

"Humph" was all Jenny answered.

Del chuckled at her and took a large sip of her strawberry margarita. Jenny had suggested she try one, and she couldn't use the excuse of driving to refuse. She had no responsibilities for the afternoon, and the frosty drink had sounded appealing. So here she sat with a large and definitely delicious drink in front of her, with the top of the glass becoming more exposed as she was irresistibly drawn to it again and again.

Del hoped Jenny wouldn't draw her into a repeat of her early morning exchange with Jessie. She didn't want to think today. She didn't want to delve into her feelings now. It was just too hard. The margarita was much better to concentrate on, and another large sip went down easily.

Before she finished her quesadilla, the glass was empty. She excused herself to use the restroom, and when she returned, the waiter had brought another one. "Wait a minute. I can't drink that, Jenny. My feet are already thinking about whether they'll listen to me or not." She sat down awkwardly in the booth as if to prove her coordination was impaired.

"I'll make sure you get home safely. Don't worry," Jenny reassured her.

Del had every intention of limiting herself to no more than half of the second drink, but Jenny continued to chat long after they had finished eating. When she lifted the glass and found it was empty, she looked at Jenny in surprise.

"Want another one?" Jenny asked.

"No," Del answered quickly. "You may have to carry me out as it is."

Jenny chuckled. "You needed to relax, Del. You've been wound pretty tight for a long time."

"Had to stay wound to keep going. Hope you don't have much more shopping to do. I'm not sure I still have my walking legs."

"No. I'm done for today. Is there anything you wanted to do while we're out and about?"

Del shook her head.

"Well, let's get out of here, then." Jenny moved faster than Del to reach for the bill when the waiter placed it on the table. "You leave the tip, the rest is my treat for going shopping with me. And don't argue."

Jenny's tone permitted no room for discussion, and Del wisely didn't try. When she slid out of the booth and tried to stand, she found her legs less than dependable. She leaned her thigh against the table for support. "Whoa," she said. "I think someone moved the floor."

Jenny laughed and firmly grabbed her arm. "Come on, lightweight." She steered her to the counter, where she paid for their food and drinks, then led Del out the door and to the passenger side of Jenny's Camry. "Do you need help getting in?" She was laughing as she leaned Del up against the car just behind the door.

"No. I can make it." Del spoke confidently, but she wasn't steady when she turned to open the door, and Jenny watched her closely as she clumsily sat down in the car. "See? All in." She grinned as Jenny laughed at her again.

"You are a mess, Del Smith."

"Don't forget it's your fault, Jenny Andrews."

Jenny didn't drive straight home. She stopped once at a small liquor store downtown and wouldn't tell Del what she was after. After a few minutes, Jenny emerged with a brown paper bag, which she placed behind her seat.

"What's that?" Del asked.

"That strawberry margarita looked good, so I thought I'd fix me one when we get to your house. You do have a blender, don't you?"

"Of course."

"Ice?"

"Yes."

"Good. Then we're all set."

"Okay." Del smiled and shook her head. Jenny was a hard one to figure out, she decided.

Ten minutes later, Jenny sank back into Del's couch, a tall glass of red, frosty margarita in her hand. She placed her shoeless feet up onto the coffee table and sighed a deep sigh. "This is a wonderful way to spend the afternoon."

Del looked at the glass Jenny had placed in her hand, wondering why Jenny thought she needed another when she still hadn't recovered from the first two. "You've already confirmed I'm a lightweight when it comes to alcohol, Jenny. What are you trying to do to me?"

"Del, have you ever thought about how much like Gus you are?"

"No." Del drew the word out, a bit worried about whether Jenny might be making a strange pass at her. She looked over at Jenny suspiciously, and Jenny laughed.

"No. Not like that, goofball. I meant emotionally. You know, the way you deal with things. You and Gus are just alike. You bottle things up inside and pretend like nothing is wrong while you quietly spin yourself into insanity."

"Huh. Gus does that too?"

"Yes. And I learned quite by accident when his mother died that alcohol loosens his tongue and he spills."

"So that's the plan. Get me drunk and I tell you all my troubles. That will make me all better." Del's voice brimmed with bitter disbelief.

"Maybe. But if that doesn't work, at least we get to enjoy an afternoon of margaritas."

Jenny's response eased her initial concerns, so Del took her first sip and decided to try to relax. "Mmm. Good stuff, Jenny. You may have the Mexican place beat." Another sip confirmed it. She could visualize diminutive figures of her mother and brother racing ahead of a strawberry-red wave as they escaped the corners of her mind. Widow popped up in a variety of ways, riding a surfboard, floating lazily in a canoe and doing a backstroke through a margarita sea. "Only good thoughts," she said aloud.

"Were you speaking of anything in particular or just good thoughts in general, Del?"

"Oh. Did I say that out loud?"

"Yes. And you didn't answer me. Any good thoughts in particular you were referring to just then?"

Del grinned, picturing Widow wishing her a good night less than twenty-four hours earlier in the doorway just a few feet away. "No," she lied. "Just in general."

Jenny narrowed her eyes and shook a finger at her. "I saw that look. You're not telling me something, Del. I have plenty of experience getting things out of my boys. Don't make me use my interrogation skills on you."

"Waterboarding is illegal, you know," Del quipped.

"Don't worry. I don't need waterboarding. I have ways that even the CIA doesn't know about. I missed my calling, you know. I should have been a spy."

Del laughed. "You're crazy, Jenny."

"You doubt me now. Just wait. So Del, how was your dinner with Widow last night?"

Del had been taking another sip of her drink, and she almost choked with surprise. After coughing and getting her throat clear, she was able to answer. "How did you know I had dinner with Widow last night?"

"She called me while you were asleep in her recliner."

"Oh."

"Well...did you have a good time?" Jenny probed.

"Yeah. Sure. Widow's a fine cook. Beats the hell out of what I can do."

"And that grin I saw a few minutes ago had nothing to do with food. I'll bet money on it," Jenny insisted.

Del tried to refrain from grinning again, but too many margaritas prevented her from stopping it. She couldn't help but join Jenny as she laughed at her. The drinks made her laugh much more than she normally would have, and she was unable to control it. Soon she was wiping tears from her eyes with the back of her hand. "Stop! You're killing me!" she protested.

"Talk Del. I've known you and Widow have had the hots for each other since Jessie's birthday party. You might as well tell me. I'll get it out of you sooner or later," Jenny promised.

"Really?" Del was surprised. "You knew that long ago? I don't think I even knew then."

"You were lying to yourself then. I saw how you looked at each other."

"How?" Del was curious now. "How did she look at me and why didn't I notice it?"

"You didn't notice because she was watching you when you weren't looking. And she had one of those foolish grins on her face like you had a while ago. She didn't have any memories of you to be remembering, so she must have been dreaming of what could be."

"Oh." Del hoped she remembered this conversation when the tequila wore off. She wanted to ponder that a little more but didn't seem to be able to keep her thoughts on track long enough at present to do so. "Well, maybe Widow and I..." Del tried to finish but couldn't figure out how to explain what they had without getting into territory she wasn't comfortable with.

"Maybe Widow and you...?" Jenny waited a few seconds, then continued, "It's okay to admit you like her, Del. Remember, I'm on both of your sides."

"Yeah. I like her." Del was much quieter, feeling more pensive now. "I like her a lot."

"Good. Good for you both," Jenny said.

"I just…I'm just scared, Jenny. I'm scared to let myself go there." Del forced the words out through a throat that suddenly felt tight.

Jenny reached over and placed a hand on Del's knee. "Just take it a day at a time, Del. Widow is a pretty special woman. She knows you're still hurting, and I'll bet she's willing to wait until you figure it all out."

"And what if I can't get past it, Jenny? What then? Then I hurt Widow, and I don't want to do that."

"Hang in there, Del. You'll get past it."

Del took a large gulp of her drink. "I hope you're right. I wish I could just let go and try again. But I don't think my heart came through the loss of Sarah in one piece."

"I know you'll always have Sarah in your heart. And I know it will take time for you to risk it all again. But I think that time will come, Del. Just don't give up."

Del sat quietly for several minutes, and she and Jenny sipped their drinks in silence. Finally Jenny broke the stillness with a change in direction. "So Del, are you ready for the funeral tomorrow?"

There. I knew she'd get to it eventually, Del thought, almost relieved now that she had. "Yeah. Everything is taken care of. Cindy's going with me. You guys don't need to come. I know my mother wasn't on your favorite-person list." That was the argument she had practiced using in her head; now she only hoped it would work.

"Your mother's dead. She won't care who is or isn't there. Don't you get it, Del? You *are* on our favorite-person list, and you are the one we would be going for. Funerals are more about the living than they are the dead. And we want to be there for you, our friend."

"But it's just going to be a mess. I don't want Glen…" Del stopped. She wasn't supposed to let slip that Glen would be there. That would just lead to more questions. Damn the tequila for messing with the brakes on her tongue.

Jenny's eyes widened at Glen's name. "Is Glen going to be there, Del? Is Glen out on bail?"

"I think so," she admitted. "His lawyer made it sound like he would have him out today."

Jenny sat for a minute saying nothing, then Del saw sudden understanding cross her face. "Del, when did you talk to his lawyer?"

Damn. "Yesterday," she admitted. "I might as well tell you and get it over with. You've managed to get everything else out of me." Del didn't try to hide her frustration. "I went to see Glen and told him he was inheriting all of Mom's estate after bills are paid. He should at least get the house free and clear. Anyway, he should be able to use the house as collateral for bail, and I took his lawyer a copy of the will so he could arrange it all for him." She left out that she had been the one who initiated the whole plan.

Jenny looked at her closely. "So, Glen will be there tomorrow."

"Probably. That's why I was trying to get you guys to not go. I don't want a confrontation."

Jenny sat back and mulled over Del's confession. "What do you think about Glen going?"

"I think he should. She was his mother too. You know, I'm kind of glad he has a chance to go. I would've felt bad for him if he wouldn't have had the opportunity to be there." The final admission escaped her faulty brakes. *Damn tequila.*

"Ahhh." Del's confession was obviously shocking to Jenny. "You know what, Del? Your family didn't deserve you. They treated you like dirt and you still look out for them, even after they're dead."

"You don't understand, Jenny. I had to do something. This whole thing happened because of me. Glen being in jail, Mom dying, none of it would have happened if I wasn't involved." She tossed the remnants of her drink back, barely tasting it as it went down.

Jenny's disbelief showed on her face. "Help me out here, Del. I'm not following you. How is it your fault Glen's in jail?"

"If I hadn't moved back, if I hadn't told him we'd be out of town, if I hadn't helped the cops catch him. Admit it, Jenny."

"I can't agree with you, Del. Glen stole those cattle. Glen used you to find out the best time to take them. Glen deserves to pay for his actions. If you hadn't lived here, he would have stolen cows from someone else's pasture."

"It doesn't matter anyway. Besides, I killed Mom," Del finally admitted.

Jenny moved over to sit on the arm of Del's chair and put an arm around her shoulders. "Why would you say that, Del? You know you didn't kill her."

Del wanted to shrug her arm away but sat motionless, knowing when she told her, Jenny would probably recoil. "Mom was fine when I went to see her. I'm the one who made her angry. I knew better. I knew her health was fragile and she shouldn't be upset. But I did. I made her mad and she died. See. I did it."

But Jenny didn't recoil. When she responded to Del this time, her voice was soft. "I wasn't there, Del, but I know in my heart that you didn't make your mother angry. Your mother became angry all on her own. You cannot take on responsibility for her feelings. No Del. You did not kill your mother. She decided to get upset. Instead of appreciating you for everything you did for her, she chose to become angry, probably over something that wasn't even your fault."

Del dropped her head into her hands. She was trying to sort it out in her mind, but the alcohol was making it harder. She stood and staggered, nearly falling. Jenny grabbed her by the arm to steady her, then released her when she regained her balance. "I need to take a walk, clear my head."

"Let me go with you," Jenny said.

"No. I need to be alone, Jenny. I gotta go." She pulled the door open and weaved onto the porch. Jenny stayed close by until she was down the steps safely, then sank down onto the top step, watching Del make a crooked path along the driveway and up the hill.

* * *

Gus was five minutes away when Jenny called for reinforcements. When he pulled off the county road onto Del's lane, he could see her walking toward him about fifty feet ahead. After passing through the gate, he pulled his truck to the side so he wasn't blocking the way and turned off the engine. He swung the gate closed and fastened it before turning to walk toward Del.

Del stepped through the barbed-wire fence along her lane and headed off into the pasture. Gus wasn't deterred by her obvious attempts at evasion and followed, then jogged a few final steps to catch up with her. They walked together without speaking. Gus sensed Del would talk when she was ready.

When they reached an outcropping of large rocks, Del circled around them then appeared to clamber up onto them easily, considering her intoxicated state. Gus waited until she sat down with her feet hanging over the edge of the highest boulder before he climbed up as well. He sat down next to her and waited.

"Remember when we were kids? We used to walk for miles through the fields, climbing up on rocks and down into sinkholes." Del's first words were a surprise, but he wasn't really sure what to expect. "Yeah. It's a wonder none of those sinkholes ever fell in with us."

"Maybe. Maybe it would have been better if I would have gotten swallowed up by one." Del tossed a pebble into the pasture, and Gus watched the grasshoppers jump away from where it landed.

"I'm glad you didn't."

"Why? You've got Jenny and the kids. You've got other friends. You don't need me."

"First off, if you would have fallen into a sinkhole, I would have been left behind to try to get you out, or at least to explain to all the grown-ups why we'd been playing around it in the first place. Second off, you were my best friend. Things wouldn't have been the same without you."

Del snorted. "Some best friend. I took off and you didn't hear from me for years. I even suck at being a friend."

"You know, Del, the road goes both ways, and so do the phone lines. I could have found you if I would have tried. I wasn't any better at staying in touch than you were."

Neither spoke for several seconds, then Gus continued, "You know, I was so glad you got away. I hoped you had made a clean break and would leave it all behind you. I was a little disappointed when you called and said you wanted to come back. I was afraid all the shit you grew up with would somehow start again and drag you in."

"Is that what's happened?" Del sounded tired.

"Del, you're a good person. Your parents were never happy with anything. They thrived on misery and weren't content unless everyone around them was just as miserable as they were. Glen is definitely their son. He turned out just like them. But you...you were always different. You always had a spark of light to you. They tried to kill your spirit, but somehow you made it out. You got away and made a good life with Sarah."

Del sniffed and nodded. "Yeah. It *was* good."

"You deserved a lot better than what fate dealt you, after what you grew up with. You deserved to grow old with Sarah. But you got screwed. And that just wasn't fair."

Del nodded again and blinked several times. "It was pretty rough growing up. All I knew was that I didn't want my life to turn out like theirs. I decided I couldn't hurt someone else just to get my way. When I met Sarah, she was full of light and happiness. She was everything I needed. Our years together overflowed with laughter...until the end, when it all shattered. That's the best way I can describe it. Everything shattered and I had to start again, this time with a broken heart."

"It's so hard, Gus. When I left here all those years ago, I was young and strong. I was so determined then to make something of my life. But I'm not strong anymore. When I lost Sarah, I lost part of me."

Gus paused several seconds, mulling over her words. Finally he spoke. "Del, maybe you should try to think of it this way. You didn't lose all of Sarah. You'll always carry a part of her in your heart. That, and your memories, will always be with you. That makes you stronger, not weaker. When you left home, you were a kid and you were alone out there. You're not alone this time. You have your friends and, more importantly, you have Sarah showing you the way."

"Things are such a mess, Gus. What am I going to do?"

"First, I wish you would worry about what you need to do for Del a little more. Your compassion for others is commendable, but at some point you need to ask yourself if the other person deserves it."

Del looked at him sharply. "Gus, I can't just ignore someone who's down. I don't care whether they deserve it or not."

"Okay, okay. Let me finish. I don't mean you have to ignore someone. Just be aware of the consequences to you. Glen is a good example." Del opened her mouth, but Gus held his hand up to stop her. "Jenny told me you helped Glen get things together for his bail so he can be at the funeral. Right?"

Del nodded.

"You were so busy thinking about him, you never considered how it would affect you."

"That's not true. I know it's going to be hard with him there. But I don't know what else to do about it. He has a right to be there."

"So do you. You have just as much a right to be there as he does, maybe more. You're the one who's been watching out for her, not him. He hasn't even seen her since before she went in the nursing home."

"He said nursing homes bother him."

"So it's all about him. I'm sure not seeing her only son bothered your mother more than going into a nursing home for ten minutes would have bothered Glen."

Del nodded.

"So, tell me this, Del. Does Glen have more of a right to bid farewell to his mother, to be comforted by his friends and family, than you do? Don't you have a right to be able to mourn the loss of your mother instead of having to be vigilant every second, watching Glen for an ambush of some sort?" Gus turned his gaze from the pasture, where he had been focused while he spoke, and looked at her in concern.

Del dropped her head. "Uh, I don't know. I guess, maybe."

Gus put his arm around her shoulders, and she didn't draw away from him. "When you moved to the city, you were able to do it. You lived for you. I know losing Sarah has thrown you for a loop. But right now, Del, you need to put *you* first. And, whether you want me to or not, I'm coming to that funeral tomorrow. I'm standing right beside you the whole time. There is nothing you can do about it. And if Glen doesn't like it, he can leave. That building is big enough for the two of us."

Gus could feel Del tense. "Don't worry. I won't let him start anything there," Gus promised.

"Now, there's something else I really need to tell you, Del." He smiled at her serious expression. "I'm not as young as I used to be, and this rock I'm sitting on is killing my keister. Can we please get up and walk again?" He smiled and squeezed her with his one arm before releasing her and standing up. He reached a hand down to her, and she took it and pulled herself up beside him. "Thanks Gus."

"Come here." Gus reached for her and enclosed her in a tight hug.

"Let's go home." Her voice was muffled against his T-shirt.

* * *

They walked in silence back to Gus's truck, and the short ride down the lane to her house was just as quiet. Del was surprised when they passed over the cattle guard and she saw Widow's truck parked in front of her house and Widow sitting on the porch next to Jenny.

"I'm surprised she didn't call out the National Guard too," Del said in exasperation.

Gus laughed. "Sorry Del. I married a woman who thinks she knows what is best for everyone." He winked at her. "Just be glad you don't have to live with her."

Del rolled her eyes. "Well, guess I had better go face the music."

"Just let me do the talking, Del. I've learned how to handle her." Gus sounded confident, but Del doubted his assurance was well-founded.

Del was steadier on her feet when she walked from the truck to the porch. She glanced behind her in time to see Gus give Jenny a thumbs-up, which she found only slightly annoying.

"Are we interrupting a party?" Gus said, indicating the two half-empty margarita glasses encircled by condensation rings on the wooden porch deck between the two women.

"Not interrupting…joining. Would you like one?" Jenny offered.

"Not for me," Del spoke quickly. "I think I may have had my annual limit on tequila already today. Good afternoon Widow." She smiled in an attempt to erase the lines of worry she saw crossing Widow's forehead.

"Hi Del," Widow said simply.

"Is there another drink choice? I'm not much of a strawberry fan," Gus explained.

"Come on inside, Gus. I'll fix you up," Del promised, stepping between the two ladies and entering the house. She made her way to the bottle of honey whiskey over the refrigerator, then pulled two small glasses out of the cabinet. She dropped ice into both of them, then poured the amber liquid over the white cubes in one of them. After putting the bottle away, she took the other glass to the sink and filled it with water.

Gus picked up the whiskey glass from the counter. "Thanks Del. Shall we join the ladies?"

"Do we have a choice?" Del joked.

"No," he answered, a grin splitting his face.

They returned to sit on the porch on either side of the margarita drinkers. "What a way to spend a summer afternoon," Jenny said. "Sitting on the porch with your friends drinking margaritas. The only thing that would make it better would be a pool. You really need to get a pool, Del."

"I just got the house to the point it's not falling down around my ears and now you expect a pool?" Del said, incredulous at Jenny's remark.

"Sure. Why not? Gus never has got us one. So I have to count on one of my friends to get one instead."

Widow laughed, so Del turned the conversation to her. "Widow's your friend. She should get one."

"Actually, I've been thinking about it," Widow said. "Maybe I will. And maybe, if you all are nice to me, I'll invite you over for a swim."

"Sounds like you're my new best friend, Widow," Del teased.

"I see," Gus kidded in return. "Years of friendship mean nothing when a pool comes along."

"Don't worry Gus. I don't think it's just the pool Widow has you beat with." Jenny looked at Widow and Del and smiled. She paused a moment before adding innocently. "I hear she cooks better than you too."

Neither Widow nor Del could stifle their blushes. Gus lifted his eyebrows. "Now I'm curious. Is there something I should know?"

Not knowing how to describe her feelings for Widow, Del said nothing. Widow must have sensed her inability to define things, because she answered gruffly. "Gus Andrews. You are as nosy as an old woman. And to answer your question, no, there is nothing you should know." She continued in a gentler tone. "I promise we'll tell you if there's anything you do need to know."

Gus grinned, apparently unable to resist the chance to tease them a little.

"Let's talk about something different," Del suggested. "I hate to bring it up and ruin the mood, but I would really like to know what to expect tomorrow. Widow, I told Jenny and Gus today that Glen will be at the funeral. I don't expect you'll want to be around him, and you don't need to go. Cindy will be there, and Gus told me today he will be there regardless of what I say." She smiled at Gus, grateful for his insistence. "Why don't you two skip the funeral? There's no need for you to miss more work anyway." She looked at Widow and Jenny, waiting on their response.

"I have an idea," Jenny proposed. "Widow and I can fix a dinner for you all after the service. The two of you and Cindy can come to my house or Widow's afterward and we'll have a feast. It'll be good for you to have your friends around, Del."

"That's a great idea, Jenny," Widow agreed. Del could have sworn she saw the wheels turning behind her eyes, already assembling a menu.

Del nodded her approval, relieved she would only have to worry about Glen offending Gus and Cindy now. Oh, and me, she thought, trying out Gus's advice to consider herself.

"Let's meet at our house," Gus said, and Widow and Jenny nodded in agreement.

"Cindy and I can meet you there at about nine thirty if you want to ride together," Del suggested. "It would probably be easier if we were all together."

"Fine. Then we're all set. When does Cindy get here, by the way?" Gus asked.

Del looked at her watch. "Probably be another four hours. Eight thirty or so."

"Anybody up for a few hands of pitch?" Gus asked.

"Sure," the three women agreed in unison.

"I'm calling the house and sending the boys on a pizza run," Jenny announced. "They can bring us our pizza and get some for themselves too."

It took a few minutes for the four to decide on pizza toppings, then Jenny called and relayed their order to Jim. Del cleaned off her kitchen table and found her deck of cards. Jenny and Widow sat across from each other, forcing Gus and Del to be partners. By the time Jim and Gary arrived with their food, she and Gus had lost the first three games in a row.

After breaking for pizza, Del chose a moment when Jenny was out of her seat to steal her place. "Switching teams!" she announced. "I want on Widow's team. Jenny, you can have Gus."

After initial protests, Del finally won out. When Cindy arrived several hours later, she found empty pizza boxes on the counter and Gus and the three women battling it out with the cards. They greeted her briefly, then returned to their hands.

"Sorry Cindy, but we've been going back and forth all evening. One team wins, then the other does, every game. If Widow and I win this hand, we'll win the game. It'll be two games in a row and we'll be the overall winners," Del explained.

"And if Jenny and Gus win?" Cindy asked.

Del shrugged. "I guess we have to keep playing."

"It doesn't matter," Widow said. "They aren't going to win." She used her ace to pick up the three Gus had been forced to play. "That should do it!"

Gus dropped his head down onto the table, and Jenny tossed her cards haphazardly into a pile. "I demand a rematch." She rubbed her eyes and yawned. "But not tonight. I'm beat. It's been an emotional day, and I'm running on empty."

"We probably all need to get some rest," Del agreed. "It's going to be another long day tomorrow."

Gus and Jenny said their farewells to all and headed home. Widow stood beside Del and watched them go, then looked at Del inquiringly. "Walk me to my truck?"

Del nodded, and Widow took her hand, loosely intertwining their fingers. "See you tomorrow, Cindy," Widow said as she pulled Del along to the door.

"Uh, yeah. See you tomorrow." Cindy shook her head in apparent confusion. Del could feel her eyes on them as she watched them stroll across the porch in the growing dusk.

Widow leaned her back against the driver's door of her truck and grabbed both of Del's hands. She looked closely into Del's eyes as if searching for an answer. Finally she asked, "Are you okay? I mean, really okay?"

"Yeah. I think so." Del thought about what to tell her, how to explain her fears and learned behaviors from her childhood. "I guess I just let my mother and Glen get to me." She still felt shaky and unsure when she thought of them and wasn't sure her resolve was strong enough to keep her from falling into the darkness of their misery again.

"I just want you to know I'm here for you. I want you to come to me if you need me for anything. Do you hear me, Del?

Anything." Widow placed her hands on either side of Del's face and stopped Del's sudden attempt to look away.

"I hear. Thank you. For everything." She glanced down briefly. "I guess I'll see you tomorrow." Her heightened awareness of Cindy's presence inside the house made her suddenly uneasy.

"I don't care if Cindy is watching," Widow astonished her by apparently reading her mind. "I'm not leaving without a kiss."

Del smiled foolishly. She did want to kiss Widow. She meant for it to be a brief kiss but forgot about the immediate rush of heat that coursed through her body every time their lips met. It demanded more—more fire, more closeness, more…everything. She forgot about Cindy. She forgot about the funeral and her brother. All the world revolved around a pair of lips moving against hers, a tongue teasing her own, arms wrapping around her neck, and hands working their way through her hair.

"No," she protested quietly when Widow began to gently push her away instead of pulling her closer.

Widow smiled. "As much as I would like to keep kissing you, I think now is not the time. Good night Del. I'll see you tomorrow."

"See you tomorrow," Del promised. She released Widow and backed away.

Cindy feigned innocence when Del returned to the house until Del gave her a look that said she knew Cindy had been watching.

"Old lady," Cindy said. "Sit down and make yourself comfortable. Catch me up on everything. And I mean everything too." She grinned at Del and chuckled as Del felt a light blush creep across her cheeks.

"Are you sure?" Del said. "It's a long story. I've been a real mess the past couple of days."

Cindy was immediately more subdued. "Of course. How can I be your best friend if I don't know what's going on? Talk to me, Dec. Use me as a sounding board."

Del had taken for granted having best friends, but after today she was glad she had not one, but several. She retrieved another glass of water from the kitchen and settled into her recliner, eager to tell Cindy everything so she could hear it all again herself and maybe make more sense of it all. "Okay Cin. Here goes."

CHAPTER TWELVE

Thursday morning the alarm went off at eight. Del awoke and rolled over to stop its incessant jangling. She sat up in bed and listened to the house, smiling when she heard the coffeepot brewing loudly in the kitchen, sounding as though it was gasping its last breath. "Cindy's up," she said quietly. She felt an odd sense of peace this morning. Cindy had helped her to analyze it all, even her talks with Jenny and Gus. Her confusion and her dysfunctional reactions to her mother's death made more sense to her this morning, and she vowed to not let Glen drag her down into the mire again. Cindy and Gus would be with her, she reminded herself, and she would be strong.

"Going to the shower," she called out loudly, knowing Cindy would hear her from her post in front of the TV, where she was undoubtedly watching the morning news.

Thirty minutes later she made her way into the living room. "Morning," she said to Cindy, who was, as Del predicted, sipping coffee and watching the news.

"Morning. Hope you're going to wear shoes with that outfit," Cindy advised. Del wore black slacks and a short-sleeved, dark green blouse. She had black socks in her hand but no shoes.

"Of course I'm going to wear shoes. I just have to find them. I'm not sure I've unpacked the ones I want."

"No." Cindy groaned. "Don't tell me they're in the boxes."

Del smiled. "I won't tell you, then." She had meant to unpack the boxes that filled a closet in her spare bedroom in the weeks following her move, but the process of making the house livable again had taken priority. Now she needed shoes that she would likely find in the box most difficult to get to.

"Go take your shower while I look for them," she ordered.

"Gladly," Cindy agreed.

Del removed six boxes and rifled through each of them before finding the misplaced shoes. She pushed the boxes to the side of the spare bedroom, not bothering to put them back in the closet. Maybe having them clutter up the room would give her enough incentive to unpack them.

When Cindy returned, she found Del in the kitchen, a half-eaten banana in one hand and a glass of apple juice in the other. "Is that your breakfast?"

"Jenny and Widow are fixing a big spread after the service today, so I thought I'd have just enough now to get by. Want a banana or an apple? Or I can fix you an egg or something really quick," Del offered.

"An apple sounds good." Cindy grabbed one from a basket on the counter and rooted around in a drawer for a paring knife. "So, how are you feeling, Dee? Are you ready for this?"

"Yeah. I think so. Besides, with all of my good friends backing me up, how could anything go wrong?" But as she said this, Del felt a little flicker of warning not to get too self-confident.

Cindy smiled. "That's the spirit, Dee."

"Well, let's go. We don't want to keep Gus waiting, do we?" Del motioned toward the door, and they made their way out of the house, Del sighing audibly as she pulled the door closed behind her.

Cindy turned to her before stepping down the porch steps. "You've got this, Dee."

"Yeah." Del wished her voice would indicate the courage she was trying so desperately to feel. She shook herself mentally, then stepped away from the house, determined to make it through the day.

* * *

"Gus, are you ready?" Jenny called down the hallway to their bedroom. "Del and Cindy just pulled up."

Gus donned his suit jacket and checked his tie in the mirror for the third time. "Coming," he yelled, then stumbled to a stop as Jenny popped around the corner of the doorway in front of him. "'Bout stepped on you," he said.

"I just wanted to tell you how much I love you," Jenny said, encircling his shoulders with her arms.

"I love you too," Gus said, wrapping his arms around her waist and pulling her close so her head rested against his shoulder.

"You be careful today. Take good care of Del and Cindy, and take care of yourself too, Gus Andrews," Jenny cautioned.

"You know I will, Jenny. Don't worry about us, okay?"

"Don't tell me that, because I can't not worry. He's dangerous Gus, and he wouldn't think twice about hurting you."

"I know. I promise I'll be very careful." He leaned down to kiss his wife, then tapped a finger lightly on the end of her nose. "We'll be back as soon as it's over. Then it's your turn. You and Widow get to impress us all with your cooking." He grinned at her.

"You better act impressed regardless," she threatened lightly.

"Yes ma'am."

Jenny turned to answer the knock at the door, and Gus watched her walk away, allowing the concern he had hidden from his wife to express itself as he frowned with worry.

* * *

The parking lot at the funeral parlor had only a couple of cars in it when Gus pulled in and parked. "Nine fifty," he announced, looking at his watch.

"Might as well go in," Del said. Del, Gus and Cindy exited the truck and made their way to the entrance. The funeral director met them inside and ushered them to the room where the visitation and service would take place. Del looked warily at the casket centered in the front of the room, afraid of what, or who, she might see inside. Contrary to what she'd thought, she realized she must have retained some memories of Sarah's funeral, because she now pictured her face pillowed against the white satin of her final resting place, pale but no longer marked by the pain and fatigue that had ravaged her final days. Her knees were suddenly weak, and Cindy steadied her with a hand on the back of her arm.

"Easy there Dee," Cindy whispered.

Del nodded and swallowed deeply, dragging herself back to the present. She took determined steps to the front of the room and looked at the woman resting inside the dark, shiny wood of the casket. She was struck by how serene her mother seemed. Del realized she couldn't remember a time when her mother had a peaceful expression on her face. Anger, yes. Disgust, yes. Disappointment, yes. Hatred, yes. Tranquility, never.

"She looks good," Del noted inanely. "Uh, the dress I picked out looks good on her."

"May you have one less demon to haunt you now," Gus said seriously.

Del nodded, saddened by the truth. "Let's go sit in the front row. I don't know if many people will be here or not."

The next hour passed slowly with a trickle of her mother's old neighbors and friends passing through. Some of them knew Del, some did not. All of them spoke to her courteously but without warmth. Cindy and Gus stayed at her sides as each mourner approached, a hand on her arm for reassurance.

At eleven, the funeral director approached her. "The minister is here. Are you ready for us to begin?"

"I'm sorry. My brother isn't here yet." Del looked toward the door, but there was no sign of Glen. "Let's wait another ten minutes and if he isn't here, we'll start. Is that okay?"

He nodded but looked at his watch impatiently. Apologizing for my brother again, Del thought.

"Maybe he didn't get bail posted," Gus said quietly.

"Yeah, or maybe he just didn't have the decency to show up," Del replied.

There were probably ten to fifteen people scattered among the chairs behind them, waiting for the service to begin. Five minutes later, Del heard the outside door open and turned to see her brother enter the room. He wore stained blue jeans and a torn flannel shirt, but at least he was there. Several of the people seated behind her stood and shook his hand and extended heartfelt condolences as he passed by. She shook her head in wonder. What made people show respect to someone like Glen when they could only summon basic courtesy for her? Was her mother right all along? Was she a bad daughter, a bad person? She hated that they made her question herself.

"Don't let them get to you," Gus warned, speaking closely into her ear. Glen had briefly made eye contact with Gus when he scanned the room upon entering but had avoided looking toward Gus since then. Del could see Cindy looking behind her in obvious confusion. She wished she could explain it to Cindy, but she didn't know how.

Glen finally neared the front of the room, and Del rose from her chair, Cindy at her left side and Gus right behind her as she stepped to the center aisle to greet her brother. "Glen" was all she said by way of greeting.

To her surprise he pulled her into a rough hug. She remained stiff in his embrace. After a few seconds, Glen released her and she backed quickly away from him. "They are ready to start the service as soon as you are," she said, her voice as stiff as her body still was.

"Okay sis. Give me a minute with Ma, then we can start." He spoke loudly so those seated in the back could hear him. He walked slowly toward the casket and made a show of pulling a white handkerchief from his back pocket, then he blew his nose loudly. Del never saw any indication of wetness on his face, but he dragged the handkerchief under his eyes several times, as though to wipe away profuse tears. Finally, either having gotten control of himself again or satisfied he had convinced the other mourners of his grief, he made his way back to the front row of seats. To Del's consternation, he sat next to Cindy, who was on Del's immediate left.

"Glen Smith," he introduced himself gruffly to Cindy, holding out his hand. From a seat away, Del could smell a faint hint of beer on his breath, but it was nearly masked by the sour smell of sweat. His clothes, although stained, appeared clean and dry, so she could only surmise the source of the odor was his body. Cindy took his hand calmly. "Cindy Collins. I'm sorry for your loss."

Del saw the funeral director approaching out of the corner of her eye and nodded to him as she caught his gaze. He turned and left the room, then returned moments later with a graying, nearly bald man carrying a Bible and a few other papers. This man placed his Bible and papers on a small podium to the left of the casket, then began speaking hesitantly. He soon settled into a rhythmic drone that did little to hold Del's attention. After he finished a short, nondescript sermon, the few people behind them filed past her and Glen to the casket, then out the door. She hadn't known who to ask to be pallbearers, but the mortuary had reassured her they could provide the manpower. The funeral director asked Glen and Gus if they would like to assist with moving the casket to the hearse, and both did as directed, accompanied by staff from the mortuary.

Glen wanted to ride in the limousine behind the hearse and insisted Del join him. Del stood her ground and rode with Gus and Cindy instead. The trip to the cemetery was over in minutes, with Del saying little and staring out the window most of the time. When they arrived at West Memorial Gardens, the funeral director managed to place Del next to Glen in the chairs under the heavy maroon awning. The preacher from the funeral parlor opened his Bible and read a few more verses, thanked everyone for coming, and, mercifully, it was over. The few people who had accompanied them to the graveside scattered quickly, and soon only Glen, Gus, Cindy and Del remained standing around the gravesite. The mortuary personnel stood nearly out of sight, trying to be unobtrusive as they patiently waited for the family to leave.

The day was hot like a typical Missouri summer day, but Del felt cold. She shuddered slightly, and Gus wrapped an arm around her.

"So sis," Glen said, "anyone having a dinner for us?"

"Look around Glen. There is no one. Sorry to disappoint you." Del wasn't about to invite him to Gus and Jenny's house. "I'll meet with the lawyer who drew up Mom's will next week and try to get everything settled for you."

"No need sis. I talked to my lawyer, and he says he can handle it all for me. You know, since you weren't in the will and all. He said you could come by and he would have you sign something, then it's all taken care of."

"Thanks Glen. I really appreciate that." Del was relieved to have it off her hands.

"See sis? I look out for you. You don't give me enough credit." Glen leered at her. "You shouldn't believe everything your friends say about me. I'm one of the good guys."

Del looked over at Gus and saw his face redden with anger. She answered her brother before Gus could speak. "Glen, I don't have to listen to my friends to know you're not one of the good guys. I've had enough experiences of my own to figure that out." Del started to walk toward Gus's truck. "Let's go, guys."

Glen followed close behind her. "You want anything out of the old house, Del? We can negotiate if there's something you want, any antiques or anything."

"No Glen. I don't want any of it. It's all yours." Del slid into the backseat of Gus's truck. "I'll stop by your lawyer's office and sign the papers."

"That's it, then. You won't even stay to talk to me? You act like you can't stand to be around me. You've got a lot of nerve. You act so self-righteous, so high and mighty. Well, maybe you should wake up and smell the coffee, Delilah. Everyone at that funeral home today knows what you are. They know you abandoned your parents and your brother for a woman, and then you came back and got your only brother thrown in jail for something you can't prove I did. You rubbed our mother's nose in it until she got so upset she had a stroke and died. Probably figured you'd get half the house at least. She showed you, Delilah. Left it all to me, didn't she? Didn't think I'd find out, did you? But I know one of the aides at the home, and she told me the whole story. You killed her, Delilah."

Glen's taunting voice was muffled when she slammed the door, but she could still hear it.

"Gus, let's go," she said frantically. "I need to leave, now."

Gus started the truck and pulled away as fast as he could, with Glen shouting insults as they drove away. Del sat in the backseat alone, tears spilling down her face unheeded. A couple of miles down the road, Gus turned into a parking lot and stopped the truck. Cindy wordlessly stepped down from the front passenger seat and made her way around to the backseat. She scooted in next to Del, pulled her toward her and held her as close as the cramped conditions would allow. Del sobbed on her shoulder, unable to stop herself, hating herself for losing control.

After several minutes, she became calmer and the tears finally slowed. Her mind rolled with thoughts, blaming herself for things she had no control over. She tried to shut it all down. She knew how to hide those thoughts, how to control those unwanted emotions. All she needed to do was breathe deeply and stop thinking long enough to push them down into that little corner of her brain where she could lock it away. *Breathe, breathe, breathe.*

Del cleared her mind forcefully but couldn't speak yet without choking up. Continuing to breathe deeply, she pushed herself upright in the seat and stared out the window at the lamppost Gus had parked beside, focusing on getting herself under control. It seemed like an eternity before she could finally croak out some words. "I'm okay. Let's go home."

Cindy grabbed her hand and squeezed. She returned the squeeze briefly, then pulled her hand away. If she was going to keep it together in front of Widow and Jenny, she needed time to lock her emotions down. By the time they pulled into Gus's driveway, Del was breathing normally. She was relieved when she tried out her voice and it sounded normal. "Thank you Cindy. Thank you Gus. For everything."

Gus responded first. "You don't need to thank me, Del. I love you like a sister and I was honored to be there for you."

Del smiled and nearly sobbed again.

Cindy saved her with humor. "You should thank me, Dee. You owe me, you know. I sat next to that smelly brother of yours for twenty-two-and-a-half minutes. I timed it. Holy crap. Did you smell him, Gus? I guess they don't let them bathe in the pokey." Cindy grinned at her and laughed, but her eyes were full of love. Del hugged her in response.

"Let's go in before they come out looking for us," Del said.

The aroma of food nearly had them floating into the kitchen, where Jenny and Widow were finishing up lunch. They both gave Del quick hugs before returning to their work.

"Sit down at the table and give us a blow-by-blow," Jenny said.

Gus and Cindy both looked at Del expectantly, so she tried to recount the highlights. "Not very many people were there. Glen arrived at five minutes after eleven, and we waited for him to get there before starting the funeral. He expected a dinner for us afterward, but I didn't tell him about this." She left out the final outburst by Glen and hoped Gus and Cindy wouldn't mention it either.

"Sounds like it went okay, then," Jenny commented. She looked at them as if for reassurance but instead received noncommittal shrugs from Cindy and Del. Gus nodded slightly. "So Cindy, are you staying tonight, or do you have to go home?"

"I'm heading home this evening, I guess. I only took one day off work."

"Are you going back to work tomorrow, Del?" Jenny asked.

"Yes," Del said emphatically. "I'll be glad to get back to work. There are too many idle hours in the day when you're not working."

The others laughed.

"I have a honey-do list here a mile long if you have to take a day off again, Del. You can help me knock a few things off it," Gus teased. Jenny shook a finger at him in mock anger, and he pretended to tremble in fear.

"Maybe I'll just call Jenny and have her take a day off so we can drink strawberry margaritas all day," Del responded. "You can take the day off too, Gus, and we'll watch you work on the honey-do list."

Gus took the brunt of the teasing from the four women for the rest of the afternoon. Del joined in from time to time, but it was interspersed with periods of quietness as they ate and later as they cleaned up and returned to the table to sit and talk.

At four o'clock, Cindy looked at her watch and reported it was time to head home. She had driven Del to Gus's house that morning, and her bag was in her truck so she could leave from there. "Do you need a ride home, Del?" Cindy asked.

Widow spoke up quickly. "I'll take her home, Cindy, if that's okay with you, Del?" she asked, looking at Del for approval.

"Yeah. That'll be fine." Del nodded to her, then stood to walk Cindy out to her truck.

"Cindy, can I get your cell number before you leave?" Widow asked.

Cindy recited it, and Widow and Jenny entered it into their phones. "Thanks," Jenny said. "You never know when we might need to reach you."

After a chorus of goodbyes, Cindy and Del made their way outside. Cindy climbed into her truck and leaned out the open driver's window. "Dee, are you going to be okay?" she asked. "I can stay tonight and tomorrow if you want me to. Or I can come back tomorrow night and stay the weekend."

"No. I'll be okay, Cindy. Today was the worst of it, and it's over now. It'll be all good from here."

"I hope you're right, Dee. Promise me you'll call if you need anything, even if it's just to talk."

"Yeah. Okay. I promise I'll call."

"And keep me up-to-date on you and Widow," Cindy ordered with a twinkle in her eyes.

"Cindy," Del warned, but then she smiled. "Drive safely."

Widow met Del inside the front door. "I'm good to go whenever you're ready," she told Del. "Or I can stay and visit as long as you like."

"I'm feeling pretty tired. It's been a trying day. If it's okay with you, I'm ready to go." Del rubbed her neck.

They followed the sound of Gus and Jenny's voices to the kitchen. "Gus, Jenny. Thank you again for everything today. I don't know what I'd do without friends like you. You guys are the best," Del said. "I'm exhausted, so I think I'm going to go home and try to get some rest. I hate to say good night to good company, but I'm afraid I must."

"Yeah, sure." Gus stood and held a hand out for Jenny, and they walked together with Del and Widow to the front door. "You two have a good night," they said in unison.

"Good night," Widow said as she looped her arm around Del's waist and walked with her to the truck. Once inside, Del reached her hand across the center of the truck toward her. Widow grasped Del's hand, and Del was immediately comforted by the connection.

She parked in Del's driveway and reached her left hand around the steering wheel to turn off the ignition, never loosening her grip on Del's hand. "Mind if I come in for a while?" Widow asked.

"I might not be very good company," Del warned.

"That's okay, I'll take my chances."

Del waited for her to make her way around the truck, and they walked to the house together, each with an arm wrapped behind the other. When they entered the house, Del sat down in her recliner. Widow didn't move to sit on the couch as she had expected, but stood in front of her, waiting. Del reached for her and guided Widow to sit across her lap, legs dangling over the low arm of the chair and an arm behind Del's neck.

"Would you mind just holding me?" Del whispered, allowing Widow a glimpse of how vulnerable she was feeling.

Tears welled up in Widow's eyes. "Of course. I would love to just hold you."

Widow cradled Del's head against her chest, stroking her hair gently above and around her ear. Del held Widow loosely around the waist, tracing small circles on her back with one hand. For a time, Del was content to sit calmly, comforted by Widow's soft touch. She allowed herself to forget, to release the anger, the pain and the frustration.

The sound of a vehicle approaching didn't penetrate Del's tranquility until the metallic slamming of a door startled her. Widow had apparently been as unaware of the visitor as Del, and she scooted to her feet quickly, then moved to the door. Del was a step behind her, looking over Widow's shoulder in surprise at the man making his way toward her porch.

"Oh hell," she muttered. "What does he want?"

Her brother stumbled at the first step but regained his balance and climbed to the porch safely.

"Excuse me, Widow," Del said, stepping past her to get to the door. "Why don't you stay inside? I'll talk to him."

Widow said nothing but stepped back into the room away from the window. Del walked onto the porch, and Glen stopped in front of her, swaying slightly. She could smell the whiskey and he hadn't even spoken yet.

"Glen."

"Hiya sis. How's it goin'? Thought I better come check on you and make sure you're okay, what with burying Ma today and all."

The words on their own could have been taken as well intentioned, but the leering grin and the chuckle he couldn't contain told her that he wasn't there out of concern for her well-being.

"Don't worry, Glen. I'm fine." She kept her anger in check, hoping he would grow tired of whatever his game was and leave.

"Yeah. I saw that when I walked up. Got a hot little mama in there keeping you company, huh little sis? I'd be fine too." Glen looked over her shoulder at the door.

Del hoped Widow wouldn't take the bait and would stay inside. "I think you'd better leave, Glen."

Glen took a half step toward her. "Maybe I'm not ready to leave yet. Invite me in, Dee-li-lah. Big brother will give you a few lessons in hospitality."

At his advance, Del had automatically stepped back. She realized she wasn't going to be able to talk him into going away easily. Now the question was, how to keep him from escalating? "Let's sit out here on the porch. It's a nice evening. We can talk."

Glen took a full step toward her, causing her to back up to the door. "I want to meet your friend, sis. Is she one of your lesbo friends? Maybe I can show her what a real man's like."

Del wasn't sure what to do, but she knew she wouldn't willingly open the door for him and let him harass Widow. She put her hands up defensively, hoping he would back away. "Glen, I want you to leave. You've been drinking. Go home and sleep it off. We can talk about it tomorrow."

"I already told you, sis. I ain't ready to go yet." His slurred voice hardened as he grabbed her arms and pulled her close to him. "Now, I think you should invite me inside."

Del cringed at the roughness of his grasp, and the sudden rush of anxiety nearly paralyzed her as she waited for his fist or his open hand to strike her.

Glen froze when a click echoed loudly behind him, easily recognizable as a gun being cocked. He made no move to release her, but neither did he try to harm her.

"Let her go, Glen!" Widow stood at the bottom of the steps, her shotgun trained on his back. Del wondered how she'd been able to sneak around the house and into her truck without either of them noticing.

Glen released Del's arms and held his hands up beside his head, but he didn't seem concerned at being held at gunpoint. He smiled and laughed when he turned and recognized Widow. "Well, well. If it isn't my old girlfriend, Widow. You knew that, didn't you, sis? Things were just heating up between us when that greedy-ass Gus got in the way. Guess one woman wasn't enough for him. He had to have mine too. See sis? The folks you've been calling friends have treated your big brother badly over the years."

His version of things was so far from the truth, Del wondered if he could possibly believe what he was saying. On shaky legs, she stepped away from him, out of the path of the shotgun. "Glen, just leave. Please."

"Or what? Little Annie Oakley here gonna shoot me?"

"If I have to, I will. If you doubt me, remember how you terrified my children, you bastard." Widow stepped up the stairs, her aim never wavering as she pointed the barrel at Glen's chest. "You need to get in your truck and get the hell out of here."

Glen stopped smiling, and Del could tell he was getting angry. Fearing this, she reverted to being the peacemaker, just as she'd done throughout her childhood. "Widow, it's okay. He doesn't mean any of it. Do you Glen? It's been a long day. Everyone's tired. Glen, please, just go on home and get some rest," she pleaded. She thought she had succeeded when he started to smile.

"That's my sister. You better watch out, Widow. Delilah will never have your back. All her life, all she's ever done is kiss ass or run." He laughed harshly. "You two deserve each other."

He staggered once before he reached the steps but somehow negotiated his way to level ground safely. At his truck door, he stopped and looked at them again. "Little sis, I'll be seeing you. Widow, don't worry. I'll catch up to you someday when your bodyguard, Gus, isn't with you. I bet you won't talk so big without him or that gun. Maybe little sis will be there too. I'll show her how to treat a woman like you."

He gunned his truck loudly and scattered gravel behind him as he roared up the hill. Only after he was out of sight did Widow ease the hammer down and set the safety on her shotgun. She placed it on the small table at the corner of the porch and fell into the chair beside it.

"Whew! I thought I was going to have to shoot him!" Del stood silently, trembling as she stared off the porch toward the driveway where Glen's truck had been. "Del? You okay?"

"Uh, yeah. I'm okay. Sorry 'bout all that, Widow. Look, maybe you'd better go home in case he comes back. He won't bother me if I'm here by myself."

Del couldn't look at her, but she heard Widow walk over to her. Del stared at the porch when Widow stepped in front of her. "Is that what you want, Del? Do you want me to leave?"

"Yeah. I guess you'd better. You know." Del didn't know how to explain that Glen was right. Widow was better off without getting any closer to her. Del couldn't protect her, couldn't be the person she needed. All those years ago, she hadn't stood up to her family when she had told them she was a lesbian. Instead, she had run. She had fooled herself when she lived in the city. Looking back, she realized she had always sidestepped confrontations, had never allowed herself to be put in a situation where she would have to choose between fighting and running. Now, Glen had forced her to see her own cowardice and had exposed her weakness to Widow. There was no more hiding the truth.

Del looked up and saw the confusion and hurt in Widow's eyes before Widow turned away. Del watched as she picked up her shotgun and walked in silence to her truck. She looked toward the porch one last time before climbing inside. Del was confused when Widow looked at her with sadness, not the disgust she expected.

Del walked back into the house and sat in her recliner, feeling overwhelmed by the numbness that had started when she watched Widow drive away. The evening shadows slowly darkened the room, but she didn't move to switch on a light. As the chorus of frogs and crickets heralded the onset of dusk, she drifted into a restless sleep, haunted by a demon only she could conquer—the fear that defined Del Smith.

* * *

Five o'clock on Friday couldn't come too soon. After awakening in pain from sleeping upright in her recliner, Del had taken a long, hot shower, hoping to wash away some of the soreness and some of the memories of the evening before. She had driven to work and performed her job robotically, distracted and distant to the patients who had become accustomed to her lighthearted, joking behavior. They were aware she had been away for a few days because of her mother's death, and none questioned the obvious change in her mood.

As Del drove home, she dreaded the thought of her empty house. She would be alone with herself again, and right now she definitely wasn't her favorite person. But she didn't want to go anywhere else, so home it was.

At seven, the phone rang. She allowed it to go to the answering machine. When she heard Cindy's voice, she reached over for the receiver, knowing her headstrong friend wouldn't give in until she had spoken to her.

"Hi," she answered flatly to discourage a long conversation.

"Dee, this is Cindy. Are you okay? You sound a little off."

"I'm okay. What do you need?"

"I don't need anything. I was just calling to check on you. Yesterday was a rough day for you. I know I left you in good hands, but I still worry. You don't sound right, Dee. What's wrong?"

"I'm not feeling too well. I'm okay though." Del spoke quietly and evenly into the phone, her eyes fixed unseeingly on the juncture of the wall and ceiling in front of her.

"Talk to me, buddy. Did something happen between you and Widow?" Cindy pried gently.

"I don't really want to talk about it. I just got home and need to fix dinner. I'll talk to you later, okay?" Del ended the call before Cindy could respond. She closed her eyes and tried to silence her spinning mind.

* * *

"Is this Jenny Andrews?" A woman asked impatiently when Jenny picked up the phone.

"Yes. And who is this?"

"This is Cindy, Dee...Del's friend. Have you spoken to her today?"

"No, not today. Why? What's up?"

"I just called her and she sounded upset. She hung up on me too. I've been trying to call her back, but she won't answer. I'm probably overreacting, but can you check on her for me? It would ease my mind."

"Of course. Gus and I had talked about going out for a drive. We'll stop by and see if she's okay. I'll call and let you know."

Within minutes Gus and Jenny headed toward Del's house. The sun was just below the horizon as they pulled up behind her truck, leaving her house darkened by long shadows from the line of trees behind it. Jenny reached the door first and knocked twice. Not waiting for a response, she pushed it open and stepped inside.

Del turned her head at the intrusion, looking resigned to encounter whoever it might be. She blinked at the sudden light when Jenny flipped the switch by the door. "Oh. Hi Jenny. Hi Gus." Her voice sounded as weary as she appeared.

"Del, what happened? What's wrong?" Jenny demanded, her instincts telling her there had been an immense change in Del in the twenty-four hours since they had last seen her. Her paleness and apparent fatigue could be explained away by an illness, but the dark aura that surrounded her, the absence of a spirit of hope and life frightened Jenny.

"Just tired," Del answered.

"Cindy called us," Gus explained. "She's worried about you. What's going on, Del?"

"I'm fine. Do me a favor, call Cindy and convince her I'm fine before she gets in her truck and drives down here too." Del rolled her eyes and looked away. Jenny directed Gus to the kitchen with a look and a nod in that direction.

Jenny pulled a footstool in front of Del's recliner and sat facing her. She grabbed both of Del's hands and captured her gaze with her own. "Del, talk to me. You know you can trust me. Is something wrong?"

At first, Del shook her head. Tears slowly gathered, then streaked her face. Finally she stammered, "You know, I thought I was over it. I thought...I thought I had conquered my fears, when I left home and again when we caught Glen. I felt like all of that old stuff, that it was gone, you know. Like maybe I was finally the person everyone thought I was. I guess I was lying all along—to Sarah, to Cindy, to you, to Gus and to Widow. Even to myself."

Jenny shook her head. "I don't understand, Del. What do you think you were lying about? What happened to bring all this up?"

"Glen came over last night while Widow was here."

Jenny gasped. "Oh God. What happened? He didn't hurt you or Widow, did he?"

"No. We're fine. Widow saved us. She ran him off with her shotgun. Good thing. I would have done anything just to keep him from starting a ruckus." Del chuckled.

"I'm glad she had her gun with her. But I don't understand, Del. Why do you say that...that you'd have done anything?"

"Good old Del won't fight, she'll just take it. Sure, she might run like hell if she gets the chance, but she won't stick around when the going gets tough." The tears were gone now, and Del sounded defeated.

Gus returned to the room. "Del, I don't know where you're getting this load of crap. Sure, when you were a kid, you took it. You had to take the abuse in order to survive. That doesn't mean you were weak. It means you were a survivor. Glen survived it too, by using others and turning the hatred onto them. I think that makes you the strong one. You survived without losing your humanity."

He paused and looked at her until Del met his gaze. "Furthermore, there's a difference between running and escaping. You escaped, you didn't run. You need to get Glen out of your head and start thinking right."

Del shook her head. "You weren't here, Gus. You don't know. Ask Widow. She'll tell you. She stood up to Glen. All I could do was beg for him to leave. I couldn't stand them fighting like that. If he wouldn't have left, she'd have had to shoot him."

"You're right. I wasn't here, but I'll make a guess that Glen used you, Del. He wanted a way out, to save face. He got in your head. But you don't have to let him stay there. If push came to shove, you would have stood strong. I'm sure of it."

Jenny could see a battle going on in Del's eyes. There was a glimmer of hope, a spark of light at Gus's confident words. But it was extinguished in a blink.

"I'd like to believe you, Gus, but Glen proved he's right." Del rubbed her face with both hands. "He told Widow the truth about me, and he was right. I didn't protect her. I just begged him to leave. She deserves someone who'll stand beside her, not hide in fear. I couldn't even talk to her last night. I just asked her to leave."

Jenny's eyes widened. "She deserves to hear your thoughts, Del. She deserves to understand why you sent her away. But I don't understand why you are so convinced you're a coward?"

Del ducked her head in shame. "Don't you see? I can't stand up to him. I run like I did at the cemetery yesterday, or I cower down and wait for a beating. What does that say about me? Widow doesn't need a girlfriend she has to rescue every time someone yells at her."

Jenny shook her head. "Del, you're wrong. You don't know how strong you can be because you've always found a way to avoid being violent. There's nothing wrong with that. I would trust you to stand up to Glen or anyone if it came down to the wire, especially if you were protecting someone you loved."

Jenny could see the doubt in Del's eyes and knew she was still unconvinced.

"I guess I do owe Widow an explanation."

"Let me call and see if she's home," Jenny suggested, pulling out her cell phone before Del could protest. "I need to talk to her anyway." She frowned slightly when the phone went to voice mail, but left a brief message.

"I'm going to fix a sandwich, then I'll drive over and talk to her," Del promised.

Jenny suspected Del was trying to get rid of them so she could return to her dark thoughts. She was hesitant to leave Del alone when Glen still had such an obvious influence on her. "Gus, Widow and I need to make some plans for that benefit dinner we're helping with next weekend. Why don't I drive over to her place now and you can come with Del in a little while?" Jenny suggested.

Gus looked at Del, and she nodded in resignation.

* * *

Thirty minutes later, Del and Gus headed toward Widow's house. Del was beginning to feel less nauseous when she remembered the confrontation with Glen. She had mulled over Gus and Jenny's words but was still unconvinced they were right. The way she had shut out Widow after Glen left was as unforgivable as her cowardice. She only hoped Widow would understand when she explained why a relationship between them wasn't a good idea.

As they pulled into Widow's driveway beside Gus's truck, the house was strangely dark. A light in the machine shed drew Del's attention, and she thought she saw a tall figure pass before the lit window.

"Gus. Something's not right. There should be lights on in the house." A cold fear settled in her stomach.

"You go slowly to the machine shed. I'm going to circle the house, then come around to the back of the shed if they aren't in the house. Give me some time to get there." Apparently Gus was as suspicious of the situation as she was.

Del opened her door and stood in it a few seconds, blocking the view of the rest of the truck as Gus slid out the passenger door and disappeared into the darkness. She shut the door, then slowly made her way toward the shed. To the right of the two big bay doors at the front of the shed, a small door with a window allowed the only light out of the building. She peered through the window as she neared it but saw only equipment and workbenches covered with tools. She listened closely for any indication from Gus that Jenny and Widow were in the house. Hearing nothing, she eased the door open and stepped inside.

"Little sis, glad you could make it to my party." Glen laughed from the shadows in the back of the shed. He shoved Widow into the light of the single bulb hanging in the center of the high roof. Her clothes were torn, and the bruises on her face indicated she had been struck several times. Her eyes remained downcast, and Del wasn't sure if Widow knew she was even there.

Glen moved forward slowly, pointing a rifle at Widow's back. "Act nice, sis, and maybe I'll let her live."

Del looked from Glen to Widow, trying not to think about where Jenny might be or where Gus was. She was surprised that her initial cold fear had been replaced by a strange calmness. She needed to stall and give Gus time to get there before Glen hurt either Widow or Del, or both of them. "What do you want, Glen? Why are you doing this?"

"I think you know the answer to that, don't you, sis? You know you caused this. Your selfishness, your fucking perversion, that's the problem. It always had to be you, didn't it? The world revolved around you. Daddy's little princess. Dad never gave a shit about me or Mom after you came along. Then you abandoned us all to go fucking women all over St. Louis. All I ever heard about was how you had such potential and were throwing it all away on a bunch of damned women. What about me, Dee-li-lah? What about my potential? He never gave a fuck about me or Mom."

Glen's words angered her. He couldn't be talking about the same life she remembered. *Princess?* Del took a deep breath and willed her calm to return. "Glen, you got it all wrong. Dad never gave a damn about either one of us. He was too busy looking for the next drink. We both got a shitty hand to start out with. I decided to throw all my cards back and start again somewhere else, that's all."

"Fuck you, you lying bitch. You're a damned coward. You abandoned us. You could have changed things for us if you would've stayed. Now look at what you've caused. This is all on you, sis. None of this would have happened if not for you."

Glen grabbed Widow's arm and spun her toward him. She still didn't look up or acknowledge him.

"Turn her loose, Glen. You don't need her. I'm the one to blame. I'm the one who runs. Well, I'm not running now, Glen. I'm staying here with you. Let her go." It was clear in Del's mind for the first time. The battle that had raged in her mind had been won. A cold, calm determination fed by a deep anger she had never felt before made her take two steps toward Glen, one hand raised in front of her.

"This bitch thought she could get away with pulling a gun on me." Glen touched the end of the rifle barrel to Widow's forehead. "I guess I showed her. You should have been here last night, sis. We had a helluva party without you, didn't we, sugar?" He leered at Widow, who seemed to shrink toward the floor.

The heat of a fury like she had never felt before washed over Del, and the cold, hard sound of her voice drew Glen's attention to her. "Let her go, Glen. You've got me now; that's what you wanted, now let her go."

"I'm done with you both." Glen aimed his rifle at Del. At the same time, a shadow silently stole across the rear of the shed toward him.

Stall, stall! "Glen, wait. I'm your sister, your blood."

"My blood will never run yellow like yours, Del." He pulled the gun in tight.

This is it. She diverted her attention from Glen to a spot about five feet to the right of him. He glanced in that direction just as a blow came down across his rifle from his left. Del dove backward as it fired. The sound was deafening and made the scuffle between Gus and Glen seem surreal. She sat up in time to see Glen lying on his stomach on the ground, Gus sitting astraddle his back and tying his hands behind his motionless body. Del rushed over to Widow, who stood oddly unmoving.

"Widow, it's okay. He can't hurt you now." Del reached toward her, but Widow flinched and turned away when Del touched her arm. Unsure what to do, Del stood looking at her helplessly.

Gus finished securing Glen, then hurried over to Widow. "Where's Jenny?" he demanded.

Widow only shook her head slightly, not looking up from the floor.

"Widow, we know Jenny came over to see you. Where is she?" Gus placed a finger under Widow's chin, forcing her gaze upward. "Widow, it's me, Gus. You're safe now." Del saw a flicker of recognition in Widow's eyes as Gus spoke to her. "Widow, where is Jenny?"

In a whisper barely loud enough for them to hear, Widow gave the answer they needed. "In the house…he hit her with the gun."

Gus dashed toward the house. Del started behind him, but when Widow didn't follow them, Del turned and took her hand. She wanted to stop and hold her, comfort her, but Jenny's life could depend on her, so she placed an arm around Widow's waist and hurried her along to the house.

Jenny lay in a crumpled heap just inside the front door. Blood oozed from an ugly-looking slash on her scalp and another on her forearm, which was draped partially over her face.

"Looks like she tried to block the blow," Del noted as she quickly knelt to assess her. "Her pulse is good and strong," she reported.

Gus was on his knees beside Jenny and started to pull her to his chest.

Del reached a hand over to stop him. "Wait. She might have hurt her neck, Gus. Help me roll her onto her back while I keep her neck stabilized." Del took Jenny's head between her hands and moved in tandem with Gus to position her flat on the floor.

"Jenny," Gus called out softly, stroking her cheek. "Jenny, wake up."

"Widow, can you get a cold, wet washcloth?" Del asked.

Although she didn't acknowledge she had heard, Widow turned and walked slowly from the room. Moments later, she returned and handed the cold cloth to Del. Del placed it on Jenny's forehead, then slid it behind the back of her neck, being careful not to move her head. After several seconds, Jenny's eyelids began to flicker.

"That's it, Jenny. Wake up. You're safe now," Gus said softly.

Jenny moaned and gradually focused on Del's and Gus's faces hovering over her. She frowned at Gus, then reached up and brushed away the tears on his face. "Gus?"

"Thank God you're okay," Gus's voice broke with emotion. He kissed her forehead beside the ugly wound. "I don't know what I'd do without you, babe."

"What happened? My head..." Jenny winced when her fingertips probed the gash on her forehead. "Glen! Where is Glen?"

Jenny braced her elbows on the floor to sit up, but Del stopped her with a hand to her chest. "Wait Jenny. Lie still. Gus took care of Glen." When Jenny relaxed, Del moved her hand away. "We don't know if your neck is okay. You shouldn't move, Jenny."

Jenny probed her neck with her fingertips. Del watched her, knowing what was coming but not sure how to prevent it.

"See," Jenny said after finishing her assessment. "All good. Now I'm sitting up. You can help me or not." She held out a hand to Gus, and he took it, letting her ease herself up to sitting on the floor. "Don't look at me like that, Del. Now will somebody tell me what the hell happened?" Holding her head with both hands, she carefully looked around until she saw Widow's disheveled, distant appearance. "Widow, are you okay?"

Widow didn't answer, and Del shook her head slightly. "Glen had her captive since last night, Jenny. He must have clubbed you this evening as soon as you stepped in the door. Gus and I knew something wasn't right when we got here because the house was dark. Gus tackled Glen in the machine shed, then we found you here.

"I wish you'd lie still, Jenny. I know you think you're okay, but Widow said Glen hit you with the rifle. If your neck is hurt..." Jenny shot Del another look, stopping her. Gus looked at Del and shrugged in defeat.

Gus stood, then helped Jenny to her feet. After walking her to a chair in the living room, he knelt in front of her. "Jenny, I want you and Widow to call for an ambulance. You both need to be checked out...by a doctor. I have some unfinished business to take care of outside, but I'll be right back."

The adrenaline rush that had started when the gun went off was beginning to wane, and Del's head was throbbing. She hadn't had time to process how she'd stood up to Glen, and now she had to decide what to do next. She was sure Gus would take charge of the situation, and she would back him up in whatever he decided. But this was Glen: her brother, her problem, her fears, her responsibility. She wanted, no, she needed to take care of things. Letting Gus take over was just another way to run. The decision was firm in her mind. Then the idea hit her in a flash, and Del knew what she had to do. "If you'll help me load the trash, I'll take care of things from there. You can make sure Widow and Jenny are okay, and I guess the sheriff needs to be called." She looked at Widow and her determination wavered, the desire to stay with her, to be sure she was okay, nearly overpowering the need to protect her. Nearly, but not quite.

"Del, are you sure you can handle him?" Gus looked at her with concern.

"I need to do this on my own, Gus. Just promise me you'll make sure Widow and Jenny are okay."

"I will. How long do you want me to wait before I call the sheriff?"

"Go ahead and call him. Tell him Glen escaped and I went to look for him."

"You sure?"

"Yeah. It'll work out, Gus. I don't want Widow and Jenny to wait to be looked at."

"Jenny, I'll be back in a few minutes. Will you be okay?" Gus looked at her closely.

"Sure. I'll just hold my head together while you're gone." Gus frowned and took a step toward Jenny. "I'm trying to make a joke, Gus. I'll be okay. Go do whatever." Jenny waved him toward the door with one hand.

Del turned to Widow and noted her gaze was unfocused and appeared to be directed at a blank place on the wall. She was unsure whether she could get through to her or not, but she had to try. Del gently touched Widow's arms and winced when she whimpered and pulled away. "Widow, I have to leave, but Gus and Jenny are here. They'll take care of you. I'll be back as soon as I can, I promise. You're safe now, Widow." She took her hand and led her gently toward the couch. Widow sat with a gentle push from Del. Jenny placed a hand on her knee, and Widow remained beside her.

Del looked at her one last time as she headed toward the door. Widow's expression was fixed, void of emotion, and Del couldn't help but wonder what was running through her mind behind the mask.

Thoughts of what her brother had done to her friends focused her mind on the task at hand. Del had a plan, and she was determined to see it through.

CHAPTER THIRTEEN

Del walked into the machine shed and quickly found the items she needed while Gus checked on Glen, who had been immobilized with a heavy blow to the jaw during their struggle. She walked her equipment to her truck, then returned to where Gus waited. They carried Glen's limp, unconscious body together to the bed of her truck and covered him with a tarp.

"Gus, I've got this. Remember, he escaped and I'm looking for him. We decided you should stay and make sure Jenny and Widow are okay," she said firmly.

"If you're sure," Gus said.

"I'm sure." After a last glance toward the house, she got in wordlessly and drove down Widow's drive to the county road and finally through her own gate. She turned into the pasture and headed carefully down the hill and across a long bottom. The terrain looked foreign viewed in the tunnel of her headlights, and she hoped she could find her way. She shifted into four-wheel drive before venturing up the steep bank on the other side. At the top, the land leveled, and the truck's lights illuminated the group of trees she was seeking. She turned her truck around and backed it carefully, then turned the key in the ignition when she was satisfied.

Del walked to the back of the truck and peered closely at a dark opening in the ground with a semicircle of saplings standing guard over it. The sinkhole looked much as it had decades earlier when she had first explored this ridge. Adrenaline had carried her to this point, but now she felt a darkness rising in her. She had avoided confrontations all her life, but strangely now she found herself welcoming this. Her anger, so long bottled up inside, was turning her resolve to steel. She thought back to the events of years ago, when Glen had terrorized Widow and her children. She thought further back to when she was a child and he had terrorized her, always looking for a way to put her in the line of fire from their father or mother. The hatred he had spewed at her tonight and the suffering Widow had undoubtedly endured at his hands made her realize how twisted he had become. He attempted to justify his own evil actions by blaming everyone around him. She knew he would have killed Jenny, Widow and her if Gus hadn't hit him when he did. She also knew he expected her not to fight back. The Del he grew up with had turned the other cheek repeatedly, and he had expected nothing less tonight. He hadn't bargained on the fact she might no longer be the Del he grew up with.

The sound of her brother wriggling around in the truck bed indicated he had regained consciousness. She flipped the tarp back and exposed his head. The light on the back of the cab was dim, but she could see Glen take a deep breath when he saw his captor.

"Go ahead and yell. No one can hear you out here."

She grabbed him by the shoulders and slid him to the edge of the tailgate. "Sorry about the drop, brother." She pulled him to the ground unceremoniously, not responding to the cursing that ensued when he landed on his shoulder and neck, the rest of his body following and resulting in him lying in a twisted pile on the rocks and hard, dry ground. She reached into the bed of the truck and pulled out a lantern, a rope and a winch. She lay on the ground beside her bound brother and hooked the winch to the back of her bumper, working partly by feel in the shadows cast by the tailgate.

Del got to her feet again. She tied the rope to the lantern, then lit it and lowered it down into the abyss behind the truck. She lay on her stomach at the edge of the hole and peered inside. "Oh yeah. This will do perfectly."

She retrieved the lantern from the hole and placed it nearby to light up the area. She pulled another rope from the back of the truck and tied one end to the winch. The other end she wrapped around the ropes Gus had used to tie Glen's feet together. "Better hope you tied your boots right this morning, brother."

Del grabbed him by his arms and dragged him to the edge of the hole. She was sweating with exertion by the time she finished. "You ever think about going on a diet, Glen?" she said sarcastically.

"Go to hell, Delilah."

"You first, big brother."

After one last look at the rope length, she shoved his body closer to the hole, moving his head and shoulders, then his back and hips over the edge, watching him slide over the lip as gravity took over and the rope jerked tight. Glen's yells ensured he had stopped before he hit the bottom.

Undoubtedly no longer doubting his sister's determination and worried about what she had planned, Glen began to bargain. "Wait," he shouted. "What are you doing? Sis, it's me, Glen, your brother. You can't do this to me. I'm family."

"Any last words, Glen?" Del's voice was dry, emotionless. The anger had burned away to nothing, leaving her empty. She felt almost like a hollow shell, except she knew she had a mission.

"Del, Delilah, think about what you're doing. You don't want to kill me. I'm your brother." Glen's muffled voice was pleading now. "Del, please."

"What makes you think I'm going to kill you, Glen? I'm going to teach you a lesson you'll never forget, brother. You might beg for me to kill you before I'm done, but I'm not going to do that. That would be too easy. Next time you decide to shove someone around because you think you're bigger than they are, remember what could happen, Glen."

Del held the lantern over him and looked down. "Another ten feet should do it," she muttered to herself. She climbed into the truck and started it, then backed it up what she guessed to be ten feet. The sounds of her brother's muffled yells were obvious as soon as she killed the engine. "Guess I didn't kill him yet." She returned to the hole and tied the lantern to the second rope again.

"Glen, you've misjudged your little sister," Del said as she lowered the lantern. "All of those years, I never fought back. I tried to keep the peace, and you all took advantage of me. You treated me like shit, Glen, just like our parents. And tonight you would have killed me."

"No sis. I was just shooting off my mouth. I didn't mean nothing by it. I was just trying to scare you. I wouldn't have killed you." She could see fear in his face as she lowered the lantern toward him.

"I'm your worst nightmare, big brother," Del continued in the same flat, emotionless voice. "We're more alike than you think. The same genes run through us, and you seem to have forgotten that. You thought you could fuck me over and I would just bend over and let you. You were wrong."

She lowered the lantern to the bottom of the hole, illuminating the floor in its yellow light. "Remember what I'm capable of, Glen. Always remember."

Del walked back to the winch and began to ratchet Glen farther down into the sinkhole. She knew he was looking at the bottom when she heard his screams of terror coming from the depths. She lowered him one more notch, then stopped and sat in the dim cab light with her back resting against the bumper, listening to him scream. A strange sense of satisfaction filled her, and she tried not to question why.

A short time later, the screams began to diminish. "About done, I guess," Del said to herself. She arose wordlessly, pulled out her pocketknife and opened it slowly. Her hand shook slightly from her white-knuckled grip. She placed the sharp blade against the taut rope and held the rope steady with her other hand. The screams turned into a weak whimper that barely ascended the depths of the hole.

After standing there motionless for minutes, she pulled the knife away, folded it and placed it in her pocket. She dropped her head and stared at the ground for a long moment. Then she started the truck and pulled him slowly out of the hole.

The shaking, drooling, whimpering body she found lying on the ground behind the truck resembled her brother very little. She cut the ropes away, and he stood and climbed into the truck bed with little assistance, moving when she encouraged him, staring as unseeingly as Widow had. He lay motionless as Del gathered the rest of her gear, then draped the tarp over him again.

She tossed the ropes, the lantern and the winch into the shed at her house, then headed back to Widow's place.

CHAPTER FOURTEEN

Two hours after she left, Del drove up the lane to Widow's house and pulled to a stop between the sheriff's car and Deputy Tom Hart's truck.

The sheriff met her at the door, but Del spoke before he could ask any questions. "He's in the back of the truck." She walked past him into the house.

"What?"

Del was suddenly very tired and wanted to sit with her eyes closed for a few seconds. She entered the living room and was surprised to see Deputy Tom Hart sitting on the couch. "Deputy."

"Del. Gus and Jenny asked me to let you know they'll see you at the hospital. Jenny and Widow rode in the ambulance, and Gus followed them."

"Thanks Tom. How were they doing when they left?"

"Jenny said she had a headache, but she was acting normal. The paramedic said she needed to be checked out. A blow to the head can be serious, especially with her being unconscious for quite some time. You know Jenny, she argued with them a little, but Gus and the paramedic wouldn't back down, so she finally gave in."

"And Widow?" Del asked quietly.

Tom cleared his throat. "She was still pretty shaken up, Del. She did manage to tell us about Glen trying to kill you both in the shed."

"Yeah, Gus tackled him and knocked him out. When we went back later, he'd taken off, so I went to look for him. Gus stayed here in case he came back."

"Did you find him?"

"Yeah. I finally saw him staggering alongside the road a couple of miles from here. I pulled up beside him, but he acted like he didn't even see me. I helped him into the back of the truck, and he just lay there."

"He's in your truck now?" Tom asked incredulously.

"Yep. Unless the sheriff already helped him out of it," Del answered matter-of-factly.

Tom was up and out the door before she knew it.

Del dropped onto the couch and leaned her head back, staring up at the ceiling for a few seconds before allowing her eyes to close in exhaustion. A few minutes later, she thought she heard footsteps returning. She opened her eyes, and Tom was standing in front of her, a strange look on his face.

"Sheriff wants you to come outside, Del," he said.

In front of the house, they found the sheriff standing beside his car. Widow's motion light on the front of her garage lit up the driveway, and through the open rear door of the sheriff's car, Del could see Glen sitting motionless. The sheriff turned to look at her with a frustrated expression on his face.

"Are you going to explain this to me?" he asked abruptly.

"I found him walking alongside the road like that, Sheriff. I don't know what happened to him."

"Surely you can do better than that. I have a grown man sitting in the back of my car who pissed in his pants when I pulled him out of your truck. He just sits there and shakes. Every now and then he whimpers a little. Other than that, nothing. *He* won't tell me anything. Now I suggest *you* tell me what happened to this man, or I might just take you to jail with him."

Del shrugged and answered calmly, "It's just like I said, Sheriff. I found him like that, wandering down the road. Maybe something scared him, like a bear or a mountain lion."

"You know, Sheriff, Junior Wells over to the west of my place reported seeing a mountain lion about a month ago," Tom added.

The sheriff shook his head. "Tom, I want you to bring her into the office and take her statement. Maybe by the time she gets there, she'll decide to do the right thing and tell me what happened. I'm taking this man to the stress center to be assessed."

"Yes sir." Tom opened the driver's door for the sheriff.

"Miss Smith, think about what I said." He looked at Glen, who was still trembling and staring silently at the back of the front seat and shook his head again.

As he backed away, Tom turned toward her. "Well Del, shall we lock everything up and head to town?"

Exhausted and wishing the evening would end, she shrugged again. "Sure Tom."

* * *

Forty-five minutes later, Tom had recorded her statement. The sterile room where she sat at a white plastic table had a vent right over her chair, and the cold air blowing from it chilled her. She shivered as she waited for Tom to call the sheriff to decide whether she could leave or not. As Tom reentered the room, she looked at him questioningly.

"He's letting you go, Del. He's not satisfied. He said to tell you not to leave the area."

"Okay. Tom, could you give me a lift to the hospital? I doubt if there are any cabs running at this hour."

"Sure."

As they approached the hospital, her stomach clenched and she felt nauseous. While a part of her mind had quickly traveled down a horrific path of possibilities of Widow's ordeal with Glen, she hadn't allowed herself to dwell there long, afraid it would prevent her from dealing with her brother. Now her imagination was getting the best of her. By the time Tom pulled his truck into the ER parking lot, she was ready to jump from it and run into the building. Only years of practice controlling her emotions allowed her to maintain her composure.

She calmly thanked Tom, assured him again that she would be available if they had more questions and watched as he drove away. Then she walked into the building and asked the receptionist for information. Within minutes, a nurse appeared at the door beside the reception desk and motioned her back. Del followed her down the hallway, feeling an odd disorientation among the beeps of the machines, the spinning of wheels on the tile floors and the cold sterility she had so frequently worked among during her years in health care. She was glad to be shown into a room with a drawn curtain hiding the gurney beyond it. Gus stepped from behind the curtain and upon seeing her, moved the curtain back, allowing her to see Jenny reclined there, a nurse at her side.

"It's about time," Jenny exclaimed. Despite the nurse's attempts to keep her down, she rushed to Del and hugged her.

After a few seconds, the nurse insisted Jenny go back to the gurney. After receiving Jenny's assurance she would stay reclined, the nurse left them alone. Jenny's cheeks were pale, but Del was relieved that she looked much better than she had when she'd first regained consciousness. Del could only hope Widow would show the same degree of improvement, although she had her doubts.

Gus and Jenny demanded to know what had transpired, and she gave them the same short version she had given the sheriff and Tom. When they stared at her in disbelief, she looked at the open door, indicating their lack of privacy.

"Del, are you okay?" Jenny asked.

"Sure, I'm fine." Del's tone didn't match her words, but she wasn't willing to expand on it any more than she was willing to talk about Glen. "Have you heard how Widow's doing?"

"They've taken her to a quiet area in the ER. One of the psych nurses from the stress unit promised to stay with her the entire time. They had to do…some tests, you know."

Del swallowed with effort. "Yeah, I figured. Do you think they'll let us see her?"

"I don't know, Del. A nurse just walked past the door. Why don't you ask her?" Jenny urged.

Del was able to catch the briskly moving woman in blue scrubs before she walked around the corner and out of sight. The nurse gave her no information about Widow's status, only empty assurances that she would tell Ms. Jennings she had a visitor.

When Del returned to Jenny's small room, a balding man in his middle forties, his white jacket and stethoscope leading Del to believe he was a doctor, sat on a stool in front of Jenny, looking between Gus and Jenny as he spoke. Del was in time to hear "concussion" and "observe her in the hospital overnight." They were all relieved to hear that there was no sign of a skull fracture or hemorrhaging.

Gus caught her eye from where he sat on the other side of the doctor and nodded at her, smiling. She smiled in return but could only hope Widow's doctors would be as encouraging.

As the doctor exited, Del claimed the stool he had abandoned. She took Jenny's hand and squeezed it gently. "I'm so glad he didn't hurt you worse than he did. I'd have never forgiven myself if…if it would have been worse," she finished lamely, unable to voice the fear that had gripped her when she first saw Jenny lying on Widow's floor, bloody and unmoving.

"Del, you're talking nonsense. You have no reason to need forgiveness. You're not responsible for any of this."

"I can't help but feel if I had stood up to him at my house, maybe none of this would have happened. And now…now it's too late. Widow and you are both hurt, and there's nothing I can do to reverse time and make it not happen." Del could feel the tears at the corners of her eyes and fought to keep them from escaping.

"You're right Del. You can't undo the past, but you certainly did your part to make sure we'll all be safer in the future." The power of Gus's direct gaze didn't allow her to look away, and she could only nod in agreement.

"I'm worried about Widow. I wish they'd bring us some news," Jenny voiced Del's thoughts. "I wonder if she called Jessie yet, or if the nurses did."

"You didn't call her?" Del was surprised.

"I wanted to give Widow a little time. Jessie can be a bit overwhelming at times, and I wasn't sure Widow was in any condition to face her and the barrage of questions I'm sure Jessie would have."

"Maybe you could talk to her first...try to calm her down before she sees her mother," Gus suggested.

Jenny closed her eyes and leaned back against the pillow. "I guess it has to be done. Gus, why don't you call her? Just tell her there was a little accident but her mother and I will be okay. Ask her and Johnnie to come to the hospital and you can meet them in the waiting room. If you bring them to me, I'll tell them what I know and see if I can keep Jessie calm. I'm going to rest a little now though."

"Maybe they'll have you in your own room by the time she gets here," Gus offered.

"Mmm," Jenny acknowledged without opening her eyes.

"Let's go to the waiting room and I'll make the call," Gus suggested.

Del nodded and followed him out of the cold, white corridor to the warmer colors of the waiting room. She found a seat in the far corner and stared out the tinted windows at the empty cars in the parking lot. Gus stepped outside to get a better signal on his cell phone, and she was glad for the time alone. She dropped her head into her hands. *How did it come to this? Why did he have to attack Widow? And why won't they tell me how she is?*

She hadn't moved by the time Gus returned, and he sat beside her silently until Jessie rushed into the room fifteen minutes later, Johnnie trailing a few steps behind her. Gus looked up at the sound of their entrance and quickly rose to meet them. Del stood as well but stayed a couple of steps behind Gus.

"What's going on, Gus? Where's Mom?" Jessie demanded. She glanced at Del briefly before focusing her full attention on him.

"They're still checking her out in the back. Jenny's back there too. They're keeping Jenny overnight for observation. She had a concussion."

"Concussion? What happened? Were they in a wreck?"

"No." Gus took her firmly by both arms. "Jenny said she would explain it all to you. Let's go back and you can ask her."

Jessie looked at Gus and Del in confusion but nodded and turned to follow him. Del grabbed Johnnie by the hand before he could follow and motioned him over to the corner where she had been sitting. He looked at Jessie and Gus moving away from them, then back at Del questioningly.

"Come on Johnnie. Let her go back and talk to Jenny. Gus and I need to talk to you."

He followed her slowly to the corner and after a few seconds sat down across from her. "Is Mom going to be okay?" he asked at last.

"I think so," Del answered truthfully. "I mean, the doctors haven't said yet, but I don't think any of her injuries…" She swallowed hard "…any of her injuries are life-threatening."

"Will you tell me what happened?" he asked quietly.

Del looked at the door Gus had passed through moments before and was relieved to see him returning through it. "Yes Johnnie. Gus and I will tell you everything we can."

Gus came over and sat beside Johnnie. He looked over at Del, who nodded and began.

"Glen took your mother hostage sometime last night, Johnnie. Jenny went over to talk to her this evening, and Glen clubbed her when she came in the door. That's how she ended up with a concussion." Del watched Johnnie carefully. He didn't react at first, but then his posture changed abruptly, the slumped shoulders straightening and his eyes narrowing as he focused on her closely. She watched, waiting to let him digest everything she had said.

"Glen, Glen Smith. Your brother?' His eyes sparked with anger.

"Yes, my brother," she answered, feeling defeated.

Gus leaped to her defense. "Del and I followed Jenny over a little later in the evening, and we noticed things weren't right as soon as we pulled up. Del went to the front of the shed, where there was a light on, while I snuck around to the back door. Glen had your mom in there, and Del stood up to him, even with him holding a gun on her and your mom. It gave me a chance to get around him and shove his gun away when he shot at Del."

"He shot at you?" Johnnie asked, incredulous.

"He had your mother between us and he said he was going to kill us both, then he pointed his rifle at me, but Gus messed up his aim and tackled him. Glen was never a match for Gus, and he made short work of him. He had Glen bound up like a hog before I knew it."

"Wow!" Johnnie looked at Gus with admiration. He must have replayed it all in his head, because his expression suddenly became serious again. "So, what happened to Mom? She didn't get shot, did she?"

"No Johnnie. Nothing like that. We got her out of there safely," Gus assured him. "But before we got there, Glen beat her up pretty badly. She seemed to be in shock when we subdued him."

Johnnie's face gradually reddened with anger as Del watched him mull over everything. She wasn't surprised when he asked the question she wanted answered too. "So, did he rape her?"

Del blinked back the immediate tears. "I don't know, Johnnie. I don't know. We haven't had a chance to see her since she arrived. I hope they let us see her soon. Do you think I should go check on Jenny and Jessie?" Del asked Gus, suddenly feeling uncomfortable and looking for a reason to get away.

"Sure. I'll stay here with Johnnie. Maybe we can get the receptionist to check on Widow again." Gus's eyes followed her until she walked past. She turned and saw him drape an arm over Johnnie's shoulders, and she wondered if the young man was crying. God knew she wanted to cry.

She tapped lightly on the open door to Jenny's room before stepping inside. When she rounded the curtain, she saw Jenny sitting on the edge of the gurney, embracing Jessie. When Jenny saw Del, she released Jessie slowly. Del wasn't surprised to see Jessie's face streaked with tears when she turned to see who had entered the room.

Jessie launched herself toward Del and shoved her beyond the curtain, forcing her back against the wall beside the doorway. "I wish my mother had never met you. You've brought her nothing but trouble. You need to stay the hell away from her, Del Smith, you and your fucking brother."

Del didn't attempt to defend herself. Jessie's words were no different from what she had told herself many times. She allowed Jessie to keep her pinned against the wall with a forearm across her sternum, barely registering the pain encircling her ribs. Jenny, however, had leaped from the gurney as soon as Jessie moved toward Del and was now pulling at Jessie's other arm, trying in vain to reason with her.

The scuffle alerted a passing nurse, and she and Jenny were able to pull Jessie away from Del before the younger woman inflicted any damage. "Get her out of here," Jessie yelled. "She's nothing but trouble. We've had nothing but trouble since she moved back."

"Jessie, listen to me," Del said. "It was just a matter of time before Glen found an excuse to come after your mother. Think about it. She was always the one that got away, and he took quite a beating over her too. He's been waiting for a chance, for you and Johnnie to move out and leave her there alone."

Jessie shook off the two women holding her arms and straightened her shirt. She stared at Del, still looking enraged but apparently listening.

"I would do anything to turn back the clock and undo the past twenty-four hours, Jessie. And I know it may be a little late, but it will never happen again. I promise that."

Jessie stepped toward Del, and Del shook her head at Jenny and the nurse as they started to follow. "What makes your promise mean anything to me? How do I know you're any different from your brother?"

"My brother has bullied his way through life. Until tonight, I could honestly say I've avoided confrontations all my life. I've devoted my life to helping others, not hurting them. That makes me different from my brother." Del's voice was soft but firm. "After what he did to your mother, I faced my brother, and I'm telling you once more, Jessie. Glen will never hurt her again."

The two women stared at each other for several seconds. Del could feel the tension in the air between them as dense as fog. Jessie must have found some truth in the depths of Del's eyes because she finally turned away and stepped back around the curtain, where she sank down in a chair and dropped her head.

The nurse shook her head and walked toward the door, where she turned to look at Jenny. "You need to go back to that gurney," she scolded. "Remember, you *have* had a concussion." She added in a lighter tone, "And call me if you need me."

Jenny smiled and nodded. She grabbed Del's hand and led her around the curtain. After getting comfortable on the gurney, Jenny spoke to the other two in the same tone Del had heard her use with her teenage sons. "Widow is very lucky to have two strong-willed women looking out for her. Right now she needs you both, so make up your minds to get along. And do it quickly. I've got an unbelievable headache." She closed her eyes and placed a hand on her forehead.

"Jenny, I'm sorry. I wasn't even thinking…"

"Me too," Jessie said. "I'll go back out to the waiting room with Gus and Johnnie."

"You can stay if you want, but breaking up a fight between you two is more than I feel like taking on again. I know you're both sorry, because that's who you are. Nothing more needs to be said."

Properly chastised, Del and Jessie remained silent. When the nurse reentered the room, Del and Jessie each had their eyes riveted on opposite walls, unmoving, and Jenny appeared to be asleep on the gurney. "Now, this is more like it," the woman remarked, her voice as brisk as her movements as she walked around the room. She smiled as Jenny cracked open her eyes. "Ms. Andrews, I need to record your vitals once more, then a gentleman will be here to take you up to your room. You'll be going to room four oh two, bed one."

Del stood and moved to within Jenny's line of vision. "I'll go out and tell Gus. We'll make our way upstairs and catch up with you in your room."

Jenny squeezed the hand Del gave her. "Okay Del. See you there."

The nurse removed the blood pressure cuff from Jenny's arm just as Del walked away. "Wait," she ordered. Del stopped and turned to look at Jenny with concern.

"Are you Del Smith?" the nurse asked. "I heard Ms. Andrews call you Del," she said.

Del answered hesitantly, "Uh, yeah. That's me."

"When I finished here, I was going to try to find you. Another patient, Felicia Jennings, asked for you."

Del stepped toward the nurse as Jessie rose and moved to her as well.

"That's my mother," Jessie said.

Apparently remembering the previous scuffle between the two women, the nurse looked warily at them. "Do I need to talk to you in separate rooms?"

Del and Jessie exchanged a look of understanding, and Jessie responded, "It'll be okay. You can tell us here. How is she?"

"She's settled down and the shock appears to be nearly resolved. She is very tired but insists she wants to talk to Del Smith before she'll allow herself to sleep."

Jessie's eyes widened in surprise and she opened her mouth as if to speak, but Del interrupted her. "Is that okay with you, Jessie?" she asked. Her hands hung loosely at her sides as she opened herself up to whatever Jessie decided.

Jessie stood speechless for several seconds, staring at Del in surprise. Finally she nodded slightly. "Okay," she murmured, then turned away as if to reduce the temptation to add something she might be sorry for later.

The nurse motioned for Del to follow, and they left the room quietly.

Del's stomach began to churn again as she followed the nurse along the corridor. They turned down a short hallway, and her apprehension peaked as the nurse opened a nondescript door near the end of it. Del swallowed forcibly and wiped her palms on the sides of her pants. She also struggled to wipe the concerned and fearful expression from her face and replace it with a look of what she hoped was positivity. The nurse ushered her through the door, then closed it behind Del.

Del stood silently in a small, windowless room, empty as far as she could see, but a large curtain partitioned off about one third of the room. She listened for the sounds of another person's presence but could only hear the nurse's retreating footsteps. She tiptoed toward the curtain and peered around the edge. She could make out the outline of Widow's body under the blanket on the small bed as she lay on her side, facing the wall.

Unsure whether to risk waking her, Del waited for some indication that Widow was awake. Finally Widow rolled awkwardly on the tiny bed, her eyes widening slightly when she saw her visitor. Del hoped her expression didn't waver when she saw the darkening, purplish-black bruises over most of Widow's face. Swelling along her jaws, her forehead and around her nose showed she must have taken numerous blows. Del was unable to prevent a renewed surge of anger toward her brother. *I should have cut the damn rope.*

"Del, you're okay!" Widow sounded surprised, and Del looked at her curiously.

"I'm fine. What about you?" Del pulled a chair up beside the bed, sat and reached for Widow's hands. When their flesh met, she felt comforted in a way she didn't realize she'd needed.

"I'm bruised pretty badly, or so they tell me. No one has given me a mirror yet, so it must be pretty bad, huh?" Widow tried to smile, but the swelling only allowed part of her mouth to move.

Del gently traced a path along one cheek, feeling the puffiness under her fingertips. "Does it hurt much?" she asked.

"Not much. They gave me something for the pain. It's made me sleepy. I must have been dozing when you came in. I didn't hear the door open."

Del blinked hard to fight back her tears. "I was worried about you. I'm sorry things happened the way they did." She dropped her head to avoid Widow's eyes. "I'm sorry I wasn't there to keep Glen from hurting you."

Widow urged Del's chin upward with one finger and looked at her closely as if seeking the truth through her eyes. "I don't understand. You *were* there. Jenny told me Gus and you rescued us. Have you seen Jenny?"

"Yeah. Jenny's going to be fine. She has a concussion and they're keeping her overnight for observation." Del looked at Widow curiously. "Widow, do you remember what happened?"

"Not really. I remember taking you home from Gus and Jenny's house and…holding you." Widow's eyes warmed Del as they shared the memory of Widow sitting on her lap and holding Del's head to her chest.

"You don't remember scaring Glen away with your shotgun that evening?"

"No! I did? Good for me, then." Her smile was jagged and disfigured.

Del hesitated. "I'm ashamed of how I acted that evening. I sent you away afterward. I acted like a coward, begging Glen to leave us alone, and when he called me on it, I didn't fight it. And then I was so ashamed of myself I figured you would be too. So I told you to go home. You didn't want to leave, but I insisted. So you left. You went home and Glen took you hostage."

Widow had listened to her confession with a puzzled look. "I wish I could remember so I could convince you I wasn't ashamed of you. I know you learned very young how to survive when people are threatening you, so I'm not surprised if you reverted to that. But when push came to shove, you were there." She looked at Del closely. "So, what do you think now? Do you still want me to leave you alone?"

"No," Del answered quickly. "I was so scared I was going to lose you when Glen was threatening to kill us. I wanted a chance to tell you I was sorry; I was wrong to send you away. I wanted to tell you...how much...you mean to me."

"How much?" Widow asked, her voice so soft Del barely heard her.

"How much?" Del took a deep breath and continued. "You've quickly become a very important part of my life, Felicia Jennings."

Widow smiled through the bruises and stroked the side of Del's face. "I guess that's probably the best I'm going to get out of you for now." She put a fingertip to Del's lips to prevent her from interrupting. "I know. But your heart is healing, and when it does, I hope there'll be a place in it for me."

Widow sat up on the edge of the bed and reached for Del. Del wrapped her arms around her, careful to avoid hurting her. From the quick glance at the black-and-purple marks on Widow's arms below the short sleeves of the hospital gown, Del assumed the bruises were everywhere. "Thank you for believing in me. I'm sorry I have to go slow."

"Shhh. Just hold me," Widow said. After a few seconds, Del felt Widow begin to tremble. She cried gently on Del's shoulder for several minutes as Del softly rubbed her back and rocked her.

The tears slowed and Widow relaxed in her arms. "Are you okay?" Del whispered.

"Yeah," Widow whispered in return. "I don't know why I keep crying. I try to remember everything, and I just feel this overwhelming grief and I can't stop the tears."

"It's okay. It really is. You can cry on my shoulder anytime," Del reassured her.

Widow leaned back to look at her. "Careful, I might take you up on that." She rested her head against Del. "Tell me what happened, Del. I need to know what I can't remember."

"Are you sure you want to hear it tonight? Why don't you just rest for now?"

"I'll rest better if I know."

"Okay, but lie down and get comfortable first."

Widow did as Del asked, then looked at her expectantly. Del held Widow's hand gently between hers, rubbing small circles along the back of it with her thumbs. "I told you before about Glen coming to my house and you chasing him away. I'm not sure when he showed up at your house. He might have been waiting for you when you first got there. But whenever it was, he said he'd been there that night. Cindy sent Gus and Jenny over to check on me after I came home from work today, and I told them about the showdown with Glen at my house and how I reacted. I guess they got me thinking about it differently, and I was going to talk to you about it. Jenny said she needed to see you too, so she came over first. I guess Glen hit her when she came in the door, knocking her out. Then he took you out to the machine shed to wait, knowing Gus or I would eventually come looking for Jenny. We rode over together about half an hour later and knew instantly something wasn't right. The house was dark but the shed was lit up. So Gus went around the back, and I went to the front of the shed."

Del drew a deep breath. "When I came inside, Glen had you at gunpoint. You must have been in shock. I'm not sure you even realized I was there. He was threatening to kill us both, and I stalled to give Gus time to get to him. He had the gun pointed at me, but Gus shoved the gun just as he shot, and he missed me. Then Gus took him down. He had him knocked out and tied up before I knew what was happening. We went to the house and found Jenny, then called the sheriff and the ambulance."

"Where did you go?" Widow asked.

"What do you mean?"

"I remember you telling me to stay with Gus and Jenny. You said you had to leave. Where did you go?"

"I had to make sure he wasn't going to hurt any of us again."

Widow's eyebrows drew together, and she frowned. "I don't understand. I thought Gus tied him up."

"I knew Glen would never stop trying, Widow. It might be while he was out on bail, or if he ever got out on probation, or if he could ever talk someone into hurting one of us for him, but he would never stop. So I taught Glen a lesson he'll never forget, if he ever recovers from it."

"What do you mean?" Widow asked, looking at her in concern.

"When this all blows over, I'll tell you everything, but for now, the less you know, the less you have to worry about telling the sheriff. Just know that Glen Smith won't bother you again. I promise." Del brought Widow's hand up to her lips and gently kissed her fingers. "Now, why don't you rest? I'll stay here with you if you'd like."

"I'd like that...very much." Widow pulled the covers up around her and settled the pillow under her head, then took Del's hand. She closed her eyes, and Del felt her hand relax as she finally slept.

Del tilted her head back against the wall, closed her eyes and saw the evil gleam in her brother's eye as he sighted down the long rifle barrel at her. She cringed momentarily, then forced her mind to change to an image of Widow, smiling despite her bruises because Del was unharmed. A sudden flash of Sarah caught her by surprise, and she wondered what Sarah would think of the events of the past day and a half. The thought was somehow worrisome and comforting at the same time, and, mulling it over, she drifted into an exhausted sleep.

CHAPTER FIFTEEN

Del sat on her front porch watching the shadow of the house stretch farther across the yard and the tops of the trees turn orange as the last of the Friday evening sun sank over the horizon behind the house. The serenity of the evening settled over her and seemed strange in contrast to the roller-coaster ride of the previous month. Some of her tension about the evening ahead melted with it, and she sighed deeply. She thought about the events of the past two weeks as she waited for her guest to arrive.

After several meetings with the sheriff, he had apparently decided she would offer no further information. Tom had let it slip to Jenny that Glen had apparently recovered. Oddly, though, he had remained tight-lipped about where he had disappeared to and what may have happened to him. But the haunted look in Glen's eyes made his assertions less than believable to Tom. Neither Jenny nor Gus had asked Del for an explanation, and she was relieved. As long as she and Glen were the only ones who knew the truth, at the worst, it would come down to his word against hers.

Glen seemed willing to face three charges of first degree assault and armed criminal action and one charge of kidnapping, although he had pleaded not guilty on the advice of his attorney. The prosecuting attorney had reassured Del that a plea bargain was in the works and a trial almost certainly would not be necessary.

After only a few hours of sleep upright in a hard hospital chair early Saturday morning, Del had returned home later in the day after Widow and Jenny had been discharged and tried to sleep more, but insomnia ruled. Like a DVD spinning relentlessly in her mind, the events of the past few days replayed themselves. It started with the tragic argument with her mother and ended with a still frame of Widow, bruised and swollen in the cold, stark interior of a hospital room. She called to check on Widow and Jenny Saturday evening and twice on Sunday, but her relief at finding them doing well did nothing to stop the constant replay in her head.

Del had returned to work that Monday, but her supervisor had immediately pulled her into his office to ask about her haggard appearance. After she told him of her brother's arrest for her attempted murder, he insisted she take two weeks off. She had to agree; she probably wasn't in the best condition to treat patients.

Two weeks at home had given her time to think, and as the spinning DVD slowly lost its hold on her mind, she had found in herself a new determination. She had taken the first steps toward advancing her degree, researching the details and realizing she could afford to return to college if she worked part-time. She had intended to take this step years earlier, but life had been good and the stress of college was more than she wanted to inflict upon her relationship with Sarah.

Sarah…Sarah had also colored her days but less in the darkness of pain and loss and more often in the bright memories of love and happiness. The heartbreak was lessening, and memories of laughter, love and even the occasional spat between them would cause Del to suddenly smile. She had wondered at the switch in her emotions but decided to ride this high as far as it would take her without questioning it too deeply.

She had been shocked when, earlier that morning, she finally went through the lockbox she had taken from her mother's home. She had sorted through the jumble of papers her mother had stacked inside it over the years and had wondered at the reasoning behind most of them. A receipt for a pair of boots likely given as a gift at one time had been tucked in an envelope along with her father's last driver's license and social security card. A lifetime warranty on a garden hose had joined many other strange items in Del's wastebasket as she dug through the stack. In a small white envelope, folded in half at the bottom of the lockbox, she had found a tattered and faded birth certificate. In bright light, she had been able to discern her name and date of birth, but the mother's name had been smudged as if someone had tried to erase it. She hadn't been able to make out the letters, but something about it had seemed wrong. The first name had appeared to be about five or six letters long, unlike Beatrice, her mother's name. The surname, however, had been the most noticeably different. It had clearly been twice as long as Smith.

She had assumed it must be a mistake and had called the courthouse to verify it. Although they wouldn't share any information with her on the phone, she had learned she could get a new copy of her birth certificate by showing up in person or requesting it by mail. She had tried not to jump to any conclusions, but a kernel of doubt grew as the day progressed. Her omission from her mother's obituary had seemed spiteful at the time, but Del wondered if the truth had been there for her all along. Doubting her roots had left her mind whirling with possibilities, and she was eager to look into it further. But not today. Today she had other priorities.

Jessie and Johnnie had made it clear to Del as they helped Widow from the hospital wheelchair into Jessie's car that they would be staying with their mother for at least a week and Del shouldn't worry about her. The look from Jessie that had accompanied this had spoken volumes. Despite being warned away, Del had checked on Widow each day with a brief phone call.

Her reaction to what Glen had done to Widow still surprised her. She thought back on the incident and had tried to put other people in Widow's place. Only with Sarah could Del imagine herself fighting back as she had. She loved Jenny and Gus like the family they had so quickly become, yet she doubted her courage enough to think she could have overcome her fears for them.

She was giving Jessie and Johnnie space, understanding they needed this time with Widow as well as time away from Del. But Del still wanted to see for herself that Widow was okay and that no one could harm her.

Now, two weeks after the attacks, Del was relieved to know she would soon see Widow in the flesh. So many things between them had been left unfinished, so many of her own questions unanswered, some of which she wasn't sure she wanted to know the answers to. Widow sounded stronger every day when Del talked to her on the phone, but had Glen left scars so deep in her heart that she would turn against Del in time? And what about herself? Del needed to know if this *thing* she wasn't ready to label yet was strong enough in her to change Del's future, to give her the courage to sustain this determination that had carried her through the past two weeks.

Del felt suddenly short of breath when she heard the distant sound of gravel popping that signaled the approach of a car. She couldn't stop the foolish grin from spreading across her face as Widow's truck slowly made its way down the hill. She slowed her steps with effort as she bounded toward her driveway and opened the door just as Widow stilled the motor.

"Hi." Del was suddenly shy and couldn't find any of the words that had run through her head when she imagined their reunion.

Widow turned to smile at her through the open door, and Del's shyness melted as concern took over. The tinted windshield of the truck had disguised her appearance, but now the evening light was bright enough to show everything. The swelling was gone from Widow's face, but the yellow-and-purple bruises, although fainter, were harsh reminders of the trauma she had suffered.

"Don't worry, Del. I'm okay," Widow admonished.

"Sorry. I guess I forgot about them."

"Yeah, I do too. Until someone stares and gets that look on their face you just had."

"What look?"

"That 'you poor thing, are you okay?' look I've been getting every time I go out of the house."

"Sorry. I'll try not to let it happen again. Why don't you get out and come to the porch? You've had supper with your kids, right?" Del held out a hand, which Widow took, and she followed her up the steps to the chairs Del had set out for them.

"Jessie picked up fried chicken on her way home from work. She's staying this weekend. I think this shook up both her and Johnnie quite a bit." Widow waved her hand in front of her battered face. "I'm trying to give them time to realize I'm okay and I'm not going anywhere. It's tough when you lose a parent when you're so young. You get so dependent on the only parent that's left. If something happens to that one, I think everything gets magnified."

"Yeah. I guess I can see that." Del couldn't help but contrast Widow's concern for Jessie and Johnnie to the indifference her own mother had shown her.

Widow laughed. "They even set a curfew for me. If I'm not home by ten o'clock, they promised they would both be here knocking on your door to check on me."

Del's eyes widened in surprise. "Thanks for the warning. I think I'll keep one eye on the clock, or should I set an alarm?"

"Surely between the two of us, we can keep track of time."

"So, how are you? I mean, not the bruises, but...here." Del held a hand over her heart. "And in here." She tapped the side of her head.

Widow looked out at the trees for several seconds as if seeking an answer written in the myriad of green formed by the intermingling of small branches and leaves. "Better. I'm better. At times, I'm good. Like nothing ever happened. Then a word, or a move, or something I can't even remember will make me feel...I don't know...frightened, maybe? If I could remember, maybe it would be easier."

"Do you remember...anything?" Del couldn't bring herself to ask how badly Glen had hurt her.

"The rape kit showed no signs of a sexual assault, if that's what you're asking," Widow answered softly. "But I honestly don't remember much."

Del was relieved but surprised. Her brother had made it sound like... Well, her brother was known for his lies. She was so grateful this had been another one, that Widow had been spared this most demeaning of personal violations. Del reached for Widow's hand and squeezed it gently.

"Maybe your amnesia is protecting you from what might overwhelm you."

"That's what my counselor said too." Widow nodded at Del's silent question when she lifted an eyebrow. "I've gone twice a week for two weeks, but I'm going back to work next week, so I'm cutting back to once a week."

"Back to work already?"

"Already? I love my kids and I understand their need to hover right now, but if I don't start getting things back to normal soon, I'll need more than a twice-a-week counselor. They'll be locking me in the looney bin and throwing away the key." Widow smiled, and Del couldn't help but smile in return.

After several seconds, Del realized she'd been staring and averted her gaze quickly to study the foliage. "So, are you sleeping?"

"Oddly enough, I am. The counselor was surprised too." Widow waited until Del turned to look at her again. "I just close my eyes, picture you sitting there holding my hand and I drift off immediately."

Del floated in her eyes, recalling the hours in the hospital and the peace she had felt holding on to Widow's hand as she slept. She blinked several times to break the spell. "Uh, do you...would you like something to drink?" The words tripped out, spilling over each other rapidly.

"Sure." Widow rose with her. "Let me come inside and help you."

"Okay. What do you want…to drink, that is? What do you want to drink?" Del took a deep breath, wondering where her composure had gone.

"Let's go see what you have," Widow suggested, smiling as if to ease Del's sudden awkwardness.

Del distracted herself fixing icy glasses of sweet tea and returned to the porch with Widow at her side. After a few moments of silence while they both enjoyed their drinks, Widow turned to Del, her expression serious.

"Del, I want you to tell me."

"What do you mean?"

"You know what I mean. What happened when you left with Glen that night?"

"I'm trying to protect you from being involved. If you know and don't report it, doesn't that make you an accessory?"

"That doesn't matter. I need to know, and I think you need to be able to share it with someone. I feel like I've earned the right to know through every one of these bruises." She touched her face gently. "And you know I'll never repeat your story, Del. I'd never risk hurting you."

She looked at Del so openly and with such strong emotion, and Del knew she could trust her. She took a deep breath and looked out across the yard. The lengthening shadows hid most of it, and only the tops of the trees were still visible against the darkening sky. She reached for a lighter on the small end table and lit a tiki torch at the edge of the porch to ward off mosquitoes. After settling back into her chair, she reached over for Widow's hand.

"Okay. But first I have to tell you a little about my childhood… and Glen's." Del allowed the painful memories she'd buried long ago to resurface. "Our dad…well, our dad could be pretty cruel. To put it plainly, he was a really mean bastard. He always claimed he was trying to toughen us up, but I think he just liked to see how much he could hurt us. I remember when I was about four, he lit my teddy bear on fire and tossed it out in the middle of the yard to burn."

Widow gasped and Del felt her fingers tighten around hers. "Yeah, he was mean. And he left some scars, not just on me, but on all of us, Glen and Mom too."

"But I thought your mom was…"

"Mom was mean too. She was. But not as bad as Dad. And he was mean to her too. Do you remember those stamps they used to give out at the grocery store when you spent a certain amount? They'd have some sort of giveaway if you collected enough. There was this one time Mom saved enough stamps to get a nice set of dishes for the house. We never had anything nice like that, you know. Matching plates, saucers, cups, bowls, the whole set, kept up in the cabinet where us kids couldn't break them. Dad came home one night from the bar and demanded supper, so Mom heated him up something. She pulled one of the old plates down from the cabinet, but he demanded one of the good ones. Said she never used them and accused her of thinking he wasn't good enough for them, so she relented. Sure enough, as soon as he finished eating, he stood up from the table and staggered around until he crashed into the table. Her new plate cracked into three pieces when it hit the floor. The store had moved on to another promotion, so the set would never be whole again. Mom never said a word about it. He probably would have hit her if she had. Who knows? Maybe she convinced herself it was an accident. I know he was walking steady when he came into the house that night, and he didn't stagger after that either."

"Why did she stay with him?" Widow wondered aloud.

"That's hard to say. I guess we'll never know for sure. I do know she was afraid of him. Anyway, I wanted to explain how he was so you'll understand. See, that night, when I saw how much Glen had hurt you and Jenny, it came to me. I knew how to get Glen to stop once and for all. And if I did it right, I could do it without going to jail."

Widow raised both eyebrows, but Del didn't stop.

"When Glen was about ten years old, when he was mowing, he saw a snake in the corner of the yard. He was always scared of snakes, and he ran into the house to tell Mom about it. Dad was on the couch sleeping off another hangover, and the noise woke him. When he heard what was happening, he dragged Glen out to where he had seen the snake. Dad claimed the snake was a king snake, and he shoved Glen down within a foot of it to look at it. Dad was yelling at Glen, calling him chickenshit and other things. The snake coiled and struck at Glen, but Dad wouldn't let him back away. The third time it struck, it bit Glen on the arm."

"Oh my. I hate to say it, but I feel sorry for him."

"I did too, at least I did for that Glen, the child. But that's not the worst of it. It wasn't a king snake, it was a copperhead. And Dad wouldn't let Mom take him to the ER for several hours. He was really sick and had to be in the hospital for a long time. The bite was infected, and he almost lost his arm. Ever since then, he's had a real phobia about snakes."

"I guess so." Widow looked a Del sideways. "Del, what did you do to him?"

"Let me finish. Right now you're feeling sorry for Glen, the child. I spent most of my life making excuses for Glen and my mother because of all they went through. But remember, I went through things too. So do lots of people, every day. That doesn't give us an excuse to mistreat others, to hurt others like we were hurt. I didn't make the choice to become an abuser and others don't either. I've had time to think these past two weeks, and I've finally figured that out. I've realized I can be angry at Glen if he treats me like shit. The night I sent you home, I was wrong. I was still trying to escape a confrontation with him, thinking it wasn't his fault he was the way he was. But he made the choice to behave that way."

Widow nodded in understanding. Del paused to take another gulp of sweet tea. "So, what I did to Glen, I made a choice to do. You may not approve of what I did, but in my mind it was the only way to get him to stop without killing him. Just, please, don't feel sorry for Glen, because his own actions brought it all down on him."

"I'm listening."

"Like I said, the idea just came to me. Gus had tied Glen up after he tackled him, so he was easy for us to load into my truck bed. I borrowed a rope and winch from your shed. In case Glen ever does decide to talk, I've disposed of them and will replace them with new ones."

"It's okay. I hadn't missed them," Widow interrupted.

"I drove back here into my northwest pasture where there's about a thirty-foot-deep sinkhole. When we were kids and were out wandering one day, Gus and I stuck our heads in that hole, and we counted about seventy-five snakes with our flashlights. After I checked with a lantern to make sure snakes were still living there, I hooked Glen up to the bumper and slid him over the edge, headfirst. Then after I had him close to the bottom, I lowered the lantern so he could see the snakes."

Widow's eyes widened. "Oh."

Del heard the unspoken surprise in her tone. *Better she know the real me now.*

"When he quit screaming, I figured he'd gone a little mad. I thought about dropping him in there, but I couldn't go that far. I'm counting on Glen being too ashamed of his fear and of the fact he was bested by a female to ever tell anyone what happened. He also knows he underestimated me, and I don't believe he'll ever try it again. He likes to terrorize women and children because he doesn't think they'll fight back. He knows now that I'll fight back."

Del looked at Widow closely, watching for any sign of emotion that would give her a hint of what Widow thought of her actions.

To Del's surprise, Widow looked and sounded nonchalant. "Looks like you were right. He hasn't talked yet."

Del breathed a small sigh of relief. "I think that's the last we've seen of Glen Smith. And his lawyer is handling Mom's estate, so I never have to see him again."

"Sounds wonderful."

"Doesn't it?"

"So, tell me this, Del. How are you doing?" Widow held her hand over her heart, then tapped an index finger against the side of her head.

"Better. Especially now that I've told you who I am and what I've done and you're still holding my hand."

"Were you afraid I wouldn't be?"

"I was surprised to learn I could do something that cruel to another human being."

"Like you said, his actions brought it on."

"Maybe. But I'm sure a lot of people wouldn't agree with you, including the sheriff. I think he'd call that taking the law into my own hands and, more specifically, assault and kidnapping come to mind."

"He'd have to prove it. That would be difficult."

"True. It'd be Glen's word against mine."

"Guess you'd better just keep your nose clean, then, so they never have any reason to doubt your word." Widow's voice held a teasing note in it.

Del was glad for the change in tone, eager to move on to better topics. "Hmm. I might need some help...someone to keep an eye on me to make sure I behave."

"Jenny would be a good one. She already watches Gus and the boys like a hawk. She doesn't miss anything. Remember at Jessie's birthday party, when you left Jenny and me in the kitchen to finish the gravy?"

"Yes," Del drawled slowly. "I'm afraid to ask."

"Jenny told me that you and I were interested in each other."

"She did?"

"I told you, she never misses a thing."

"I swear that woman must be psychic. She knows more about me than I do. But she sounds like she might be a little busy. I think I might be better off looking for someone else to keep me on the narrow path."

Widow grinned. "What does one need to qualify for the position?"

Del looked up at the stars and thought carefully. "She needs to have a keen mind and a warm heart. Oh, and she needs to be a good cook."

This earned a slap on the shoulder. "Del!"

"Okay, the last is optional. How about she needs to be able to capture and keep my attention completely in order to keep me out of trouble?"

"And by what means is she allowed to capture and keep your attention?" Widow was leaning toward her now, and her voice had become soft and low.

"Whatever means necessary," Del replied in a voice that had suddenly become husky.

"And how does one apply for the position of your, um, watcher, Del Smith?"

Widow had a glint in her eye that struck Del in the pit of her being. One last whisper of panic sounded deep in her mind, but the feelings Widow aroused in her easily drowned it out. Del rose to her feet and tugged gently on Widow's hand until she stood in front of Del. "Felicia Jennings, you would be my first and only choice for the position, if you're interested. You don't even need to fill out an application." She ran the edge of her thumb under Widow's eye, careful not to press on the fading bruises. "I already know everything I need to know. I know you make me strong, you make me happy, you make me... me." Suddenly concerned, Del added, "But if you're not sure, if you need time..."

Widow shushed her with a finger to her lips. "Del, I think I fell for you when I saw you struggling to keep the gravy stirred in my kitchen that day. You were so sincere, so warm. But I also saw the pain you battled with and knew you needed time."

Widow wrapped her arms around Del's neck and held her tightly. Del couldn't stop the tears from coursing down her face as she breathed in Widow's scent and nuzzled into her neck.

As the wetness cooled against Widow's skin, she pulled away to look at her. "Del, what's wrong?"

Putting one hand to her face to wipe away the tears, Del attempted to speak. "I'm...just...so...happy." She sniffed loudly and wiped the back of her hand across her face again. "Sorry..."

"No. Don't be sorry." Widow stroked Del's hair and rubbed her back, holding her again for several minutes before whispering, "I plan to always be here to let you cry on my shoulder. I'm sure there will be times I'll cry on yours as well. I want to heal your pain and share in your joys. I want to wake up every morning and look into your eyes, then tell you how much I love you."

"How did I ever find you? What did I ever do to deserve you?" Del wondered aloud, whispering into Widow's ear. "I love you too, Felicia Jennings." She opened her eyes in time to see a flash of white flutter from the porch and knew everything was right. *Sarah*.

"Stay with me tonight," Del said. "We can call, or if you'd rather I can go home with you. I just don't want to miss out on any more time."

Widow smiled and nodded. She wiped a lingering tear from Del's cheek with her fingertip. "Let me call my new bodyguards. They're old enough now that they'll just have to understand."

* * *

The morning sun blinked in and out of Del's eyes as the breeze from the air-conditioner gently rocked the window blind. She sat up, disoriented, looking at the walls lightened by the morning sun peeking through the wooden shades. The queen-size bed was empty except for her and an odd jumble of bed linens loosely piled over and around her. A few rapid heartbeats later and she knew. She was in her bed, and Widow was supposed to be in it with her. The sound of water running in the bathroom revealed Widow's location, and Del relaxed against the pillows and smiled.

New scenes replayed in Del's head now, scenes where clothes fell to the floor and hands sought curves to caress and explore. Their kisses were hungry and tongues danced with desire, teasing and tantalizing, stoking fires ever hotter. Del remembered the wonder she felt when she gazed upon Widow lying nude on the bed, reaching out her arms for Del to join her. She had nearly cried again as she carefully caressed the fading bruises across Widow's breasts and ribs. Widow had turned Del's attention away from the bruises with another fiery kiss.

The rolling as first one, then the other took charge had quickly twisted the covers, until Widow sat up and tossed them unceremoniously into a heap on the floor. The look she gave Del when she turned back to her had the same effect as if she'd touched her, and Del almost cried out. Raw desire and need stunned her with their intensity. Del wanted to give Widow the release she needed, and she moved over Widow, seeking with her fingers the satin wetness, filling her, moving her closer to the edge, then tumbling over with her in disbelief.

They made love slowly, spending time to learn every curve, every dimple of the other's body. They made love desperately, both in need, frantic for the other's touch. They slept, intermittently, but a touch or a move from the other would reignite fires and sleep would once again be forgotten. Del could hardly believe the events of the night, wondering how she'd had the energy for it.

She heard the bedroom doorknob turn, and her breath caught when Widow stepped through the door in Del's old blue bathrobe, her blond hair disheveled and framing a face that, although still marred by healing bruises, was glowing as Widow looked at her.

"Good morning," they said simultaneously.

"I started the coffee," Widow said.

"Come over here." Del patted the bed beside her.

Widow sat and leaned over to kiss her. The good-morning kiss quickly escalated, and Del reached for Widow, trying to bring her closer. A hand to her chest kept her from getting the contact she desired, and Widow chuckled as she drew away.

"I think we may have a problem," Del said.

Widow's forehead creased with concern. "Already?"

"If every time I see you, I feel like I do now, we may never be able to leave this room."

Widow whispered, "If you keep making love to me all night like you did last night, you'll have to let me leave or I'll starve to death. Contrary to popular belief, you cannot live on love."

"But I'd die happy trying," Del teased before wriggling her tongue at her.

Widow grabbed her ribs, tickling her. "You scoundrel."

"Stop, stop, please!" Del begged. "I have to pee."

"See. You'd have to leave the room too."

Del grabbed an old T-shirt she sometimes slept in from the top of a hamper in the corner, then dashed toward the door, where she turned to look at the lovely woman lying on the bed, her blue robe gaping open in places that made Del sweat. She nearly turned back, but nature was calling.

She debated when she left the bathroom, but finally turned toward the kitchen for coffee. When she reached into the cabinet for two coffee cups, a sound from behind alerted her that she wasn't alone. When warm arms slid under the edge of the T-shirt, she nearly dropped the mugs. After setting them clumsily onto the countertop, she turned in Widow's arms and enjoyed another kiss full of passion and promises, leaving her breathless. She was disappointed to notice Widow had changed from the revealing robe into her jeans and T-shirt. While the clothes did little to hide her delectable curves from Del's knowing eyes, she realized they also probably meant the night had ended.

"Don't worry." Widow must have read her mind. "We have tonight and tomorrow night and the night after that…"

"And the night after that," Del continued for her in a low tone. "If you give me a second, we may have now, because the way your hips are moving against me right now, I'm having cavewoman thoughts about dragging you back to bed."

"Oops." Widow smiled and stepped back, releasing the hold she had around her waist. "But I won't say I'm sorry."

"Me either."

"I love you, Del Smith."

"I love you, Felicia Jennings."

Bella Books, Inc.

Women. Books. Even Better Together.

P.O. Box 10543
Tallahassee, FL 32302

Phone: 800-729-4992
www.bellabooks.com